Praise for the Authors of
DARE ME

National Bestselling Author
CHERRY ADAIR

". . . is one of the reigning queens of romantic adventure." —*Romantic Times*

"[Creates] highly charged sensuality." —*Rendezvous*

National Bestselling Author
JILL SHALVIS

". . . will light your fire with her irresistible heroes . . . so bleeping sexy, you'll break into a sweat."
—Stephanie Bond, author of *Whole Lotta Trouble*

"Shalvis delivers just what readers want."
—*USA Today* bestselling author Lori Foster

National Bestselling Author
JULIE ELIZABETH LETO

". . . always delivers sizzling, snappy, edgy stories!"
—*New York Times* bestselling author Carly Phillips

"[Offers] a compelling, highly charged tale . . . [with] one of the sexiest . . . heroes ever."
—*Romantic Times*

Dare Me

. . .

CHERRY ADAIR

JILL SHALVIS

JULIE ELIZABETH LETO

A SIGNET ECLIPSE BOOK

SIGNET ECLIPSE
Published by New American Library, a division of
Penguin Group (USA) Inc., 375 Hudson Street,
New York, New York 10014, USA
Penguin Group (Canada), 10 Alcorn Avenue, Toronto,
Ontario M4V 3B2, Canada (a division of Pearson Penguin Canada Inc.)
Penguin Books Ltd., 80 Strand, London WC2R 0RL, England
Penguin Ireland, 25 St. Stephen's Green, Dublin 2,
Ireland (a division of Penguin Books Ltd.)
Penguin Group (Australia), 250 Camberwell Road, Camberwell, Victoria 3124,
Australia (a division of Pearson Australia Group Pty. Ltd.)
Penguin Books India Pvt. Ltd., 11 Community Centre, Panchsheel Park,
New Delhi - 110 017, India
Penguin Group (NZ), cnr Airborne and Rosedale Roads, Albany,
Auckland 1310, New Zealand (a division of Pearson New Zealand Ltd.)
Penguin Books (South Africa) (Pty.) Ltd., 24 Sturdee Avenue,
Rosebank, Johannesburg 2196, South Africa

Penguin Books Ltd., Registered Offices:
80 Strand, London WC2R 0RL, England

First published by Signet Eclipse, an imprint of New American Library,
a division of Penguin Group (USA) Inc.

First Printing, March 2005
10 9 8 7 6 5 4 3 2 1

Playing for Keeps copyright © Cherry Wilkinson, 2005
Nothing to Lose copyright © Jill Shalvis, 2005
Dare to Desire copyright © Julie Leto Klapka, 2005
All rights reserved

SIGNET ECLIPSE and logo are trademarks of Penguin Group (USA) Inc.

Printed in the United States of America

PUBLISHER'S NOTE
These are works of fiction. Names, characters, places, and incidents either
are the product of the authors' imagination or are used fictitiously, and any
resemblance to actual persons, living or dead, business establishments,
events, or locales is entirely coincidental.

Contents

Playing for Keeps

• • •

CHERRY ADAIR

To Rachel Kizer,
my favorite .5

You go above and beyond,
and I love you for it.

Mahalo.

Chapter 1

Danica Cross wheeled the drinks cart down the narrow aisle, heading back to the galley. The cabin of the 737 was hotter than usual, and she blew her bangs off her clammy forehead as she walked. While handing out drinks with plenty of ice, she assured the passengers that the problem with the heat would soon be resolved.

She'd reported the passengers' complaints to the captain an hour ago, but she couldn't feel a noticeable decrease in the temperature at all and tempers were rising with the heat.

She wasn't usually fanciful—and God only knew Captain Marks was an ass, but she doubted he'd leave the temperature this high intentionally. Danica hated to even think it, but something was wrong. She'd had this vague niggle of disquiet since Flight

723 had taken off from South America two hours ago, and the sensation had only become stronger.

With relief she pushed the drinks cart into the small galley and locked it in place, then tugged her white uniform shirt away from her damp skin at the small of her back.

"Did you give Monster Kid his ninety-ninth apple juice?" Angie Hotchner asked, handing Danica a cold soda.

While the more experienced flight attendant looked as hot as Danica felt, she didn't appear concerned. Danica tried to ignore the butterflies doing takeoffs and landings in her tummy. Forcing a smile, she accepted the drink, rubbing the icy can over her forehead. "Shh, someone will hear you." Popping the tab, she rested her butt on the cabinet behind her as she drank.

"Oh, like they couldn't hear the kid whining for the past ten thousand miles?" Angie jerked her head toward the cabin. "Have you ever seen anyone kiss up to a seven-year-old like that?"

"This heat's getting to everyone." All 148 seats were occupied by sweating members of President Palacios's staff. And one of those passengers was his very bored, very spoiled son. It had been a long, *long* flight from San Cristóbal to Miami with an all male, all-demanding, all-women-are-servants contingent of passengers. The heat, coupled with the loud de-

mands of a cranky, whiny child, didn't help anyone's disposition.

Dani, Angie and the first officer, Jean Harris, were
the only females on board. Lucky them. The crew
had been offered a hefty bonus to do the round-trip
from Miami to South America and back in one day.
Danica had her eye on a nice little condo in Delray
Beach. Thoughts of that bonus had kept her moving,
and biting her tongue, as she'd worked her way
through the cabin.

"He's President Palacios's only son," she finally
answered after gulping the rest of the soda and savoring the icy burn down her dry throat. "Guess the
little guy's used to getting what he wants."

"Yeah?" Angie took a lipstick out of her pocket
and uncapped it. "If he were *my* kid I'd blister his
arrogant little butt so bad he wouldn't be able to sit
down for a wee— Jay-sus! Is it menopause, or is it
getting hotter in here?"

Danica tossed her empty can in the trash with
studied nonchalance. "Everyone's still complaining.
I'll go speak to the captain again."

"May the Force be with you."

Danica grinned as she pushed through the curtain
and turned to the secure door into the cockpit. She
pressed the buzzer, then stood there with the sensation of every dark eye from the cabin checking out
her butt. *Should've grabbed a diet soda.* "Come on, you

7

guys, open up," Danica mumbled under her breath, glancing through the portal in the exit door at the blur of murky browns and faded greens thirty thousand feet below. They were already flying over the Everglades. She'd be home in just over an hour. A dip in the apartment pool sounded heavenly.

She jabbed the buzzer again.

Jon, her soon-to-be-ex, was a white-knuckle flier. Perhaps in some perverse way that was why Danica had become a flight attendant a year ago when she'd seen the writing on the wall. So much for soul mates.

"Open up, Jean," Danica muttered under her breath, frowning at the closed and locked door to the cockpit.

Dean Marks was an arrogant, womanizing jerk. And if the copilot had been any woman other than Jean, Danica would have been convinced they were boinking in the cockpit—which Marks had almost been caught doing on a flight to Singapore last year. But since Jean was a happily married grandmother of five, he wouldn't get to first base. Okay. So no mile-high club in the cockpit. Why weren't they opening the friggin' door? Bile churned in Dani's stomach.

Glancing down at the small gold watch on her wrist while she waited, she sighed. Still another twenty-two minutes and thirty seconds to go on this flight from hell. She pressed the buzzer again with a little more force than necessary. *The bonus, remember the bonus . . .*

The door between the cockpit and the main cabin didn't open, and Danica felt a spurt of something elemental in the pit of her stomach. Instinctively she knew the door wasn't *going* to open. It wasn't her imagination. Something was wrong. She pasted a reassuring smile on her face for the passengers and hotfooted it back to Angie in the galley.

"Ange, someth—"

"We're going to crash." Angie said it so flatly, so calmly, it took Danica a second to compute the words that she herself had been thinking. She strode over and touched her friend's shoulder. A small *pop* was immediately followed by the sensation of the floor shimmying under their feet. Both women grabbed the countertop to keep their balance. Their eyes met.

In the cabin, the passengers shouted in alarm. The president's son started shrieking in terror.

A terrible calm came over Dani. Her weird way of reacting to trauma. The back of her neck tingled—a sure sign of impending doom. She'd had it the night Jon had staggered into their house bleeding like a sieve a year and eight days ago.

She'd had it the day she told Jon she wanted a divorce.

"No, we are *not* crashing," she told Angie with more confidence than she felt. The more her friend panicked, the calmer Danica became. It was a gift. "Just turbulence." Wind shears were a bitch to fly through, requiring skill and attention from the cockpit crew. Which explained why the pilots hadn't responded and why—she swallowed as her stomach rushed to her throat—the plane suddenly lost about five thousand feet of altitude.

"Come on. Let's go and strap in the inmates." Just because there wasn't a cloud in the sky didn't mean the thermals weren't surging against the body of the aircraft. "Angie. Come on."

"It's a faulty rudder system," Angie said, barely moving her lips. She'd flown for Transair for thirty years. She could probably fly the aircraft herself. She grabbed Dani's arm in a white-knuckled grip. "I'm the one who's been stealing your M&M's. And I told Gracie how much you paid for those—"

Another popping sound—not nearly as happy as that of a champagne cork being released—rang through the cabin, this one louder and more ominous than the last. Dani's feet slid on the carpet as the nose of the craft dipped. Call-button lights flashed on the panel on the bulkhead above the jump seats. Off. On. Off. On. Flicker . . . Shit. "We've got to go out there and calm the passengers, Ange. *Now*. Come on."

Danica tore through the drape and into the cabin, where pandemonium reigned. Half the passengers were out of their seats. All of them were yelling, screaming like girls, or crying. Ha! Where was all that superior machismo now?

She unhooked the PA mic and spoke calmly and

quietly until the hysteria subsided a little and they could hear her. She listened to her own voice, amazed at how cool and calm she sounded when she knew, absolutely, unequivocally *knew*, they were all about to die.

"Gentlemen, please. There's no need to panic. Everyone, take your seat." She motioned them to sit down. "All seats must be in their upright positions with tray tables up and locked. Please keep your seat belts firmly fastened. We're just experiencing a little air turbulence. Captain Marks assures us there is no danger."

And while she was asking herself rhetorical questions: where were Kent and Cisco, the other two flight attendants? She glanced back to check on her friend. Angie, white-faced but professional, was helping to calm the passengers.

Holding on to seat backs to remain on her feet, Danica pulled herself row by row against the downward pitch of the aircraft, toward the back of the plane.

"Please remain calm and stay seated." She shouted without benefit of the mic. No one was listening. "The plane will level off shortly." By which time it would be too late for anyone to care. *Damn it. I'm too young to die.*

As urgent as her need to check on the aft attendants was, the passengers had to come first. She checked seat belts and stowed tray tables as she went along the narrow aisle, all the while maintaining what she hoped was a serene smile.

The pain-in-the-ass kid, spiffed up in his too adult black suit to meet his new stepmother in Miami, huddled in his aisle seat, his face white, black eyes wide and terrified. Danica crouched in the aisle beside him and took his sweaty, sticky little hand between both of hers. "It's going to be all right, little one," she told the boy in Spanish.

He flung his arms around her neck in a stranglehold, then burst into hysterical tears as the nose of the plane dipped farther, rocking Danica back. She grabbed his seat arm with a white-knuckled fist, supporting him with her other arm.

"It's okay. It's okay. It's okay," she lied in English and then Spanish to both of them. Neither she nor the boy believed it for a second. Instead of staying in his seat, he snapped the buckle open and practically climbed her torso, as if shimmying up a tree.

"No." She tried to lift him back into his seat, but he was like a little monkey, wrapping himself around her as if attached with Velcro.

An incredibly loud *BOOM* reverberated through the cabin. The plane bucked and bounced, then did the aeronautic equivalent of the hula. Lights went out, plunging the cabin into daylight gloom. The overheads popped open, spewing coats, luggage and papers about the cabin like mobile flotsam.

Oh, shit, shit, shit. Hello? Anybody? Need a little divine intervention here.

She and the boy rolled like tossed dice beneath and around the seats, and the plane seemed to go end over end, tossing humans and baggage around like a salad. She buried the little boy's face against her chest, locking her arms around him as tightly as she could while they rolled back and forth in the aisle like a yo-yo in the hands of God.

She tried to protect him from projectiles, even though she knew that when they hit that ground, thirty thousand feet below, there'd be nothing left of any of them.

Her last cognizant thought before sheer terror overcame her was that she'd lied that night her husband had come home to bleed on her new peach carpet.

She'd *never* stopped loving Jon Raven.

Chapter 2

"What the *hell* do you mean, she's *gone*?" Jon Raven demanded, intentionally looming over the doctor, who was all of five feet six inches tall in his lifts. "The FAA hasn't been in to talk to her. Hell. Forget the FAA—the NTSB hasn't even finished cordoning off the site yet. So I repeat, *where* is Danica Raven?"

Dr. Delmonico took a step back. Not backing down, Raven noted, probably just getting downwind. He knew he stunk like week-old garbage. Hell, even *he* didn't want to be near him. He didn't care. Not now. Not until he saw Danica with his own eyes.

He'd gotten the call while he was on surveillance in D.C. A few strings had pulled him a flight into Miami and the use of a chopper on arrival. It was the longest flight of his life. The helicopter had rushed him directly to the crash site. No time for

15

showers. Hell, no time to even wash the grit from his eyes.

The 737 had looked like a kid's discarded toy tossed into the trees.

Jon Raven had puked. The big, bad, obscenely expensive private security consultant had puked his guts out at the scene of the crash. Only after hearing his wife had walked out, then been rushed to Mercy General in Miami, had he managed to get his shit together and fly back to the city.

"Miss Cross was released early this morning, Mr. Raven. I'm sorry I—"

"I get that she was released." Raven took the man's elbow and marched him down the too bright, too sterile corridor and out of sight of three nurses who were pretending not to listen. He had to get a grip here. By some miracle, Danica *hadn't* been among the scattering of body parts gathered up in labeled bags and then laid out in neat rows at the scene.

"She survived a fuc—a damn *plane crash*. She didn't just walk out of here, did she?" God, knowing Dani, yeah, she probably had. When she had a stick up her ass about something, it was impossible to reason with the woman. Under "stubborn" in the dictionary was a life-sized picture of the woman he'd married. The woman who thought she was divorcing him.

The doctor gave him a patient look. The guy had probably seen it all. "She departed in a wheelchair."

"A wheelchair?" God. He couldn't *think* it. Danica crippled? Worse? Better?

"Patients must always be wheeled out of the building. Hospital policy, you know."

Yeah. He did. Been in enough of them to know what pains in the asses they were about regulations. "She didn't leave under her own power, I know that much. So? She was accompanied by—?" Raven demanded through his teeth. *A lover? A boyfriend? One of the couple of hundred bottom-feeding, photo-flashing press people outside in the parking lot?*

"I'm not at liberty to sa—"

"Now see this?" Jon whipped out his semiautomatic and jabbed it into the man's rib cage. "My friend here says you *are* at liberty to say. So talk."

The doctor, looking suitably impressed by both the size of Raven's weapon and the clear and present danger of a rank-smelling, long-haired psycho holding said weapon, actually laughed. "Sir. You're standing in the ER of one of the busiest hospitals in the country. The busiest *and* the most dangerous. Half our patients come in here wielding guns and knives. Bigger guns and bigger knives." The doctor's lips twitched. "And many of them smell almost as bad as you do."

Raven shook his head and stuck the weapon back

17

in the shoulder harness under his grease-and-God-only-knew-what-else-stained windbreaker. He'd had to pay seventy-five bucks for the damn thing off a real bum just so he could get near the back door of the restaurant he was staking.

"Look, Doc. Give me a break here, would ya? I haven't slept in seventy-two hours, you've noticed I haven't been close to either soap or water in about that long, and my wife was in a plane crash. Just tell me how she was when she left and who she went *with*."

Where are you, Dani? Where the hell are you?

"Miss Cross and a child were the only two survivors of the accident—are you all right, sir? Do you need a chair?"

Hell, no, he wasn't all right. Reality slammed into his gut with the force of a pile driver. Raven braced a hand on the wall and drew in a ragged breath.

He'd nearly lost her. This time for good. Forever. Kaput. Finito. No do-overs.

"But you said she was released. She couldn't be hurt bad." He looked up at the doctor and ground out the question. "Is she hurt bad?"

"No, sir. Other than a mildly sprained wrist and severe insect bites, both Miss Cross and the boy are, miraculously, fine. The child had a broken ankle. Miss Cross carried him to safety."

Raven thought for a sec there that he was going to pass out with relief. *A sprained wrist? Only Dani.* The woman walked under a magic umbrella. The only screwup she'd ever made in her life was marrying him. And she'd rectified that mistake PDQ, or was about to.

T minus 1day:13hours:01minute:08seconds

The last, the very last thing Danica had wanted was to get back on a plane. Fortunately, she'd been doped to the gills with some *very* good stuff. When they carried her on board, she immediately fell into a dreamless sleep. She finally woke to find herself in an opulent bedroom, with a woman in a nurse's uniform sitting beside the bed.

She blinked, but didn't bother moving. She could feel every muscle and joint in her body protesting the exertion of her eyelashes moving upward. "Where—" she croaked.

The woman immediately jumped up and brought her a glass of water and a straw. "You are in San Cristóbal, Miss Cross."

Danica frowned as she took small sips of the cool water. The last thing she remembered was some man in a suit looming over the gurney in the ER. She'd thought he was Raven, and she'd been so happy, so stupidly relieved to see him—and then . . .

"San Cristóbal? What am I doing back here?" Had the crash been a dream? How weird. She'd always thought Raven would die in the line of duty. How ironic if she'd died first instead. In a plane crash. The thing *he* feared most. Nice knowing fate had a sense of humor.

19

The brain fog lifted, and numerous aches and pains made themselves felt all over her body as she remembered. The terrifying fall from the sky. The little boy in her arms. The hideous screams and groans of the people and the shriek of metal being torn asunder. No dream. All too real.

Mostly Danica remembered the vile smell of jet fuel and the sudden realization that she wasn't dead. Yes, that was what she remembered most.

Being *alive*.

And very, very itchy. The mosquitoes in the Everglades had been the size of hummingbirds. Vampire hummingbirds. Her arm itched so badly she just had to move to scratch. It was an effort, but she managed to connect nails with . . . *eeew*! Her skin was slathered with some disgusting sticky gunk. If it was itch medicine, it was a sad disappointment.

Had she asked the woman what she was doing back in San Cristóbal when she'd only left there— how long ago? Frowning gave her a headache, and she drifted back to sleep without having a good scratch *or* getting any answers.

They had Danica sequestered on President Palacios's estate. A lush, fifty-acre parklike setting on the outskirts of San Cristóbal. It had taken Raven five hours to get past the phalanx of security at the gate, and that was only with U.S. intervention because

he'd called in a few chits to keep from killing someone to gain entrance.

Five hours, only to end up pacing this overblown,
frigging chichi sitting room on the ground floor for
almost an hour before a tall, gaunt man in a well-
fitting black suit entered. The guy was flanked by six
armed guards in starched navy blue uniforms.

Raven didn't give a flying fuck who this guy was
or how many gun-toting toy soldiers he had in his
wake. With each minute he'd been forced to wait
his temper had climbed. If *somebody* didn't produce
Danica real soon things were going to get ugly.

The doctor in Miami had bartered Danica's X-rays
in exchange for a shower and a change of clothing.
Raven might smell better than he'd done all those
hours ago, but his temper was now riding an all-time
high. "I want to see my wife. *Now*," Raven said flatly,
turning fully from his position at the window overlook-
ing the circular driveway and a fountain grand enough
for an Italian piazza and tacky enough for Las Vegas.

"Your wife is in excellent hands, Mr. Raven."
Rather than sit on one of the ugly-ass, shiny, cat-pee-
yellow sofas, the man changed direction and strode
forward, all military bearing and officious pomp,
fake smile in place. "Good day. I am Edgardo
Villalba-Vera, chief of security for El Presidente. How
may I be of help?"

"You weren't listening, pal. Unless you want me

to tear this damn place apart, take me to my wife. Pronto."

"I understand that you're very upset—"

"Man, I'm way past upset and smack-dab in the middle of *homicidal*. My wife. *Now*."

"*El médico* is with her at the moment. Her nurse will alert me when he has departed. I will then have you escorted to her suite."

Raven wasn't waiting one more minute. His need to see Dani—to touch her, to check and be sure she was whole and healthy—had become his driving force in the last twelve hours. "The FAA and the NTSB are looking for her," he told the a-hole tightly. "The authorities investigating the accident want to talk to her."

"She shall be made available as soon as she is well enough to have visitors."

Raven narrowed his eyes. "Oh, yeah? And just who is it who'll be deciding when Dani's 'well enough'?"

"Mr. Raven, I assure you . . ."

"No. I assure *you*. The Federal Aviation Administration and the National Transportation Safety Board don't consider themselves visitors, *Ed*."

Thin lips pinched, and something snapped to life in his dark eyes. "They do not have jurisdiction in San Cristóbal, señor."

"Danica is an American citizen, so *she's* their jurisdiction—and she sure as hell is *mine*. And while we're at this private little get-to-know-you chat, what is she doing here, and by whose authority was she removed from the hospital in Miami?"

The man puffed himself up as importantly as he could before saying officiously, "Miss Cross saved El Presidente's only son, Rigo. He, accompanied by his father's most trusted security staff and many advisors, was on the Transair flight to Miami. All but your wife and El Presidente's precious only son were killed in the unfortunate accident last night. When I heard of the interest of your American press regarding the survivors of the crash, I took it upon myself to mobilize my staff and have both Miss Cross and Rigo returned immediately to the palace, where they would be under my protection."

"Yeah, well, I'll feel better when my wife is under *my* protection and in the hospital under a doctor's care."

"She is, señor," Villalba-Vera tried to placate him. "El Presidente's private physician is attending her as we speak. She is receiving the best of care, I assure you."

"Yeah? Well, I'd like to see that for myself. Let's go, pal." Raven stalked to the monstrous double doors, easily two stories high, and out into the marble vestibule beyond. He turned to look at the guy, who was walking swiftly to catch up. "Which way?" Damn place was probably fifty thousand square feet.

"If you would but wait a m—"

But Raven wasn't waiting. He was tired of waiting. Hell, he'd been *waiting* for Danica for *years* in one way or another. He'd reached his saturation point. He charged across the ridiculously ornate entry hall blocking out the guy in mid bullshit.

"Hell with it." He took the red carpeted marble stairs two at a time, yelling at the top of his voice: "Danica? Where the hell are you? Dani, Goddamn it, answer me!"

Chapter 3

T minus 1day:12hours:48minutes:20seconds

Raven must've tried twenty doors before slamming open the one to a bedroom with a startled nurse who rose from her seat in alarm as he burst into the room. Ignoring both her wide-eyed fright and the army of soldiers behind him, Raven strode across the plush area rug and approached the bed.

He shut out the babble of voices behind him, his entire focus on the still form in the shadowed bed. Dani's back was to him, her shoulder and hip making barely a bump in the covers. He stood over her, every muscle and tendon, every nerve and cell in his body needing to touch her. Driven to examine her for himself, he stroked a finger gently down her cool cheek when what he needed to do was grab her up, strip her bare and check her over and over again to make sure she was truly one hundred percent okay.

She was asleep, curled on her side as usual, hand under her cheek. She'd wake up in the morning that way, sleeping on her left side. He'd slept on his right. In their three years of marriage, she'd been the last thing Raven had seen each night and his first image of the new day. A great life, he remembered. How had something so right gone so damned wrong? His chest squeezed tight as he sat beside her hip on the wide, king-sized bed and touched his palm to her silken shoulder.

Memories flooded him. They would wake up staring into each other's eyes. Then kiss lazily, then make love. Slowly, as they both surfaced into full awareness. It had been a helluva great way to start the day.

He missed her. Had missed her even before that last, final good-bye.

Her lightly tanned skin was covered with pink insect bites and shiny with some sort of salve. *Ah, sweetheart.* Not only had she survived a crashed plane in the Everglades, but survived dinosaur bug bites too. And while he sat there, staring at her beautiful face, he asked himself, what the hell happened to us? How could something so damn good turn to shit?

He slid the skinny lace strap of an unfamiliar white nightgown up her arm to her shoulder, fingers skimming her cool, satiny skin. "Dani, love," he said softly. "Wake up."

Long, dark lashes fluttered. She didn't open her eyes, but her lips curved in a small smile. "Jon." A whisper. A gift. Raven wanted to fall to his knees and bury his face in her silky black Cleopatra hair, to smell the familiar gardenia fragrance of her skin. Damn it. He needed her to open those baby blues and give him hell.

He needed all the chattering people bunched up behind him out of the damn room.

"Open your eyes, sweetheart," he said softly, brushing a wayward strand of hair from her cheek with fingers that shook. "I'm here to take you home."

Danica moaned softly, but didn't so much as stir. The small sound and unnatural stillness sent an unexpected chill up Raven's spine. If he'd been a dog, his hackles would've risen, his ears would be laid back, and he'd be growling low and deep in his throat.

He frowned. Something was way out of whack here. "Danica," he said briskly, giving her butt a shake. "Wake up. *Now.*"

Five seconds response time. *Nada.* Keeping a possessive hand on her hip, he turned to the nurse hovering on the other side of the bed. Danica had always slept hard—but not *this* hard. "What," he asked the woman with lethal softness, "did you give her?"

The woman glanced toward the door. Translation from good old Ed, or permission to tell him—*what*?

"Save time." Raven said in fluent Spanish to Villalba-Vera. "Drug and dosage. *Now.*" Moving his hand down the slope of her hip, he felt for Danica's

27

bruised wrist, then rested two fingers lightly on her pulse. Slow. *Too slow*. And a breath shy of an even rhythm for a natural state of sleep.

"Nothing, señor," Mr. Chief of Security in his six-hundred-dollar suit said in barely accented English as he cautiously approached the bed, shaking his head of thick black razor-cut hair. "She sleeps a healing sleep, according to the specialist El Presidente brought specially to tend to her."

"Nothing, huh? Call the *el doctoro* back. I wanna talk to him myself. Better yet, I want my own doctor to take a look at her. Someone of my choosing."

"But of course." Edgardo Villalba-Vera inclined his head just enough to let his hair fall forward and then shift back neatly into place when he straightened. Conceited dick. "Anytime you like."

The guy was blowing smoke up his ass. It had taken Raven hours to get past the security at the gate, and he could normally talk a mink out of her coat. "Get that doctor back here. Now. And while you're at it—my bag's in the rental out there. Get someone to bring it up while I'm waiting."

Black brows rose. "Pardon me?"

"My bag. In the rental car. I'll be staying with my wife until we leave." And not letting her out of his sight for one second. Raven's bullshit antenna was up. Way up. This situation was all wrong. For whatever reason, these people were lying. They had drugged Dani. After he found out *what*, he wanted to know *why*.

Villalba-Vera shot a brief, speaking glance at him, hesitated a moment, then nodded to one of his men. "You are of course most welcome. I shall have a room prepare—"

"I'll be sleeping right here beside my wife." *Where I belong*, he added silently. Of course, when Danica woke up to find him back in her bed she might have a thing or two to say about it, but until then he was staying put. "Right now I'd like some private time with her. You can take Nurse Ratched with you. Knock when the doctor gets back."

The minute the room was cleared, Raven stood, stripped off his jacket and sat back down on the bed at Dani's hip. "I'm here, sweetheart. Open those eyes and tell me how you feel."

Her lashes fluttered. "Me—"

Frowning, he bent closer. "What, honey?"

"dica—"

Ah, hell, what was she trying to tell him?

"t-ed."

Me-dica-ted?

"*Medicated*? They're keeping you doped up?"

"Mmm . . ."

"Damn it to hell." Scooping her up in his arms, he carried her to a nearby chair, then sat down, cradling his wife on his lap. Had she always felt this light?

This insubstantial? Her head flopped to his chest. "Stay with me, honey. Just stay with me. I'm here and I'm not leaving your side. Ever again."

She moaned and her lashes fluttered, showing a glimpse of her pretty blue eyes. *Yeah, thought that would get your attention.* "Rise and shine so you can tell me to go to hell. Followed by clueing me in on what the hell's going on around here."

She tried. He could see the struggle to swim through the drug-induced fog. Raven stroked her cheek, then gave it a few sharp taps with his fingertips. Really hated to do it, but damn it, she had to wake up long enough to give him a hint—*something*—so he could help her.

Her lashes fluttered, lifted a little, then fluttered some more as she struggled valiantly to open her eyes.

"You're doing it. Keep going." While she swam up to him, Raven slid his hand down her arm, turning her cool skin up so he could check for needle marks. Nothing on the left arm, other than dozens of bug bites. He checked the right. Same deal. Of course there were other, less conspicuous places they could've— He felt sick to his stomach. They were in South America—hell, they could've pumped her full of anything. . . . The question was, were the drugs something she actually *required*? Was she more badly injured than he'd been led to believe? Or had she been given some sort of illegal crap because—why?

Because *why*, damn it? Didn't make sense. None of this made any kind of sense.

"P-p—"

"Pills?"

"Mmm. Sleep . . ."

Pills. Keeping her sedated. Again—why?

Her head nestled against his chest, silky black hair brushing his chin. The smell of her stirred his senses despite his concerns. Essence of Dani. The most powerful aphrodisiac in the world.

Having her nestled against him like this felt so familiar, so right, so much a part of him. He held her tighter, folding her limp, pliant body into his. She'd saved the son of the president of this godforsaken country. Since when did that buy a Good Samaritan a body full of controlled substances? His mind raced, poised between fury and gratitude at finding her alive. Finally gratitude won out. God, how had he lived without her for the last year? His arms tightened around her limp body. How would he ever have survived if she'd been one of the casualties in that swamp?

Surely God wouldn't save her life only to let them remain apart.

Standing, he carried her back to the wide bed with its fancy, orangey sheets. "Don't worry. I'll get you out of here, sweetheart. Then I'm coming back to find out what these bastards are up to."

He got her settled, checked her pulse again,

checked her pupils—slightly dilated—and pulled the sheet over her shoulders. She immediately rolled back onto her left side, then started snoring softly. He bit back a smile. *That's my girl.*

Raven acknowledged that there was a possibility she'd *needed* sedation when she'd arrived. He acknowledged that he always had a knee-jerk reaction where Danica was concerned. He acknowledged that maybe he was overreacting.

Except that his gut—usually infallible—was telling him this was all a crock. *The accident. The kidnapping. The drug-induced sleep.* Something was out of whack here. Way out of whack.

No one was getting within ten feet of Danica. No one.

He checked her pulse again. Steady. Then he got down to business. Did a visual search for cameras first, since if they were there, someone was watching him right now. He searched the room and adjoining bathroom thoroughly. Nothing. He checked for bugs, listening devices, any sort of recording equipment. Nothing he could detect. Didn't mean they weren't there, however.

He picked up the girlie gold-and-white phone beside the bed. Hit zero. "Buenas tardes, Señor Raven," a polite female voice answered. "How may I be of assistance to you?"

"When will the doctor be here?"

There was a pause. "I do not know this, señor. I will inquire for you."

"You do that. Have someone check to see what's keeping my bag and send up a large pot of black coffee. Make that a *couple* of pots. And a pile of sandwiches. Thanks."

"Certainly, señor. Right away."

It would be a really nice bonus if his weapons remained in the specially designed compartment of his carry-on. But that wasn't going to be the case. Nope, not a prayer. If they were keeping their little heroine drugged into stupidity, they were smart enough to pick over his bags like vultures on roadkill. He hadn't had any trouble getting them onto the plane—even in this day and age, state-of-the-art lead beat antiquated X-ray machines every time. He'd arrived armed to the teeth—but here in San Shitabol, he'd be lucky if the little guy with the pretty hair left him his toothbrush.

"Know what my gut tells me, sweetheart?" Raven whispered as he paced the room, searching—*again*. "It tells me that before this is over I'm gonna need a fistful of weapons and a shitload of ammo."

Chapter 4

T minus 1day:9hours:14minutes:02seconds

"No more," Danica protested, as Jon tried to force her to drink yet another cup of far-too-strong Colombian coffee. The stuff not only looked nasty, it was thick as syrup, tasted vile as sin, and was strong enough to grow hair on her chest.

"Last one." He stood over her, cup poised at her lips. "Promise."

"Which means there's another gallon," Danica said tiredly, *rubbing*, not scratching, a bite behind her ear. There wasn't a muscle, a bone, a joint, or a cell in her body that didn't hurt or itch. "Hello? Tea drinker, remember?"

Of course he didn't. Jon Raven had always been one hundred percent focused on what Jon Raven wanted to the exclusion of all else. Oh, she'd always believed he cared about her in his self-possessed, it's-all-about-me way. Jon was around when *he* wanted to be. When *he* wasn't working. When *his* schedule permitted. She'd always felt as if she was little more than a footnote in his life.

Well, she'd wanted more than the few crumbs he tossed her way when it suited him. Not that Jon's crumb tossing had been anything to sneer at. Five minutes of his undivided attention equaled a year with any lesser man.

And that was the problem.

It thrilled her and annoyed her in like amounts. When he made time for her—for them—it was nothing short of spectacular. Especially in bed. In bed they'd been—Danica dragged her already soggy brain away from *that* minefield. Sex had never been a problem with them.

Everything else. But never sex.

He took her hand, wrapping her fingers around the cup, pushing it inexorably toward her mouth. His dark hair had grown since she'd seen him last—twelve months, one week, three days ago—and now brushed his collar. His eyes, blue as Mediterranean waters, looked bruised and intense. And his mouth—God, his mouth. The mouth that used to take her to places of intense delight was now narrowed with poorly veiled—what? Anger? Annoyance?

Fear?

No way. Jon Raven wasn't afraid of anything.

"Buck up and drink," he said tightly. Using a finger, he tilted the cup to her mouth. "These bastards have been *drugging* you. You have to wake up and get with the program."

Because he wasn't giving her multiple choices, and because she knew the caffeine would clear her brain, Danica chugged the coffee like bad medicine—worse now that it was lukewarm—and thrust the cup back at him. Making sure this time to avoid any skin contact. "I understand the principle. Stop bullying me."

"I'm not bullying you, I'm *saving* you."

"Well, don't save me so loudly, okay?"

She felt at a distinct disadvantage as he loomed above her. Still a tad foggy on the details, she knew he'd dragged her up, somehow positioning her against a mound of pillows before force-feeding her the coffee. Looking down, she realized the sheet was bunched in her lap, leaving the entirety of her torso revealed, clad in a rather flimsy nightie she didn't recognize at all. White was too blah for her taste, but that wasn't her major objection.

Jon's repositioning of her body had pulled the thin silk taut so it now strained against her like a second skin. As armor the nightie was useless. The lacy cups, meant to conceal her breasts—sort of—were low enough that the areola of each nipple showed. A fact made crystal clear as she felt his gaze drop to admire the view.

Not even attempting to be subtle, she pulled at the stretchy lace so it at least covered her nipples. She would have yanked the sheet up too, but he was sitting on it. Danica hated that despite suffering the trauma of a plane crash and being drugged for God knew how long, Jon don't-you-dare-smile-at-me-that-way Raven had only to look at her to inspire that sudden rush of need inside her. He was warm and solid, and smelled of Lever 2000 soap, a heady, aphrodisiacal fragrance that reminded Danica of long steamy showers and hot sex.

Sadly, she knew that when she was ninety, in a wheelchair and half blind, a mere flash of his attention would still have the same effect on her.

He glanced, she melted. Nothing changed.

But she could cover up. She had to if she wanted to protect her dignity. Not physical dignity—she liked her body just fine. Emotional dignity. She didn't want Jon to see that even in her weakened state she still responded to him in the same old way.

Nerve endings sat up and begged for attention.

Melty parts melted.

Rational thought took a vacation.

Damn him.

Body parts shrieked as Danica moved, and she couldn't help a moan of pain. He reacted as if she'd screamed at the top of her voice. Gentle hands shot out to grip her shoulders as he searched her face with eyes that glowed like the hot coals of hell. "Where does it hurt?"

Everywhere. But body aches were overshadowed—
in spades—by the ache in her heart caused by seeing
him again. She realized that she'd been a whole hell
of a lot more immune when he wasn't in the same
geographical area as she was.

Clenching her teeth, Danica put up a hand in a
wait-a-second motion. "I'm okay." Of course she was
okay. Pain meant she was *alive.* She gritted her teeth
and tried to push herself higher on the pillows. "A
few muscle relaxants aren't *druggi—Hey!* What are
y—" He slid his palms under her arms to help her
sit up straighter, then held her carefully by bracing
a hard, muscled arm across her chest as he leaned
her forward, readjusting the pillows behind her back.

She closed her eyes, trying not to breathe in the
achingly familiar scent of him. They were close
enough for her to feel the warmth of his body, close
enough for his breath to wash over her upturned
face. She felt the memory imprint of his fingers skimming the sides of her breasts. Her nipples grew
tighter and harder. She fought it for all she was
worth. *No. No. No.*

Jon lifted his head. With just scant inches between
them, his eyes held hers. And asked a question.

Yes. God, yes. "Forget it," she told him flatly.

He straightened, his mouth curved slightly in a
slappably smug smile. He, better than anyone, knew
her body. Frequently better than she did herself. He

39

knew how his touch affected her. Knew that breathing against her ear would force a groan from her lips. Knew how, when, and why her breath caught.

He indicated the pillows behind her. "Comfortable?"

"With the pillows? Yes. With you looming over me? No. Mind giving me some room to breathe here?" She kept both her gaze and tone steady.

He rose, hands up in surrender—*as if!*—and took an elaborate step back. "Good enough?"

"D.C. would be better." *Right here in my bed would be best.* She gave herself Brownie points for sticking to her promise to herself. No physical contact with him again. *Ever.* It was a life sentence. But for self-preservation she had to stick to it.

"You've been dealing with the wrong kind of people too long," she told him. "The pills were to help me sleep so I can heal. I might not have broken anything, but every muscle and tendon was traumatized by the—the—" *Spiraling out of control, heart stopping—* "crash." Her stomach lurched as her memory filled in the sounds of screaming, the hideous rending noise as the body of the craft ripped and twisted in the air like tinfoil. The stench of jet fuel—*the screams.*

"Yeah?" Her ex looked furious as he raked his fingers through his too long dark hair and stalked around the room like a caged panther. "Well, *my* every muscle and tendon was traumatized when I heard about the crash as well. And until I get you back Stateside, have you seen by every conceivable specialist, I'm going to make damn sure you don't get near anything that's going to hurt you."

"Yeah? Guess *you'd* better leave then, huh?" She didn't say it with as much heat as usual. Despite her every mental protest, she was overwhelmingly happy to have him here in South America with her. Besides—she *wanted* to go home. Even if it meant being escorted by her surly almost ex. "News flash, buddy," she added, working up a bit more heat. "This is about me. Not about you."

"No shit it's about you, Dani." He shoved both hands through his hair again, stalked to the window on the far wall, then spun around and came back again. "I heard about the crash, and all I could think about was finding you."

She refused to be moved. Refused to be touched. "You found me. I'm alive."

"Yeah, and you're gonna stay that way. So get used to me. Until I've got you home and medically cleared, I'm your goddamn shadow."

She'd take his help. She'd even take his concern, because she knew that once life was back to normal, Jon would fade away again. Disappear back into his life on the edge. And she'd go back to her life alone. But at least this time she *had* a life to go back to.

Her chest ached with unshed tears. All those people—why had *they* been dealt the death card, and she and Rigo hadn't? And here was Jon. Big and strong. Solid and familiar. She needed, *craved*, the feel of his arms around her. Needed to hear the steady beat of his heart. Needed to feel alive.

But as she knew only too well, it was good to want things. But that didn't mean the things she wanted were *good* for her. Before her stood six feet three inches of sexually charged male to prove it.

Waking up to find herself not only in a strange bed but in a strange *country* had been discombobulating enough. Waking to find her ex-husband standing over her, with an unreadable expression on his handsome face that she had never seen before, had almost finished off what the accident hadn't.

While he'd force-fed her coffee to get rid of her mental fog he'd told her how he'd heard about the accident and flown directly from D.C. to Miami and then chartered a plane to come to San Cristóbal. Most of his words had drifted inside her like smoke on a hazy day. All Danica cared about was that she'd needed him. And, for once, he was there.

Jon Raven was her drug. And she'd been addicted to him from the moment they met.

Going off him cold turkey—the move from D.C. to Florida—had resulted in nothing more than severe withdrawal pain. Seeing him again, without the buffer of a conference table and two suited lawyers, brought the clawing desire to the forefront. When she was near this man, every sensible preservation instinct flew out the window.

So—she'd let him escort her home. Politely thank him. *Not touch him*. And say good-bye. The sooner the better. "Oh, shoot—"

He scowled. "What?"

"They're giving me the keys to the city on Saturday."

"Two days from now?" He gave her an are-you-out-of-your-fucking-mind look. "Forget it! You don't need the keys to *this* city."

She lifted a brow, which would go unnoticed under her bangs. "Hello? Who made you the boss of me? The president wants to honor me for bringing his son home safely. He's already tried offering me more money than I'd see in my lifetime."

She kicked back the covers and swung her feet to the floor, then had to rest a minute as her body protested and the room did a weird dip and sway before settling again. She glanced down at the unfamiliar nightgown someone had put on her. She wondered *who* and shuddered, rubbing the chill from her arms.

"Damn it, Dani, I've got a bad feeling about this."

"Yeah, me too." She swung her hair out of her eyes and looked up at him. "Probably because of the *crash* and all."

He glowered at her.

"Jon." His name came on a sigh. "The president wants to thank me for his son's life. The least I can do is stand there and be thanked."

"Be thanked long distance. I'm telling you, something's not right here. Trust me."

43

Her hair brushed her bare shoulders as she shook her head. The movement made her feel a little woozy. "Oh, that's good, coming from you."

"Fine. Don't trust me. But trust my *instincts*."

She was a little taken aback by his fervor. Jon was a lot of things, but an alarmist wasn't one of them. His instincts had always been good. Who was she to not pay attention now? "I don't have any clothes. I can't very well walk out of here in my borrowed virgin-slut nightie."

His expression softened slightly. "I threw some stuff together for you at the airport. I figured you'd need clothes at some point."

When did Jon—her Jon—take notice of such things? But he wasn't her Jon. Not anymore. "You did?" She stood unsteadily.

"Yeah," he said gruffly, stuffing his fingers into the front pockets of his jeans when she shot him a back-off look. "Doing laps?" he inquired mildly. "Or are you heading for the chair over there?"

"Right now I just need to stand. Right here." She'd wanted to pace off the rest of the lethargy, because Jon was right. She needed to get her brain clear and her stiff and sore muscles working again before she tried boarding another plane.

If she could board another plane. The thought made her press a hand to her midriff. Of course she could, she told herself firmly. Law of averages— She absently straightened the pale peach silk sheets and pulled up the peach-, rust- and cream-colored Egyptian cotton comforter. She smoothed the wrinkles out of a pillowcase, then placed the pillow precisely so back on the bed. Then turned to look at him. Oh, God. What a sight he was. A MIAMI DOLPHINS long-sleeved navy T-shirt, a size too small—which looked perfect on him—hugged his broad shoulders and snugged across his chest and was tucked into new jeans. His hair was too long and wildly disheveled, dark circles smudged his blue eyes, and the sharp planes of his cheekbones were pale under his tan. He looked like hell.

He looked like heaven.

"I can't just leave, Jon. The man is the *president*."

"He's not *your* president. Tell him you're wiped. You need to be home. Hell, tell him *anything*."

Stubbornly, carefully, she shook her head.

"Dani, *think*, for God's sake. These guys took you off American soil, without notifying anyone. They kept me out there for *hours* while they fed you some sort of narcotic—and you want to *stay* here?"

Okay, so that bothered her. She didn't much care for being kidnapped by a grateful parent and then being doped to the gills. But she wasn't about to roll over and let Jon dictate her life just because he'd shown up in the nick of time. If she needed saving, she'd do it herself, thank you very much.

"First," she told him firmly, "whether I want to stay here or not isn't the point. The point is I'm twenty-seven years old. And *single*. I make my *own* decisions. And no, I don't particularly want to stay, but I'm going to anyway because it's the right thing to do. I refused the money, but I can't just blow off the president, Jon. It would be rude. I'll leave *after* the ceremony on Saturday. *You*, however, can hie your bossy self back to D.C. and remember we're divorced."

"*Almost*."

"Almost is good enough for me."

"For God's sake, Danica—"

"Don't *Danica* me. I'm leaving on Saturday and that's that." Unfortunately, the more insistent he became that she leave, the more insistent she would be to *stay*. Perverse. But there you go. Her typical, if not always logical, knee-jerk reaction when Jon pushed was that she shoved back. But the reality was she *wanted* to get the hell out of Dodge. She was scared because *he* was scared.

She had to get over this *reaction* to his *action* cycle if she ever hoped to live peacefully without him. She'd thought she'd mastered that little personality quirk, but apparently not. Of course, her willpower and resolve worked just fine when they were thousands of miles apart.

Annoyed that he was close enough for reinfection when she was still under quarantine, Danica started the million-mile walk to a pair of chairs across the cream-and-rust-colored, inches-thick, big-as-a-football-field area rug. Her legs were shaky. Hell. Her entire body trembled from the tension in her muscles.

"Need help?" he asked, quietly coming up to walk beside her.

Her jaw ached from clenching her teeth. "I want to do this on my own."

"Don't you always?"

She shot him a puzzled glance, noticing the tightness of his jaw and the way his hair brushed his broad shoulders. "No. I enjoyed doing things with you. Whenever you were home. Which wasn't often. I learned pretty damn fast to be independent."

"Dani—"

"I *know*." This was an old argument, and one she really wasn't up to having at the moment. "You were starting the security business and had to baby it to get it off the ground. Wasn't it off the ground when you cleared your first million? How about the second? No? What about the third? How many millions did you need to make to prove you could do it? And do it well? How many damned millions did you need to remember our big fancy house and me there waiting? *Alone*. Ten? A hundred? A billion?"

"You always came first with me."

She snorted. "Yeah. And pigs fly. Even if I believed you, that's small comfort. I walked around a six-thousand-square-foot house decorated by a New York decorator flown in especially to surprise me, and I felt nothing but alone and lonely."

"I thought it was what you wanted."

"I wanted you. And—never mind. That part of our lives is mercifully over." Him. *He* was what she'd wanted. And his babies to love.

Instead, over the three years the houses and the cars had gotten bigger and bigger, and the lonely place in her heart had become an aching cavern that not even spectacular sex could fill.

She finally reached the chair and clutching a fabric-covered arm, lowered herself into it like a little old lady with chronic arthritis.

He sat in the chair beside hers, then stood again and started to pace, his long legs moving with animal grace as he walked off his—what? His mad?

"You're making me dizzier. Can't you sit down for a second?"

"Yeah. Sure." He sat. She'd never known a man with so much energy. Intense. White-hot. Burning. He was always in motion. Always—*doing.*

"Relax," Danica said dryly.

"I am relaxed." He rested his forearms on the silk-covered arms of his chair. His booted foot tapped, his finger drummed on the chair arm, his eyelids moved as he scanned the room. Danica gave a mental sigh. All that lovely energy going to waste.

Stop it, she warned herself. *Just stop thinking about what it would be like— Aw, come on! One more time.* A little devil sat on her shoulder, egging her on. *No fair when I promised myself I'd never— Go on. Double-dare you. Just one quick— Stop!*

All she had to do was move her elbow and they'd touch. She stayed exactly where she was.

As the caffeine finally started working, waking up her groggy brain cells, Danica realized that she'd almost bought into Jon's paranoia. She mentally brushed that little devil off her shoulder and away from her far too attentive ear.

"You know you're overreacting, don't you?" She glanced at him, changing her depth perception a little, so he was slightly out of focus. "Because we have a . . . history. You were afraid for me, and now you're seeing some sort of conspiracy around every corner. I'm sorry you were—" Danica made the mistake of touching his arm. His *bare* forearm because he'd shoved his sleeves up.

A bolt of pure, white heat zinged up through her hand, causing her to instinctively curl her fingers over rock-hard muscle and heated satiny flesh covered with crisp dark hair.

Their eyes met.

And just like that, she knew she was in deep trouble.

Chapter 5

T minus 1day:7hours:53minutes:0seconds

"Don't—" she started to say, her voice, in achingly familiar husky tones, dying away as Raven slid from his chair beside her to kneel between her knees. White, feminine-scented silk pooled around his hips as he pressed in closer between her parted thighs.

He'd held himself in check for hours. Controlled the ache. The panic. The fear. He shook with the last ragged edge of restraint.

Eyes the same baby blue of his first car, and more familiar to him than his own, stared back at him. Shadows filled them, like storm clouds flitting across a summer sky as she sat very still beneath his inspection. He reached up and bracketed her face, his scarred, beat-up hands dark and ridiculously large against her delicate bones and creamy complexion.

His gaze raked her face, automatically registering,

in the space of several erratic heartbeats: a bruise marred the sculpted perfection of her left cheek. A small abrasion scabbed her stubborn chin. Insect bites gave her clear complexion small pink freckles. The sexy fall of glossy black hair, and the way it curved slightly beneath her stubborn chin; the slightly annoyed frown just visible beneath the straight curtain of her bangs.

"Jon . . ."

He closed his eyes. Because as much as he enjoyed sparring with her, right here, right now, he was just overwhelmingly grateful she was alive. "Shh . . ."

She might look as though she was a lightweight. But Raven knew better. His lady had a will of steel and a backbone to match. Danica Raven—he would never think of her as Danica Cross—was a hell of a lot hardier than she looked. He opened his eyes and filled his vision with her. Then, unable to resist, plunged his fingers through the heavy black mass of her mussed hair, tilting her face up to the light. He used both thumbs to caress her high cheekbones.

"I—" He had to clear his throat to push the words out, and tried again. "I died when I heard about the crash, Dani. I. Died. My heart stopped beating when I thought I'd never see your beautiful face again, never get to hold you. Never ever hear you laugh again—"

He closed his eyes, chest tight, throat aching, and pressed his lips to her forehead, savoring the smooth texture of her flushed skin beneath the brush of his lips. He heard the catch of her sobbed breath, then felt the warm brush of her fingertips over his mouth. Breath ragged, heartbeat going haywire, he straightened and opened his eyes, tightening his fingers on her scalp as he drank in her expression. Ah, hell—her lips were parted, her eyes dark with desire. Raven groaned, bringing his arms down around her slender body, holding her tightly against him as he dragged her out of the chair, bringing them both to their feet.

He buried his face in her hair, losing himself in the scent of her. In the warm, living wonder of her. He knew he should loosen his grip so she could at least breathe. But a part of him was afraid that this was just another goddamn dream, that she'd disappear in a puff of smoke. And a blaze of regrets.

He crushed her mouth beneath his, no warm-up, no gradual buildup, spearing his tongue into the warm, coffee-flavored cavern. Not just hungry— *starving* for the taste, the feel, the texture of her. *Dani. Dani. Dani.*

Her arms came up around his neck, pulling him closer. He tasted the salt of tears. An indication of narrow escapes and near misses. Of second chances.

He slanted his mouth over hers and kissed her more deeply, nothing held back. Dani shuddered, standing on tiptoe, drawing him tightly against her body as she kissed him back with everything she had. He wanted her now, more than ever. She

53

wanted him back. That was all he needed to know right now.

Pulling his mouth from hers, dragging in what oxygen he could, he pressed hot kisses along the line of her jaw, his fingers cupping the back of her head as she flattened her breasts against his chest so that he felt their hearts beating in tune. She grabbed hanks of his hair, pulling him back to her mouth, holding on for dear life.

Oxygen intake was highly overrated. He went back in, greedily plunging his tongue into the dark, rich cavern of her mouth. Reveling in the scrape of her teeth, and the pleasure/pain of her nails digging into his scalp, he sucked on her tongue the way she liked it and had the satisfaction of hearing her breath quicken as her nails bit into his neck.

He cupped her breast, sliding his hand beneath the lace to find the hard point of her nipple waiting and eager for his touch. "God, I missed this. Missed *you*." Flames of lust incinerated what was left of Raven's brain. "I want you. I never stopped." He squeezed the hard point of her nipple between his fingers and gloried when her back arched in response.

He needed her naked. *Now*.

He slid his thigh between hers, rocked it higher. Imagined the wet heat he knew was waiting for him, and almost came at her sharp cry of pleasure. *Home*, Danica thought, dizzy with longing. *I'm home.*

Craving the familiar, sensual assault of his mouth

on hers, Danica pressed her aching breast against Jon's hand, against the urgent fingers bringing her such sharp, sweet pleasure. Their tongues played a sweetly familiar game as she rode the hard, muscular thigh pressed between her legs. *More*, damn it. *More. Now.*

She was ready to explode like a supernova and they were still vertical.

And, damn it, he was still fully dressed. She brought a hand down to tug the hem of his T-shirt out of his pants. *Offoffoff.*

Her fingers encountered satin skin. She raked her nails lightly up his side in retribution.

His mouth broke away from hers, leaving them both gasping for air and damp with perspiration. His arms loosened infinitesimally. "I'm hurting you—"

Danica wove her fingers through the long strands of hair brushing his shoulders and brought his mouth back to hers. "Stopping would hurt me more," she whispered before going in for a full assault. The hunger inside her felt almost savage in its intensity. She was no more gentle than he.

She needed him. His strength. His power. His vitality. She needed him to make her whole again, and knowing that, she held nothing back.

His hands skimmed the narrow silken straps from her shoulders, but because her arms were around his neck, he had to use brute force to snap each thin ribbon without lifting his mouth from hers. She moaned into his mouth as he freed her breasts from the stretchy lace with a brush of his calloused hand.

She keened, a low, pleading murmur, when his large warm fingers closed around the globe of her breast. Rubbing the hard pebble of her nipple between his fingers, he devoured her mouth with sexy nips and sensual lavings of his tongue.

Danica's heart pounded like a trip-hammer in her chest as he tore his mouth from hers to swing her up in his arms. His hands gently supported her back and knees as he crossed the room in a few giant strides of impatience.

She heard the hard throb of his heartbeat beneath her ear and laid her splayed fingers over his chest next to her cheek, feeling the unsteady *thump-thump-thump* as his blood flowed through his veins hard and fast.

He knelt, one knee on the bed, lowering her among the pillows, then followed her down. She reached for him, but he shook his head. Catching her wrists with one broad hand, he curved her hands over her head and held them there. "I need to look at you."

"Later." She arched her hips and rubbed herself against the hard ridge straining against the zipper of his pants.

"Cruel woman."

"*Impatient* woman," she assured him thickly. "Do something with those two thousand and one body parts of yours."

He raised a brow. "All of them?" he asked, kissing her palm.

"Get naked and I'll let you know which ones I want."

Jon smiled, a wolfish grin that had her heart doing the tango. "In a minute." His hair fell over one eye as he stared down at her, and Danica pushed the strands back, then let her fingers linger to stroke the hard planes of his face. He needed a shave.

"Now, pal. Right now."

"What happened to patience?" He took a handful of sheer silk and slowly drew the fabric a few inches down her body.

"Over—ah! Overrated." Danica moaned at the sinuous slide of cool fabric against her sensitized skin. "Touch me," she demanded, aching for him.

"In a minute." His eyes, hooded but intense, skimmed down her torso. He touched a finger to a sore place just under her ribs. "Bruise." And bent his head. The satiny strands of pooling hair were cool on her breasts, in contrast to the scrape of his stubbled jaw. He kissed the spot gently, then lifted his head again to tug a few more inches of nightie down her body in a frustratingly slow glide.

Cool silk, followed by his hot hand.

"I need both hands," he told her hoarsely. "So you just keep yours right there."

Danica obeyed, curling her fingers around a pillow as he continued his maddeningly slow reveal.

He kissed the bruises and bug bites all the way down her arched body with lips that made promises. Down the slope of rib to waist, around her navel, over her hipbone, first one, then the other. Danica flexed her fingers in protest, but didn't break the invisible hold he'd put on her. He dragged the fabric down a few more maddening inches.

A rhythmic throbbing pulsed deep inside her as his lips followed his hands. Across the bridge of her collarbone, down the slope of her chest . . . Danica cried out as his mouth, hot, wet, eager, closed around her nipple. She arched up, internal organs tightening unbearably. She was on fire. Burning.

Teeth scraped the overly sensitive bud, and she shuddered, sobbed out his name—a curse, a plea—as her body tightened another notch. "I . . . need . . . you," she managed to gasp as the scalding wetness of his mouth worked its magic. "*Now.*"

"Soon," he promised. The single word came out in a rush of hot breath against her other breast.

Powerfully impatient and wonderfully frustrated, Danica pressed her head back into the soft mound of pillows, hands balled into fists as the need he'd created consumed her. "Jon." His name was an impassioned plea, spilling from her parted lips.

"You're so beautiful." His voice was a husky whisper, more a breath than a sound. He moved up her body to kiss her mouth again. Hard. Hungry. Hers.

Everything about Jon Raven was hard: his body,

his erection, his head. Yep. That was almost as hard as his willpower.

She'd fix that—

As soon as she could move without shattering into a million pieces. "At. Least. Take. Off. Your—shirt."

With barely a pause he yanked it up and over his head, tossing it behind him onto the floor, then bent to run the slick heat of his tongue across her waist to dip into her navel. She curled a leg around the back of his knees and tried to pull him down to her.

The vibration of his chuckle against her tummy sent ribbons of desire shooting through her at the speed of light. Forget keeping her hands restrained. Danica grabbed his shoulders, curling her nails into solid muscle. His skin was hot, blazing hot, damp and smooth.

She was breathing so fast she felt light-headed and giddy. She lost her train of thought as his mouth slid down her belly, shivering. She twisted her hips as he came close to the heart of her. Her body ached and burned. Hot, then hotter, then on fire. His open mouth trailed down her thigh, leaving her shaking and close to desperate. The weasel dog.

"Don't stop—" she begged as he drew the last slithering wisp of fabric off her legs, leaving her bare to his intense gaze.

His eyes glittered as he watched her from his position near her feet. He looked up her body, then he lowered his head and opened his mouth, gently taking her toes into the hot, wet cavern of his mouth and stroking the underside with his tongue.

Sensation shot in a blinding spear from her foot directly to her womb. Her hips arched off the bed as he sucked and nibbled. Her toes literally curled with the sharp/sweet sensation of his open mouth. He knew how to play her body like a violin. No, not a violin. A *Stradivarius*.

"You . . . still have on too many . . . clothes," she said desperately, trying to sit up, trying to stay marginally sane while her body reacted predictably to his ministrations. Feeling as juicy as a ripe peach, she braced her other foot on his shoulder. "Jon—" He tongued each toe, licking, nibbling, sucking until Danica's head thrashed on the mattress and her fingernails bit into her palms. "I want you inside me. *Please*—"

He splayed a broad hand on her stomach to hold her thrashing body still. "All good things come to those—"

"I'm going to kill you."

His eyes crinkled at the corners. "Yeah. But what a way to go." He plucked her foot off the shelf of his shoulder and went to work. But this time, the sneaky bastard slid his hand down her stomach and brushed the apex of her thigh with his thumb. Her entire body vibrated with anticipation. "Jon, please. Make love to me now. I want to feel you inside m—"

She was wet and swollen, ready for the real thing,

but when his thumb stroked her, Danica gave a garbled cry and arched into his hand.

Her body convulsed violently as she came.

He surged up her body, cradling her as his fingers
brought her to a series of small climaxes that rolled
together in a wave so intense, so blinding, that tears
of fulfillment rolled down her temples into her hair.

He held her, stroking her face, her neck, her breasts
as she shuddered in his arms.

Limp, replete, she managed to open heavy-lidded
eyes and bring a hand to his smugly smiling face.
She pinched his lower lip between her fingers, nar-
rowing her eyes in warning—or she thought she did.
She didn't have much sensation anywhere but where
he'd touched her. "Get your clothes off. *Now*."

"Yes, ma'am." He rolled off her body, leaving her
heated flesh to cool a little.

That didn't last long, as she watched him. His torso
was tanned, gleaming with rock-hard muscle and
made more interesting by trails of crisp, dark hair.
Her mouth went dry as he brought his hands to his
waistband and popped the button.

She wanted to lick him everywhere. Kiss and bite
and scratch. She felt wildly out of control.

Always had.

But for some reason, tonight she wasn't afraid that
their passion would consume her. Tonight she felt as
if the Fates had given her a reward for surviving that
horror. Somehow or other, she was owed this night

with the one man she'd ever loved. The one man who meant more to her than life.

In those tense, spiraling moments, when she hung between life and death, it had been Jon's eyes she'd seen. Jon's face she'd ached to touch again. She'd faced death, and her only real regret was losing Jon.

Now, tonight, she had him again.

If only for now.

He struggled to get hold of the tab of his zipper over the bulge of his erection. The silver button sprang free, and he pushed open the V of fabric, then dragged his jeans down his strong runner's legs.

How could she have forgotten the stark male beauty of his body? The breadth and length of him. Every female organ contracted in greed just looking at him. So ready. For her.

He was a prime example of the species. Alpha male at his peak.

Danica lifted her knees, flattening her feet on the bed. He bent to pick up a pillow from the floor, then pushed it beneath her hips, leaving her open to his heated gaze.

"Incredibly beautiful," he said, voice thick, as he stood there looking down at her. "This gorgeous white skin, the pink of your nipples . . ." He brushed a hand that shook slightly over her breasts. "I wish I were an artist. I'd paint you like this. Exotic and naked . . ."

She smiled and lifted her arms to welcome him.

"Come to me. Now. Please. I can't wait another second."

With a groan of intense need, he slid his body over hers. Her hips came off the mattress to greet him, and her hands found and gripped the smooth globes of his bottom as he pushed deep inside her with one thrust of satin over steel. She whimpered. Too intense. Too incredibly wonderful. She couldn't move because she knew she'd shatter at the first stroke. And Jon, being Jon, and knowing her as he did, stayed still as her body adjusted and welcomed him. Two perfect pieces of a puzzle. Ying and yang.

She slid her hands up his back, rocking up to draw him even deeper. Risking losing her mind and losing her soul.

"We should take it slow and easy so I don't hurt you."

Slow? Easy? Was he nuts? "Haven't we . . . *had* . . . this conversation?" She was beyond ready.

"Yeah. Oh, Lord—" He pushed deep, then held perfectly still, allowing himself one perfect moment to revel in being back where he belonged. But need clamored inside her, urging her on. He started thrusting, and once he'd found his rhythm, Danica knew nothing could hold him back. Gentleness had no part here. Tonight was about tasting life. Reminding them both that they still lived. That they still loved.

"Jon," she moaned. "Oh, God. Jon. Jon. Please—"

His hips pistoned, slamming into hers as if he

wanted to impale her on the mattress. Danica loved it, wrapping her arms and legs around him tightly so she could hold on for the ride.

He bent to kiss her hard, desperate for more contact. More. More. More. They rose and fell, faster and faster, sweat gluing their bodies together as they moved in concert, their bodies remembering all the nights they'd moved together, just like this.

They climaxed together in a blinding flash of bone-melting intensity that took them into uncharted territory. It took years for Danica to come down off the ceiling. She struggled to draw more air into her heaving lungs as her heart pounded with manic intensity, and her body shuddered and shivered in the aftermath.

"Holy orgasm, Batman! Just when I thought you couldn't get any better at this," Danica gasped and rubbed her face against his, loving the feel of his whiskered jaw on her skin. "You've been working out, haven't you?"

"No. Just waiting for my shot to get back inside you." He moved against her, sending electrical charges arcing through her body. Burying his mouth against the dampness between her shoulder and neck, he breathed hard, his body still sensitized and shuddering with the intensity of his own release. "Give me ten seconds and we'll go again."

"Really?"

"Sweetheart, for you I'll make it five." He brushed a kiss against her temple. Wrapping his arms around her with a fierce intensity that hadn't abated one iota with their joint multiple orgasms, he stroked her hair in gentle, soothing, almost hypnotic, glides. Her heart, never healed, melted with tenderness. She couldn't remember the last time Jon had just held her after sex.

He'd either wanted more or he was asleep. Off and on.

Black and white.

Wired or unconscious.

No middle ground. But this. This was nice . . . She drifted.

Her hair felt cool on her shoulders as he lifted the strands and let them sift through his fingers. "Your hair always reminded me of a night sky. Did I ever tell you that?"

"No," she said and hoped he never realized how many shades of Miss Clairol she had to use to get her color just right.

"Well, it does." His voice was low, husky with want and tenderness. It brought tears to her eyes. "One of those really black nights—no stars, no moon. Just the open sky, going on forever."

"Sounds pretty," she admitted.

"I should have given you pretty words before," he murmured.

"Jon . . ."

"They were always there, Dani," he said. "Inside me." He rested his forehead against hers.

"I know," she whispered and pressed a kiss to his breastbone. Beneath her lips, his heartbeat throbbed and she shivered at his response to their lovemaking.

And experiencing this tenderness along with the amazing things he could do to her body made Danica ready for more. Ready to be a part of him over and over again. Ready to feel his body invade hers and stay there.

She trailed her hand down the center of his body, from the crisp hair covering his pecs, down his six-pack, then closed her fingers around him, loving the way his body reacted to her touch.

He groaned, turning to her to cover her mouth with his.

They made love again. Slowly this time, as if they had all the time in the world. Outside, that world moved on. Here, in this room, time stood still. For this one night, they were together, as maybe they'd always been meant to be.

But Danica knew from experience that she couldn't count on anything more than this one perfect moment. She had him in her arms right now. It would be really, really stupid to wonder for how long.

Chapter 6

T minus 1day:3hours:36minutes:18seconds

The bedside phone rang. Danica, sprawled on Jon's chest, lifted her head. His eyes were closed, but she knew he wasn't sleeping. She'd never met anyone who needed as little sleep as he did.

Jon reached over her head and snatched up the receiver, putting it to her ear, but in such a way that he could hear as well. Not sleeping and nosey as hell. *Situation normal*, she thought wryly. "Yes?"

"Your uncle is on the line, Miss Cross," the operator said in accent-inflected English. "He's quite insistent that he speak with you immediately. May I put him through?"

Danica frowned, still holding Jon's gaze. "My uncle?" Unless her only uncle was calling from his grave, she had no idea who— Jon nodded. "Ah, sure. Put him through."

"Danica?" An unfamiliar male voice spoke in her ear.

"Hi, Uncle . . . ?"

"It's Samuel, sweetie. Your aunt Martha and I are just worried *sick* about you. How're you doin', baby?" Without waiting for the answer, he said briskly, "Never mind. Put that husband of yours on the line. We don't want you getting all upset after your ordeal."

She glanced at Jon but made no move to shift position. *Both* of them would keep listening. "It's Uncle Samuel, *honey*."

He figured it would be. The State Department, the FAA and NTSB must be spitting nails by now. Join the crowd. "Yeah?"

"Hey, my boy," the guy said with forced jocularity. "Just wanted to say take damn good care of our girl there. She's become a valuable commodity right now, ya know what I mean? The family is right concerned about her after that ac-ceedent an' all. In fact, we want her home *right now*, this very minute so we can get her to our own physician toot sweet."

"Is that right?" He lifted one eyebrow, and Danica smilingly shook her head at her "uncle's" accent.

"You betcha. They say the doc back in Miami doesn't want her to get overexcited by too many visitors, ya know what I mean?"

Hell, no, Raven thought, absently reaching out to take Danica's hand in his to prevent her from scratching a welt on her neck. The problem with talking in code was that most of the time the speaker made no sense at all. Of course, it didn't help that Danica was mouthing questions at him while scratching. Jon shook his head at her, then deliberately concentrated and sifted through what the guy was trying to tell him.

He guessed their benevolent "uncle" was military. Planning an extraction, perhaps? Which made his own suspicions valid. He didn't give a shit who they were if they could get Danica clear of the highly guarded palace and out of this little shithole of a country. "Yeah, well, she'll be out of here on Saturday. Guess you heard they're giving her the keys to the city?"

"Fuc— *No way*, boy. No way. Her aunt will be just devastated if she doesn't see her *right now*. Like, I *mean* right now. Why, it might just kill her if that doesn't happen."

Danica frowned at him, but Jon didn't have time to reassure her at the moment. He was too busy fighting a soul-jarring surge of tangible fear. Enough of this two-on-a-phone thing.

Gripping the phone in a white-knuckled fist, he gently moved Danica aside so he could sit on the edge of the mattress and focus. "Is Aunt Martha with you?"

"Son, we're *all* here. The whole family got into the act to come down here and check on little Danica. This is a big deal to us."

"And where is 'here' exactly?" Jon muttered, stretching the cord of the phone so he could reach down and pick his clothes up off the floor where he'd tossed them. He started dressing one-handed, a sense of urgency making his heart pound and his brain go a mile a minute.

"Why, boy, the whole family's right here in San Cristóbal," Uncle Sam said tightly.

Jesus.

Jon shot Danica a glance, and he saw the worry on her features. A ping of regret staggered through him. Seemed that no matter when they were together, something always happened to stir the pot. Damn it. He wanted Dani. And he wanted her safe. *Now.*

"Her aunt got all upset during our plane trip down here," Uncle Sam was saying. "She reminded me of all the times we told Danica that flying in a plane was a dangerous job. There are some places people just don't belong. With what's happened fresh in her mind, you should tell her to get out and come home with us. Uh-oh, Dani's aunt's rubbing her chest agin. Her poor heart cain't take much more. Bring her to Martha as soon as you can, boy."

Crap. He got it. Subtle this guy wasn't. His fingers tightened around his T-shirt. "You're in town?"

"Not too far from you, son. We're real anxious to meet up with you and our girl. And I know none of us will eat or sleep 'til we get to see Danica with our own eyes."

"Breakfast good enough?" Not that he planned to hang around until then. The feeling of urgency was crystal clear. And if this guy, whoever he represented, was nervous, *Jon* was ten times more so.

"Hell, no. We're pretty dammed hungry *right now*. What say you two come on over and we all head *right out* for a late supper?"

Raven glanced at the dial of his watch. Twenty-four hundred hours. "How will we find you?"

"There's a real nice little place on Route 84, just north of town. Why don't we meet there?" The line went dead.

Followed by a small *click*.

Great. Just fucking great.

"What did Uncle Sam want?" Danica whispered.

He motioned for her to get out of bed, and she nodded. Staring around the plushly appointed room, Jon wondered if, despite his search, the damn place was bugged. Maybe he'd missed something—in which case they'd certainly given somebody an earful. It was the presidential palace in the country of Paranoia, so he was willing to bet it was. Either way, no point taking chances.

"He's worried about you, honey," Jon said tightly, and wagged a finger at her to get her to come to him. Guiding her into the bathroom, he turned on the water while he said, "Why don't you take a nice hot shower? Helps with the aches and pains."

With the water running loudly, he closed the door and bent his head close to hers.

"I don't know who that was, but I sure as hell recognize a warning when I hear one."

"About *what*?"

"We don't know and we're not sticking around to find out. So follow me and keep quiet. Let whoever might be listening think you're in the shower."

Then he opened the bathroom door as quietly as possible, strode across the room and grabbed the duffel the tin soldiers had brought up at the same time as their coffee and uneaten sandwiches. He hadn't needed to check for his weapons; he'd known by the weight of the bag that they were gone. Pulling out the jeans and dark blue T-shirt he'd bought at the airport, he thrust them into her hands. "Get dressed," he whispered. "We're leaving."

"It's the middle of the night." Her voice was hardly more than a breath.

"As good a time as any to make a run for it," Raven told her grimly, moving about the room to collect what he'd chosen earlier as possible weapons. They'd taken his guns, but they hadn't taken his creativity. Simple things, even a phone cord, could be a lethal weapon. "Chop-chop, sweetheart. Time's a-wastin'."

* * *

"It would've been nice if you'd thought to buy me some underwear," Danica mumbled as they ran across the manicured lawn like thieves in the night. Jon, having adjusted his speed to accommodate her shorter legs, held tightly to her hand, preventing her from falling half a dozen times. She'd never seen such blackness. Not a star, not a glimmer of a moon. The enormous palace behind them was dark. How he could see where he was going she had no idea.

"No Victoria's Secret at the airport," he said very quietly. "Veer to the left, then straight for another two hundred feet."

Heart in her throat, as it had been for what seemed like hours, Danica glanced behind them. Every step of the way she'd expected to hear dogs barking or gunshots. But other than the *cick-cick-cick* of a distant sprinkler and the soft shushing of fronds in the hundreds of palms and shrubs on the grounds, everything was quiet. So quiet she could hear the pounding of her own heart.

The balmy night air was redolent with the thick, sweet scent of jasmine, citrus blossoms and the green smell of the jungle just beyond the city. Jon's hand in hers was warm and strong, and despite the fear trumpeting through her body, she felt safe with him. She always had. He was infuriating and frustrating and had the innate ability to irritate her like no other human on the face of the planet.

But she trusted Jon more than anyone else she'd

ever known. With her life at least. Trusting him with her heart was a little trickier.

The palace guards might be prepared for anyone breaking *in*, but it never occurred to them that someone would break *out*. Or that's what Jon had assured her as they sneaked out of her room. They'd moved through the empty, dimly lit corridors, down the wide marble stairs, through the kitchens and out of the building. Undetected—or so she hoped.

She wanted to believe him. But she still kept waiting to feel a dog's canines embedded in her leg. Or the slam of a bullet in the back of her head as they ran.

Keeping close to the thick tangle of foliage bordering the gardens, they were, according to her partner in crime, heading toward a side gate and freedom.

She'd love to believe that he was overreacting. She'd like to think that "Uncle Sam" was reading danger that wasn't there. But either her own intuition was kicking in big time or Jon's paranoia was contagious. An elevated sense of urgency had completely trumped her personal sense of propriety. Under normal circumstances, she would never rudely dash off without so much as a farewell. Especially when she was the reluctant guest of honor. Until she'd seen Jon's eyes. Looked deeply and seen danger. Real, immediate danger.

"Okay?" Raven whispered.

"Define okay," she whispered back, sarcasm in her voice.

"Almost home." Metaphorically, if not in reality. The black wrought-iron fence enclosing the estate was only a couple hundred yards away. They'd managed to elude the palace guards without breaking a sweat. The best he could say about them was that they wore cool uniforms. He'd debated taking down one of them to get a weapon, but doing that would bring attention to their departure earlier than necessary.

They passed beneath an arched arbor, its shape defined by the pale blobs of spicy-scented roses flowing over it.

Danica was breathing heavily, and even though he knew she must be in some discomfort from the crash, she hadn't uttered a word of complaint. And she hadn't slowed down. He knew she was scared. This was as far away from her element as it was possible to get. She was a Sunday-with-the-*Miami-Herald*, walk-on-the-beach-at-dusk, cuddle-up-on-a-rainy-day kind of girl.

How had she of all people ended up in a plane crash, kidnapped and drugged?

And more important—why?

As a security specialist, he rarely encountered violence, although he and all his employees were certainly highly skilled and trained for any eventuality.

Up to and including terrorism. But most of his clients were Fortune 500 companies, museums, technical and medical installations that required state-of-the-art security hardware. Valuing brains above brawn.

Even so, it made him sick to think his business might have had anything to do with why Danica had been targeted. But the fact that Uncle Sam knew about Danica but asked for him by name made sense only if he was an important element in all this.

Still, it just *didn't* make sense. No matter how he looked at it. However, he did not believe in coincidence. So if it wasn't his present security business that had drawn them into this mess . . . maybe it was something from his past.

Something to think about once they were clear.

Once Danica was safe.

He wished to hell he carried a weapon. A real weapon, not a makeshift shiv and a travel-size can of frigging hair spray.

A movement up ahead caught his attention. In a heartbeat he swung Danica behind him, the shiv readied, protruding between his index and middle fingers. Every nerve and tendon in his body poised to fight.

"Jon Raven?" A male voice whispered.

"ID yourself," Raven demanded in a low voice. There were seven men that he could see. Barely. But they were there, blending in with the vegetation. Raven smelled their sweat, gun oil from their weapons and the black grease stick on their skin. Yeah. Military for sure.

"DSS. We have a vehicle waiting to transport you and Miss Cross. This way, sir."

T minus 1day:2hours:09minutes:23seconds

"No," Raven told the Diplomatic Secret Service guy ten minutes later. "We travel together or not at all." They'd run a mile to a secure location where several beat-up trucks were parked. Now these guys wanted to separate him and Dani. Uh-uh. Wasn't gonna happen.

"We need to get Miss Cross to the clinic ASAP. Our orders are to take her there. You'll be—"

Raven wrapped an arm about Danica's shoulders. "Right next to her, pal." His eyes narrowed as the man moved off, then spoke quietly into a radio. DSS was under the auspices of the State Department. What the hell did *they* want with *him*?

Or was it *Danica* they wanted?

Something around here stunk. Something was . . . *off*. He should be feeling relief that they'd been picked up by the good guys. But his uneasy gut feeling warned him that things weren't what they seemed.

The second the soldier came close enough, Raven stepped up to him and demanded, "*What* clinic?"

"I'm not at liberty to—"

"Then take us to someone who *is* at liberty to tell us what the hell is going down."

Danica had never seen *this* Jon Raven. She wasn't

the least bit afraid that his fingers were cutting off the circulation in her hand where he held it so tightly. It was the expression on his face that chilled her blood and made her fiercely grateful that the expression wasn't focused on *her*.

The soldier looked as though he wanted to refuse. Instead, he nodded briefly. "We'll take you to Uncle Sam."

"That'll do. For starters."

Flanked by half a dozen men, they walked to the first truck, and he helped her inside, then got in beside her in the front seat. His eyes, reflecting the dash lights, looked almost demonic in their intensity as the trucks moved smoothly onto a dirt access road behind the palace.

"What's our destination, soldier?"

"I'm not at liberty—"

"I'm going to liberate you with my fist in about ten seconds," Jon stated. *Too calmly*, she thought. *Deadly calm*. "I'm not in the mood to screw around with you."

"Yes, sir," the soldier replied. "I appreciate that, sir. But I have orders."

"Which are?" Danica asked, trying to angle in order to see more clearly and make out the painted face of the driver. Up to this point, she'd been largely ignored by the soldiers. "Why are they so hell-bent on taking me to a doctor?"

"Just a little while longer, ma'am."

Fifteen minutes later—or it might have been five hours; Danica was so tired her head had rested on Jon's shoulder most of the way while she rested her eyes—they pulled up at a two-story warehouse on the outskirts of town.

Escorted by the men who'd come to get them, they followed their driver into the building. The large doors clanged shut behind them with an ominous thud. "What is this place?" Danica whispered.

"Let's ask this guy," Jon said flatly as a man in a dark suit emerged from a room down the corridor.

Even to her inexperienced eye, the man was every inch a soldier, although he wore no uniform, nor was he carrying a gun like the others. At least not one she could see.

He came forward, hand extended to Jon. "I'm Special-Agent-in-Charge Donovan."

"In charge of what?" Jon countered.

"For the moment, *you*. Please," he began in a tone that bordered between evasion and condescension. "Come this way. Can I get you something to eat or drink while you wait?"

"Wait for *what*?" Jon demanded, halting Dani's automatic footsteps as she started following the man to . . . wherever.

In a hurry, and clearly annoyed by the questions, the man continued striding down the corridor, but turned to glance back. "Wait while Miss Cross is prepped for surgery."

Chapter 7

T minus 1day:0hours:57minutes:56seconds

"Surgery?" Danica repeated blankly at the same time Jon said, "Whoa! Say *what*?"

Donovan stopped in his tracks, glanced around, then slammed open a nearby door with the flat of his hand. "In here."

"*Here* is just fine," Danica said firmly, stopping on a dime in the corridor. Jon's fingers tightened around hers. "I'm not having any type of surgery, Mr. Donovan." The soldiers behind them moved back at Special-Agent-in-Charge Donovan's nod.

"It wasn't an invitation, Miss Cross," he said, voice low. "Not only is the surgery imperative, time is of the essence."

"Turn up your hearing aid, pal," Jon snapped. "The lady just said *No surgery*. She's already been checked out by the presi—"

"If you'll come inside where we can be . . . private." Donovan paused, turned and spoke directly to Jon, which Danica found irritating as hell, since she was the one they were talking about opening up.

"I'm not going anywhere," she said unequivocally.

Donovan's eyes reflected compassion and an equal measure of annoyance. "If you'll follow me, I'll explain the seriousness of the situation."

She grabbed Jon's arm and moved with him to the far wall. "Give us a minute."

Donovan nodded, then signaled the soldiers behind them to stay where they were. "We—*you*—don't have much time." He marched into the room, leaving the door ajar.

"What *kind* of surgery, for heaven's sake? I walked in here. My arms work—nothing's *wrong* with me. Oh, God, Jon. What's going on?" Danica whispered, pressing a damp palm to her midriff, where butterflies were practicing takeoffs and landings. Her heartbeat still hadn't returned to its normal cadence of before leaving the palace. Now it throbbed uncomfortably against her rib cage.

What was Jon thinking as he glanced around so casually? What was going on behind his hooded gaze? His mouth looked grim, and he was holding so tightly to her forearm that his fingers were sure to leave bruises. A muscle ticked in his cheek.

"There's something really creepy about this." Danica tried to swallow, but all her spit had dried up hours ago. "This place. Donovan." She absently scratched a bite on her arm, then *all* the insect bites all over her body started itching like crazy. She wanted to cry with frustration. She was scared. Really, really scared.

Like Alice dropped down the rabbit hole, she had no idea what she'd stumbled into, only that whatever it was, was way beyond her comprehension. "I want out of here. Right now."

Jon wrapped an arm around her shoulders, pulling her in close. She saw that he was back with her from wherever he'd just been. Thank God. "Yeah," he whispered, cupping his palm briefly to her cheek. "I'm with you on the creep factor."

He rubbed his hand up and down her arm in a soothing gesture that made her even more nervous. Because, damn it, she could tell from his expression that he too was freaking out at this new development.

She dropped her head to his chest with a thunk. "Oh, damn. I was hoping you'd tell me this whole thing didn't creep you out as much as it does me."

"Sorry, sweetheart," he said against her hair as he held her tightly against his chest. "There's a whole lot of wrong going on here. Hang tough while I try to figure out how the hell we get us out of this mess."

Danica wrapped both arms around his waist. "Speed-think."

Dani's face was white as Raven led her into the

room—and Donovan. The glow of fluorescent lighting made the setting surreal. A metal table was pushed up to a large plate-glass partition. Two chrome chairs faced the room behind the glass. On the other side, an operating room filled with equipment had been hastily prepared. What looked like a couple of doctors and several male nurses stood at the ready.

Scared shitless, Jon gave Donovan a cool look. He'd left the door to the room open. For whatever good that would do. The soldiers stood outside. All six of them, AK-47s locked and loaded. "All right," he told Donovan, keeping his gaze steady. He calculated how many seconds it would take him to get to the older man, overpower him and relieve him of the Sig tucked into a holster beneath his jacket. "We're here. What the hell's going on?"

He kept Danica tucked beneath his arm, not wanting an inch of space to come between them. He'd feel marginally better if he were wearing Donovan's sidearm. Which he would be, given half a chance.

"Transair Flight 723 had a series of small bombs on board," Donovan said flatly, motioning to the medical personnel on the other side of the glass that he needed another minute.

Minute, my ass, Raven thought, his mind flashing vivid images of Danica being subjected to some Frankenstein-ish operation. Ice traveled in a chill streak down his spine. Wasn't going to happen. He needed a plan. Actually, he needed a lot of things. Other than his wits, a shiv and a small can of frigging hair spray, he was weaponless.

Donovan started pacing—marching—around the small room, hands clasped behind his back. "Security Chief Edgardo Villalba-Vera was behind the attempted murder of the president's heir, and the murder of most of his cabinet. Plan A was the crash, rigged to look like nothing more than an unfortunate accident."

Dani's arm tightened about Raven's waist. "Other than my wife being on board," he said, hugging her to his side to give them both a modicum of Dutch courage. "I don't see what this has to do with us."

The other man turned and started pacing back the other way. "Vera has already tried a coup. Didn't work. He wants Palacios dead. Because he doesn't want the public outcry to screw his own chances of the presidency, he can't be seen to be involved in assassinating the president. As far as the people, and the president, are concerned, Villalba-Vera is a hero for bringing Miss Cross back here to San Cristóbal to honor her for saving young Rigo. Your saving the boy," he snapped as though it was an accusation, "has activated Vera to move to Plan B."

"Well, gee, I'm sorry I survived and saved the president's kid. What was I thinking?" Danica said with only a slight tremor in her voice. "This is all very interesting, but still, nothing to do with us." She tugged Raven toward the exit.

"Sadly, it does," Donovan replied, though she didn't get any genuine feelings of regret or remorse from his tone.

"Villalba-Vera brought you to San Cristóbal, Miss Cross, because he plans to use *you* to assassinate El Presidente."

"That's ridiculous."

"Unfortunately not," Donovan snapped, resuming his pacing. "Two months ago a . . . device was stolen from our top-secret R&D labs in— It doesn't matter where. Suffice to say it's imperative that we retrieve said device ASAP."

"What kind of 'device'?" Jon demanded before she could form the words to ask the same thing.

She rubbed at the persistent itch behind her left ear, then rubbed a bite on her elbow, then another on her hip. If this guy and his convoluted story didn't drive her insane, the itching from all the insect bites would. None of Donovan's problems had anything to do with her and Jon. She'd just promise not to assassinate anyone and they could go.

"Let me just say that the device was something we were working on to eliminate enemies of our country," Donovan said grimly. "A small explosive chip—"

Raven had to support Danica as her knees gave a

little dip when the implication hit. Jesus Christ. "*How* small?" he demanded.

"Tiny. A microelectronic chip encapsulated within proven inert biocompatible—"

"Implanted in *Danica*?"

Special-Agent-in-Charge-of-Terror nodded. "We suspect soon after her arrival, which explains why she was kept sedated. All that was required was a standard 3 cc syringe in order to implant the microchip. A modified Monoject syringe is used to facilitate a subcutaneous injection procedure.

"And before you ask, *yes*," Donovan said. "We're positive she's wearing the chip. My man detected it behind her left ear when you were picked up. The reader has manual, remote or computer-controlled operational capability and is battery-powered, using a 9-volt alkaline or 110/220-volt AC adapters. It also transmits via a standard RS232 interface to a computer. A low-energy radio signal energizes the device, which transmits a signal. The reading time is less than forty milliseconds."

The damn thing was in her *head*? "Tracking capabilities?" Raven asked, cold to his marrow. The question wasn't only "Could Vera track them?" It was "Could Vera remotely detonate the micro bomb implanted in Dani?"

"Yes." So Vera knew exactly where they were. Caught between Scylla and Charybdis. There were no good guys in this. "What was his plan?"

"Detonation of the bomb when Miss Cross receives the keys to the city from the president tomorrow afternoon."

No one would suspect her. And even if they *did*, a search wouldn't reveal the microscopic bomb. She would have been within touching distance of President Palacios. Ingenious.

Diabolical.

Not frigging going to happen.

"How do we block the signal?"

Donovan hesitated.

Raven put Danica gently away from him, then in a lightning-quick move kicked the door shut, locked it, and whipped around to wrap his fingers about Donovan's throat. He spoke directly against the man's ear. "Before those guys come in here, I'll kill you with my bare hands. So for the last time, is there a way to block the signal without removing the implant?"

"Tests show—adrenaline and endorphins mute it somewhat," Donovan choked reluctantly.

Just as reluctantly, Raven released Donovan with a shove. He and Danica could power a small country with their adrenaline at the moment. Now not only did he have to get them the hell out of Dodge, he had to find a doctor, a *qualified* doctor, a doctor he could trust, to remove a prototype microscopic implant, in the middle of the night, in a strange country. Piece of cake.

Raven had contacts, people he could call for help. But it was getting the right people, and the right kind of help—*immediately*—that concerned him.

"Mute it? Somewhat? *Without* removing it?" Danica demanded, eyes wide as she stared at him. "Screw somewhat!" She stepped forward and glared at Donovan. "Get it out of me. *Now!*"

Raven grabbed her by the arm, pulling her back against him where he could hold on to her, trying to still his own panic so she wouldn't see it. "Hang on," he said calmly, rubbing his palms up and down the goose bumps on her arms. "Nobody's cutting you until we have all the answers." *Yeah. As if.*

"What's the real goal here?" he asked Donovan rhetorically. "Retrieving the chip, or my wife's continuing good health?"

"Of course both are equally important to us—"

Yeah. Right. The damn chip was the star attraction. One small American woman who happened to be the unfortunate carrier was expendable. "Can the bomb be reused once it's been removed?"

"Well—"

"A simple yes or no."

"Yes."

Ah, man. This was as bad as it got. They didn't give a damn about Dani. Once they had their frigging prototype, that would be it.

He had to ask, even though the chances of them getting anything like a scalpel near her were slim to go to hell. "How safe is the procedure?" Nothing less than two hundred percent guarantee would be acceptable, and even then Raven would hesitate. He didn't trust this bastard farther than he could throw him. "The truth."

"Five percent," Donovan admitted.

"Five percent chance that something could go wrong?" Jon shook his head grimly and thought about grabbing the guy's throat again. *Nobody* was getting near Danica unless they could guarantee that she'd be fine afterward. Even if it meant he had to kill every living soul on this godforsaken spit of land.

"Forget it," he said, already thinking about an escape route. "Tell your medics to stand down, because it's not happening—not with a five percent failure rate."

"Five percent chance of *success*," Donovan corrected, albeit reluctantly. "Ninety-five percent probability of terminating the patient."

Chapter 8

T minus 1day:0hours:41minutes:02seconds

Black dots danced in Danica's wavering vision as she felt every vestige of blood drain from her head. If she fainted, Jon would have to carry her out of here while trying to fend off the soldiers. And she knew, without a doubt, that she and Jon would be getting out of here soon. *How* soon, and exactly *how*, she wasn't sure. She locked her knees and concentrated on her breathing. *Buck up*, she told herself. *Do not fall apart. Think.*

"It's a lose-lose situation." Jon sounded as grim as Danica felt. And she was feeling pretty damn grim. Oh, God. A bomb inside her? Not just inside her. Inside her *head*?

Do. Not. Freak.

"There's absolutely no choice, Raven. None," Donovan told him. "Without the removal of the bio-chip,

Villalba-Vera can, and assuredly *will*, activate it. *That's* a hundred percent death warrant."

"It was apparently easy enough to insert. *Reverse* the procedure," Jon told him tightly. "Surely to God we don't need an operating room and a surgeon?"

"There's a fail-safe built in. The device can't be exposed to oxygen." Donovan's tone was terse. "It's us or Villalba-Vera. And be assured, in the unlikely event that he *doesn't* detonate the device while it is still contained, he *will* find you and remove it himself. The race is on to see who gets you, and it, first. Time is of the essence. Surely you can see that."

"I do," Jon agreed, sounding reluctant. "But I'm going in with her."

Danica spun around to stare at her nearly-ex-husband, who'd clearly lost his mind. "Are you out of your freaking *mind*? He wants to *cut* into me! How do we even know he's telling the truth about this—this—*thing*?"

Jon cupped her face in both hands, his palms as dry as hers were damp, his dark eyes glittering with—what? Regret? Determination? "Listen to me, Danica. We don't have any choice but to go into that room. The longer you drag your feet, the longer we'll be here. Once the chip's out, we'll be on our way home."

Every cell in her body shrieked a resounding "no!" She searched his face with eyes that burned. Terror grabbed her by the throat, but instead of giving in to it, she held on to the protective gleam in Jon's eyes. He would be with her. He wouldn't let anything happen to her. The one thing she'd always felt with Jon was *safe*. Even though they'd drifted apart, their marriage crumbling around them, the Jon she knew would protect her.

Please God, she prayed, *let me know this man as well as I think I do.* "If I die in there, I'm coming back to haunt you," she told him as a terrible calm came over her. She'd crossed the line from unmitigated fear to a place where she'd stepped outside her body to observe herself. Her other self was escorted to the adjacent sterile room by two men, trailed by four armed soldiers. With Jon right beside her, holding her hand.

Sounds muted. The floor felt unsubstantial beneath her feet, and the air smelled imperceptibly of antiseptic as she, Jon and Donovan went inside. The door shut behind them. Danica was aware of each individual, slow, dirgelike thump of her heart as Jon led her to stand beside a linen-draped operating table. It was a blessed relief to feel nothing at all.

Except that, in some dim recess of her brain, she knew she had to shake this lethargy. It was hard for her to read Jon's signals.

T minus 1day:0hours:07minutes:00seconds

He turned her to face him, sliding his hand down her numb arm to take both her hands in his. His eyes scanned her face, and he frowned, looking worried.

"I'll be with you every second. Trust me, sweetheart. I'm not going to let anything happen to you, or let anyone or anything take you away from me ever again." She could see their fingers entwined, his hands large and dark, hers ridiculously small and pale, but she didn't feel the contact.

He bent his head slightly and looked directly into her eyes. She didn't blink. Jon had lovely eyes. A deep rich blu—"Ow!" She jerked when he pinched her forearm. *Hard.*

"With me now?"

Danica blinked like a sleepwalker after a rude awakening. "Oh, yeah."

"Ready?" A guy in a cap and face mask asked as he snapped a rubber glove onto his left hand.

What an irritating sound that is, Danica thought, annoyed. The brightly lit room pulsed with the low hum of machinery as Jon turned her to face him, his hands on her shoulders. "One kiss before she goes under."

"Or my head explodes," Danica murmured with gallows humor.

"Ah, sweetheart, you're one in a million." He wrapped his arms around her, pulling her tightly against him, his face buried against her neck. "Trust me," he whispered on a quiet breath. "Give it a count of five and start bawling. Make it dramatic, and make it *loud.*"

He lifted his head to brush his lips over hers. Danica felt a small spark of life as she parted her lips to greet his. But the spark was short-lived as he mouthed, "Four," brushed his mouth over hers again, lingering a little, then "five—"

Danica burst into noisy faux tears and shrieks of terror. Her own screams grated on her ears, but she kept it up, getting louder and louder and storming about the room, distracting the men while Jon did—whatever he was doing. She was too busy playacting to look.

All eyes turned to her—then a second later toward the door as it burst open, slamming noisily against the wall. Four guns clicked as the soldiers spilled through, some standing, some kneeling in the open doorway—weapons drawn.

"Oh, for—" Donovan snarled, striding toward them. "She's just hysterical, not being murdered. This room is sterile. Get out and close the damn door," he ordered the soldiers. Their weapons clicked as they backed out of the room and shut the door behind them. Donovan turned. "Keep her quiet, for God's sake, or we'll have—" He turned to find Jon standing directly behind him, a tank of ether raised at shoulder level.

Jon's shoulder—*his* face. He reached for his gun, but Jon was faster, slamming the heavy tank into Donovan's nose. The accompanying sound was like the snap of a stalk of celery. Then a thud as Donovan hit the floor. Danica didn't even wince.

She ran to the door, slamming home the lock, then

spun around to see Jon, a gun in each hand. Face expressionless, he motioned for the medical personnel to close the gap between them, which they did with stunned, robotic precision.

Danica bent to pick up the heavy tank beside the unconscious and profusely bleeding Donovan. Feeling no sympathy for him, she hefted the tank, staggering for a moment under the weight. As a weapon it was unwieldy, but no one was going to shoot at her when she was holding it. She hoped. "That looks like a closet over there." She nodded in the general direction of a door across the room.

"Move it." Jon motioned the four men with a wave of the barrel of one of his guns. They trooped inside and he shut the door, then wedged an IV stand into the handles, sealing them in.

Danica blinked, glancing around the room, wondering what the next step should be. Then her eyes caught Jon's and her calm returned. She wasn't trained, but *he* was. "How do we get past the soldiers?" she asked, adjusting the tank to rest some of the weight against her thigh.

"Guns blazing," he said, winking as he checked the magazines on the guns, then chambered a bullet in each weapon.

"Isn't that a little dangerous?" she asked, then felt an amazing urge to laugh. "More dangerous than this bio-bomb ticking away in my head?"

He ran the tips of his fingers along the line of her

jaw. "Soldiers first, bomb second. Assuming Donovan was telling the truth, you're loaded with adrenaline at the moment. That should keep the bomb from detonating for now."

"And later?" They both knew how she handled stress. With unnatural calm. A *bad* thing, given the ticking bomb in her head.

"One step at a time, honey." He positioned the tank in her arms so that it partially obstructed her vision but covered all the vital points any decent marksman might target. "Keep this up. They won't risk shooting you."

"I'd feel better with a gun," she remarked wryly. "But I'll settle for a well-armed ex-husband."

"Not ex yet. Here." He handed her the small can of hair spray he'd found in the bathroom back at the palace.

"You think this'll work, MacGyver?"

"Aim for eyes," he told her, his face grim. "We can't afford for there to be any shooting. Can you manage the tank and the can?" Danica nodded. He brushed a fingertip briefly across her mouth. "That's my girl. Okay—stand aside. I'm going to open the door and stick my head out."

She followed him across the room, then flattened herself against the wall out of the way, holding the tank up on her shoulder and her finger on the trigger of her spray can. "Do you think it's smart to stick your head in the way of a bullet?" she whispered.

"They won't shoot. Especially when they see you holding that tank of ether. One spark and we'll all get blown to hell."

"What a cheerful thought."

Jon grinned. "Trust me."

Danica gave him an arch look, but she did trust him. Completely. She knew with every cell in her body he'd do everything in his power to keep her safe. God only knew, she'd do the same for him. That would be enough. If not, then she could only hope there'd be enough time to tell him she loved him one last time. To hear the same from him.

Jon positioned himself and opened the door. "Hey, guys? Can you get in here a sec? Donovan needs some help." Using his foot and leg as a brace, Jon made sure the opening was only large enough for a single soldier to rush in at a time.

The moment she saw the soldier's face, Danica pressed the little white button on the aerosol can. The guy shouted as the spray hit him full in the face. He doubled over. Jon felled him with a hard blow to the back of his neck, then propelled him into the room with a heave of one hand.

She watched in stunned amazement as he picked each man off like it was an arcade game. A smashing karate chop, then a shove. One, two, three. The soldiers piled up like discarded toys, strewn facedown and motionless on the floor.

Soldier four apparently didn't get the playbook because he barreled inside, AK poised to shoot. Danica sprayed him. *Ffffft*—The container was empty. Damn. Tossing aside the can, she held up the tank so he got a good look. Blanching, he staggered back a step, looked confused, then swung around to see Jon. He swung his weapon, but it was too late. Jon grabbed the barrel of the rifle and used it to drag the guy closer. The soldier released his hold, coming forward into Jon, causing him to stagger.

They tumbled to the floor, rolling around, grunting and cursing as they fought.

If fear was a great motivator, Danica was in peak form as one of the downed men staggered to his feet behind Jon. "Oh, no you don't!" With strength and determination, she brought her knee up, catching her guy in the chin as he started to rise. He reeled back, and she brought the tank around, smashing his temple. With a wince at the sickening crunch of metal on bone, she watched as he crumpled to the floor.

Eyes darting between Jon and his opponent, Danica cringed every time bone met bone. She rushed over, lifted her trusty tank of ether and brought it down on the last soldier's skull. Crack. Grunt. Silence.

Jon shoved the guy off him, got to his feet and offered Danica his brightest smile. He gently took the tank and set it aside. "You're full of surprises." He leaned forward to place a kiss on her open mouth.

Tucking the pistols in the waistband of his pants,

he grabbed two of the AKs, then took Danica's hand and raced from the building.

Surprised that dawn had broken while they'd been inside, Dani clutched the stitch in her side and kept pace with Jon as he ran.

They reached the first truck. "Get in," he yelled, tossing the guns on the bench seat before reaching for the steering column. In under three seconds and with only a ballpoint pen at his disposal, he had the engine purring to life.

T minus 23hours:19minutes:07seconds

"Where are we going?"

Raven glanced over and saw, in the milky dawn light, how the color had drained from her face. Typical reaction. The adrenaline rush from the fight was wearing off. *Shit.*

"Gotta get to a phone." He gunned the engine, checked the rearview mirror for a tail, and peeled down the dirt road back to town in a rooster tail of dust. He ran through the cards in his mental Rolodex. "Donovan and I agree on one thing," he told her grimly. "That chip's gotta come out."

Danica grabbed the dashboard as the truck bounced in the deep ruts in the dirt road. "That makes three of us. But there was that little addendum about ninety-five percent probability of the patient's demise, remember?" Her knuckles were white as she clutched the dash, but her voice was steady.

"I know what he said," Raven acknowledged as he stomped the accelerator all the way to the floor. "But the chip was what he wanted. You were . . . expendable." He reached over and closed his fingers over her knee. "There has to be a way to remove the chip without harming you in any way."

"And until then?"

Yeah. Until then . . . He narrowed his eyes against the brilliance of the rising sun. He'd let this incredible woman down more times than he could count.

His security business had always been his 24/7 priority, to the exclusion of all else. He hadn't realized that she'd trip over his ambition on her way out. Nor had he realized Danica needed him too. He'd simply assumed she'd always be there. He hadn't blamed her for leaving him when she had. But now he had a second chance. And he sure as hell wasn't going to screw *this* one up.

He was *not* going to let her die, and when this was over, he was going to tell her exactly why they belonged together. Most of all, he'd tell her the truth. He'd been an ass to let her slip out of his life. She'd always been his number one priority, he'd just stupidly thought she'd sit on the sidelines waiting until he'd amassed enough money, enough power to make them both happy. It wouldn't happen again.

On either side of the narrow track, the jungle closed in around them, a hot, green, impenetrable wall of vegetation. His fingers gripped the wheel as he took a corner too fast on the dirt road. "We're winging it here," he told her grimly, swerving to avoid a ragged boy and two goats who'd emerged from nowhere into the middle of the road.

"I have a contact in D.C., I'll call and see what he knows about the chip. In the meantime, I know someone here who'll hook us up with a reputable doctor ASAP."

"We still have an immediate problem," Dani said, her voice amazingly calm, considering. "This thing can blow up at any time."

Like he could possibly forget. "Not if I can help it," Raven said, feeling grim and manic and as though time was spinning out of control while his brain raced like a rat in a maze to come up with a viable solution.

T minus 23hours:19minutes:00seconds

Danica unsnapped her seat belt. "I think I have a way around it."

She was too calm, he thought with rising panic. He knew his girl. The more pissed and afraid Danica became, the calmer she always got. This was a bad, bad, *bad*, freaking time for her to be calm and collected.

"Which is what?" he asked, mouth dry as he started praying like he'd never prayed before. *Help us out here, God.* For the first time since he'd left the tutelage of Sister Mary Angelica, Raven said the Our

Father, followed immediately by the Act of Contrition. Hell, he'd recite the Gettysburg Address forward and backward if he thought it might curry favor with the Almighty.

The truck swerved as she whipped her T-shirt over her head, exposing her pretty, bare breasts, then lifted her butt off the seat to pull down the zipper on her too tight jeans. "Pull over."

Chapter 9

T minus 23hours:18minutes:30seconds

"You are nuts," Jon murmured, spearing the truck into the overhanging trees like a hot knife through butter. The jungle closed in around the vehicle with a rustle of leaves and the snap of branches, cocooning them in verdant green. He shut off the engine and silence rushed at them. "Do you have any idea how *insane* this is?" His voice was thick as he turned to look at her.

Danica smiled, and her heart started pounding as if his hands, rather than his gaze had touched her. "Do you have any idea how messy it would get in here if we *don't*?"

He cupped the back of her head and brought their heads together, touched his forehead to hers. "Ah, Jesus, sweetheart. Don't—"

"Shhh. Shhh. Keep me safe, Jon. Make love to me."

The inside of the army surplus truck was hotter than sin, despite the thick jade canopy. Danica intended to make it even hotter. Naked, already damp with equal amounts of perspiration and desperation, she reached for the hem of his T-shirt. "Clothes off. *Now*." She dragged the damp fabric up his body and over his head and tossed the garment over her shoulder.

Just seeing the heated desire flare in his eyes as he looked at her made her adrenaline race. She grabbed his hand, placed his fingers at the base of her throat. "Feel that? You, touching me—anywhere—gives me the biggest rush. You make my heart race and my blood sing."

"I've never stopped wanting you," he said in a ragged voice thick with urgency. His fingers glided down, caressing first her throat where her pulse pounded, then trailing down her chest in an almost lazy caress. Danica looked down, watching as his lean, tanned fingers curved around to cup the weight of her breast.

Her breath caught and her body shuddered with anticipation as he bent his head, the long dark silk of his hair brushing her skin in its own caress. She squeezed her eyes shut, threading her fingers through the skeins, holding his head to her, dizzy at the exquisite pull of his wet mouth on her painfully erect nipple.

"Nobody—" she tried to say. But his tongue

stroked the distended bud in slick, rapid movements that sent her heart slamming erratically into her ribs and shuddered through her entire body, scrambling her thoughts. She fumbled with the top button of his pants, feeling his furnace heat and clenched muscles against her fingers. An electric current zinged through her, Come *on. Come on. Come on.* "Ah— could ever make me ache as you do, Jon Raven." And nobody else ever would.

He skimmed out of his jeans, shoving them aside, all hard, sinewy muscle and bronzed satin skin as he slid to the center of the bench seat, taking her with him. He lifted his head, and Danica shuddered as this beautiful man, this primal male, gently cupped her jaw, tilting her face up to meet the hard pressure of his mouth, and kissed her as though they'd been apart for a hundred years.

"You are my water in the desert." He lifted his mouth from hers long enough to murmur it. "My reason for being." Then he lowered his mouth again to gently bite the fullness of her lower lip, tugging at it to access the inner softness, before he crushed her mouth beneath his in a kiss so raw, so desperate, Danica moaned, feeling the power of it all the way to her toes.

Arms around his neck, fingers gripping his hair, she straddled his lap, opening her body to him. He glided his hands around her waist, neither insisting nor holding her back. Simply—holding her. Still kissing her as though there was no tomorrow. His thumbs moved in lazy circles, dipping into the creases at the juncture of her thighs.

Taut with anticipation, she stayed poised there, braced on her knees, feeling the jut of him, so hard, so ready, against her eager core. Liquid heat filled her, surging and rushing through her veins. The sensitive tips of her breasts rubbed against the solid plane of his chest, teased by the wiry hair arrowing down to his groin. Every part of her yearned for him, while the kiss went on and on.

She tore her mouth from beneath his as she impaled herself, then had to stop because the sensation of having Jon inside her was so sharp, so unbearably sweet, she couldn't move. And Jon, being Jon, and knowing her so well, let the pleasure build and build as the muscles in his neck corded and his body shook with the effort to remain still while buried deep inside her.

The magnitude of his control stunned and humbled her.

Then, when her nerves quivered unbearably and her muscles jumped with the strain, when the urgency encompassed her entire world, only then did Jon grip her hips in his strong hands and set a rhythm that had them both panting and gasping. Everything seemed to tighten inside her in concentric circles. Danica's vision blurred. She went deaf, blind.

Nothing could compare to this—this driving compulsion. This overwhelming race to the finish.

Jon cried her name in a garbled voice, his sweaty face buried against her equally sweaty throat as they came together in an apocalyptic finish that left them both weak and shaken.

T minus 23hours:11minutes:20seconds

"We made it even hotter in here," Raven murmured against her temple. Their bodies were glued together, and he was still deep inside her. He had to get to a phone. Now. But Dani was a limp, gloriously satiated limpet on his chest and he didn't want to move any more than she did. As relaxed as her body felt, her heart pounded in a comforting, rapid, erratic beat beneath the hand he had cupped around her breast.

"Hmmm," she murmured, not moving.

Unfortunately, move they must. "There's a spider the size of my Porsche on the hood of the truck."

The lashes of one eye brushed his chest as she stirred. "What color?"

"Silver."

With a grin Danica lifted her head. She gave him a not-so-gentle punch to the ribs. "The spider, you idiot."

His throat closed, aching with how incredibly beautiful she looked as she sat up, pushing her hair off her face. Her stick-straight bangs fell into place above her sparkling eyes like black silk. Her cheeks were hot pink with the heat, her mouth slightly swollen and still damp from his kisses.

She lifted her leg over him, leaving him bereft at the loss of her slick heat, and felt around in the foot well for her clothes. "Guess we'd better go and do whatever it is we've got to go and do before my head explodes. Right?"

"Jesus, Dani, don't even joke about it. Nothing's going to happen to you." He needed to *make* that promise. The amazing sex had sent a healthy dose of adrenaline and endorphins through her system. But how long would it last? How long before Villalba-Vera decided he wasn't getting her back, and therefore she was expendable? How long before Donovan and his soldiers found them and forced Danica to undergo surgery so they could keep their damned prototype of the smallest assassination tool ever made?

Raven pulled his T-shirt over his head, then bent to retrieve his pants from the floor. "I'm prepared to pull over any time you feel the least little bit calm," he offered magnanimously, doing up his pants while keeping an eye on the rapid pulse at the base of her throat.

"A prince of a guy." Dani smiled. Not the wide Danica smile that always made his pulse go from zero to eighty in a second, but a knowing smile that sliced right into his heart. She reached out, cupping

110

his cheek. Raven buried his face in her soft palm as the pressure in his chest built. Her other hand came up and stroked his hair back off his face.

"I'm not going to let that bastard make me explode. Got that, Jon Raven? The only person allowed to make me explode, and in future I'll use that term with due seriousness, is *you*." She stroked his hair, his cheek, her heart in her eyes.

His throat ached. *Jesus, Dani—*

"You still take my breath away," she admitted, touching the corners of his lips. "I—I want to tell you something before . . . just in case . . . I mean, if—"

Raven silenced her by pressing two fingers to her mouth. "There'll be plenty of time for this later. Let's book so I can call my contact and resolve this once and for all." He started the truck and backed back out onto the road, cracking the window open once they started moving to dissipate the fog on the inside.

Danica finished straightening her clothes, then moved the guns and slid across the seat to tuck herself against his side despite the stifling heat. Raven looped an arm about her shoulders and drew her hard against him, then rested his fingers lightly on the pulse at her throat as he drove.

Dense jungle eventually gave way to the poverty-stricken outskirts of San Cristóbal proper as the sun rose higher in the sky, heralding another hotter-than-hell day in paradise. The smoky smell of open fires mingled with the scent of spicy foods as Jon steered the truck into a rutted parking spot in front of a corner service station. A decades-old telephone booth stood guard over the antiquated pumps beneath a tattered awning.

He placed one of the guns on the seat next to her. "Shoot anyone who isn't me."

"That's a little drastic, isn't it? What if it's someone who has nothing to do with—"

"Then we'll apologize profusely." He made her pick up the weapon. "Here. Safety's off. Point and shoot." He hopped out of the truck, locked and slammed the door, and jogged over to the booth. Danica watched him through the grimy windshield as he made his call.

The interior of the truck was sweltering, and she prayed there wasn't a temperature-sensitive component to the thing in her head. Absently, she brushed hair away from her face, lifting it off her neck in an attempt to let the pitiful breeze cool her flushed skin. A bite on her neck itched like crazy, and she reached up to rub at it. Her fingers moved across the small bump that had been driving her nuts for days. A small—minute actually—welt just behind her ear. Could it be . . . ? Grabbing the rearview mirror, she tilted it in an attempt to examine the spot.

It looked like a pinprick. *"We're positive she's wearing the chip,"* Donovan had said. *"My man detected it behind her left ear when you were picked up."* Danica felt sick to her stomach as she moved her fingers gently around the slight bump.

Fear welled inside her, mixing with the annoyance, frustration and other emotions that threatened to erupt at any moment. Jon's call continued. He vacillated between periods of animated hand gestures and attentive listening. What was taking so long? Maybe there wasn't a way to get this *thing* out of her. *Oh, God!* Maybe Donovan was telling the truth. Maybe—

A bullet shattered the windshield, sending a rain of safety glass pellets into her lap.

Chapter 10

T minus 22hours:33minutes:17seconds

Before Donovan's man took his first shot, Raven was sprinting across the weed-infested parking lot toward Dani. Running interference between their truck and that of Donovan and his men.

Everything happened in slo-mo. The windshield shattering, bullets freaking flying and the sun blazing down on his head as if holding him in place. *"Da-aaaa-ni!"*

Squeezing the trigger of his automatic, he laid down cover fire as he ran like his life depended on it. He got one man, clambering out of the diesel, in the chest, the next in the right shoulder. As he ran by he scooped up the fully loaded AK-47 from the fallen guy and sent a barrage of bullets toward the truck holding Donovan and more of his men.

He kept firing, using both weapons, until the Sig

Cherry Adair

clicked empty. He tossed it aside and reached for the door handle still letting fly with the assault rifle.

Danica yanked on the lock, pulling up on the button, then flung open the driver's-side door, shouting, "Hurry, hurry, hurry!" He got off a kill shot over the door, then climbed in, slammed the door and peeled out of the parking lot in a spray of gravel, Donovan's bigger truck right behind them.

"Were you hit?" he yelled over the sound of gunfire.

"I'm fine. Turn left." Dani, his quiet, pacifist, glorious Dani, turned around to kneel on the cracked leather seat and started firing out the back window. The glass shattered and splintered, then fell off in a sheet. No safety glass there. Raven grinned as he turned left.

The back tire exploded, tilting the truck ominously. He didn't pause as the large vehicle shimmied and swerved, just flattened his right foot on the accelerator, gripped the wheel and kept going. It wasn't the smoothest ride, but they were still ahead of Donovan. If only by feet.

Danica kept firing, until her weapon, too, ran out of ammo. "Damn it—"

"Here," Raven shouted against the din of racing engines and the *thump-clop-scrape* sound of driving on a rubberless rim. He handed her the AK-47. "Take mine. It's nice and big, and full of extremely accurate bullets."

116

With a wide grin, Danica picked it up, braced it on the back of the seat and started firing. "From your lips—" Even with her inexperienced aim, *eventually* she'd hit someone, or something. Right now the covering fire was preventing Donovan's people from driving right up their tailpipe. "You are heading to the palace, right?"

"Hell, yeah," Raven shouted, rocking and rolling down the streets of San Cristóbal, bullets flying all around them. "We're about to become Vera's best friends."

"My thoughts exact—Hey! Did you *see* that? I hit the front tire! Yahoo! They're running off the roa— no, wait. They're back on again," Dani shouted, clearly disappointed she hadn't run them into the ditch alongside the narrow street. "Oh, my God! Incoming!"

Yeah. He saw them. Two more vehicles barreling down on them from side streets and closing *fast*.

People jumped clear of the trucks hurtling down Avenida del Sol, with its flowering, brilliant yellow mimosa trees and picturesque sidewalk cafés. Kids, chickens, goats and bicyclists scrambled to clear the way.

"Are we close?" Danica demanded, getting the hang of the rifle, and feeling like G.I. Jane without the bad hair and terrible shoes. They screamed past City Hall, flanked by a pretty little park, and turned with a screech of three tires onto Presidente Avenida.

"Gate's closed."

She vaguely remembered the high black wrought-iron monstrosity, about a mile wide and half a mile high. "Is that a problem?"

"No. Brace yourself. Now!"

She let go of the rifle, allowing it to drop behind the seat, then braced herself as Jon aimed the truck through the heavy iron gates like a guided missile. Danica, teeth almost jarred from her head, turned to face front as the truck hurtled past the openmouthed uniformed guards, and flew—*hobbled*, up the grand staircase leading from the sweeping gravel driveway directly into the public rooms of the palace. People poured out of various wings like ants at a picnic as the vehicle came to a shuddering, smoking stop, wedged partially inside the giant double doors.

"Very dramatic," she said admiringly as the truck gave an exaggerated death rattle and spewed up a plume of steam from the gaping mouth of the hood.

"Wasn't it, though?" Jon said, turning to run his gaze over her. "Any damaged body parts?"

She held up a finger. "Broken nail. You?"

"My nails are just fine." He jerked his head toward the front of the hissing, smoking, pinging truck and the horde of men striding toward them. "Check out who's coming this way to greet us in all his pompous, sleazy glory." Danica tucked her hair behind her ears with fingers that shook. Just seeing the monster, knowing what he'd done to her, what he planned to do to the president, made her breath hitch and her palms sweat. "He looks a trifle cranky, don't you think?"

"Oh, yeah," Jon said with satisfaction. "That bemused guy next to him must be the president. Why don't you hop out and go give old Ed a big hug?"

"Why don't I?" Unfortunately it was a little hard to "hop out" since the truck was wedged firmly between the heavy wooden doors of the palace. Vera broke away from the president and his entourage and started drifting backward. "Oh, damn. Lookit, he's slithering away!"

"Come on." Jon stood on the seat and held out his hand. "This way." And helped her through the broken windshield, onto the front of the truck, and then, assisted by some very confused gentlemen, onto the ground. Jon jerked his head toward Vera, who had his back to them as he tried to squeeze through the various palace personnel and make a break for it.

"Let's go." He grabbed her hand and ran after the chief of security. People parted for them like the Red Sea.

As he ran, Jon started shouting in rapid-fire Spanish. With much screaming and drama, everyone scattered. "Hey! Ed!" Jon yelled, closing in on the man, Danica trying to keep pace with his long strides.

There was a small flight of shallow marble steps leading off the grand entrance to the bowels of the palace. Vera's shoes tapped out an imperative beat as he ran. Danica eyed the back of his shiny black head, then launched herself off the landing, slamming into him. She clung like a monkey, arms and legs wrapped about him as he crashed to the floor face-first. They sprawled there, Danica on top as if the entire move had been choreographed, her thighs straddling his butt. Her knees stung like fire, and she'd bitten her tongue as they landed hard, but she punched the air with a fist and gave a rebel yell.

Then, leaning close to the terrified man beneath her, Danica said, "Let's see you blow me up now, hotshot."

Jon jumped lightly down the stairs and held a nice big black gun to Vera's temple. *Then* he roared with laughter.

T minus 21hours:00minutes:54se . . .

Raven wasn't laughing an hour later as he paced outside Dani's bedroom door. The musty-smelling corridor, with its funky-colored wallpaper, lined with useless antiques, was crowded with people—from El Presidente's weird-looking kid and several of the surviving members of his cabinet to a dozen dark-suited men from the FAA, the NTSB, Interpol and other assorted agencies.

Raven stormed the length—194 paces—to the end of the long corridor and back again. For the fifth time.

What the *hell* was taking so long?

The president of San Cristóbal had been in there—alone—with Dani, for thirty-four minutes. Thirty-*five* minutes. He sure as shit didn't want to speak to the alphabet soups in their official-issue suits who kept trying to question him.

He tilted his wrist to see the face of his watch in the gloom. Thirty-*seven* minutes.

She could've borne the next freaking royal *heir* by now. Raven raked his fingers through his hair as he paused outside the door. Hell, no. If she was going to bear any heir it would be— The door opened.

The president shot him a smile as he emerged. "Your wife, she is a remarkable woman, señor."

"Yeah, she sure as hell is. All done?" he asked, striving for polite, but pretty damn sure he sounded as surly as he felt. The man stepped back to let him into the room.

Without a backward glance, Raven kicked the door shut behind him, then moved to the high, canopied bed, his heart in his throat, on his sleeve and in his mouth. That about covered its calisthenics. "Hey, look at you, all pink and clean."

And heartbreakingly beautiful as she lay there, sweet-smelling and sleepy-looking, watching him with shadows in her pretty eyes, and a small smile on her luscious mouth. The white Band-Aid on her neck looked completely innocuous. Just seeing the damn thing made bile rise to the back of his throat.

He could've lost her. Again.

How many chances was God going to give him to make this right?

He sat down carefully on the bed beside her. Wanting to gather her close but mortally afraid to touch her. Afraid he'd blow this chance, this last reprieve, of getting it right. "How're you feeling?"

"Like someone stuck me in a bad action movie without a script," Danica said wryly, watching the uncomfortable shift of his gaze, and painfully aware of the awkward silence that stretched between them.

Apparently they could communicate just fine when fists and bullets were flying, but stick them in a room and expect a meaningful conversation—that was apparently beyond their capabilities.

The thought made her throat ache.

"How's your neck?" He started to reach for her, then clearly thought better of it and dropped his hand to the bedspread, curling his fingers into a fist.

"You were in here the whole time they removed it," she said, keeping the wobble out of her voice with an effort. "You know how I am." He'd held her hand tightly as she'd been given a local anesthetic to deaden the site. He didn't leave her side until the device had been successfully removed by the president's personal physician. He'd talked to her, sung a bad rendition of "Margaritaville," and distracted her from thinking her head was going to explode at any minute.

"You had a shower, I see." His hair was still damp at the ends and he smelled of an unfamiliar soap. But beneath it he still smelled like Jon. He was warm and brave and strong and he loved her. She knew he did. Just as much as she loved him. All she had to do was wait him out and make him say it.

"Yeah." He pinched a corner of the lace-trimmed sheet between his fingers and started unraveling a thread. Danica had never, in all the years she'd known him, seen Jon Raven nervous. "Nice chat with the president?" he asked, not glancing up from untatting the probably priceless sheet.

Danica wanted him to look at her. Wanted him to *see* her. Instead, she could tell he was itching to get out of the room, already feeling stifled by the weight of what he would perceive as obligation. He would want to get back to his uncomplicated computers and fail-safe security systems. His "people," and his ordered life. She'd been too unpredictable for his well-structured world. Well, too damn bad.

"He's very grateful to both of us," she said thickly.

The doctor had wanted her to rest for seventy-two hours before she flew home. The president still wanted to award her the keys to the city. Rigo wanted to introduce her to his dog, and barring the one itch that hadn't been an insect bite after all, she still itched like crazy.

How was it possible for a heart to break *twice*?

Could she really just lie here and let him weasel

out? Should she really let him leave? Pretend that they didn't share the connection that was so strong between them?

But the other option was to force him to admit his love. And then what good would it be?

"Jon, would you—" Just *go* before she started begging him? For what? Another shot at being ignored? Of feeling like the loneliest, neediest woman on the planet?

Not true, she reminded herself. Okay, the loneliness part was accurate. But that was as much her fault as his. She'd sat in that house, expecting him to entertain her. Never seeking out a life of her own—never cultivating other interests. No wonder he'd stayed at work all the time. He walked in the door and she'd clung to him like a barnacle. But she wasn't that woman anymore.

Only he didn't know that, she realized. Unless she told him, he never would.

Dangerous.

Necessary.

There was an awkward moment of tension as Danica mustered her courage. "I need to say something."

"Me first," Jon interrupted. Small beads of perspiration formed on his forehead.

He was sweating? Her heart leapt at the mere possibility. She tapped her finger against his lips. "Not this time."

His eyes rose from the unraveled lace to meet hers. "Danica, I—"

"No." She scrambled upward, meeting his intense gaze. "Me first. I got it wrong before," she began on a rush of breath. "I was immature and stupid. I expected you to *be* my life instead of sharing my life. I—"

"Had every reason to want that," Jon insisted, gently cupping her face.

"I want us to try again, Jon. I love you. I never stopped."

His thumb brushed her cheek. "I was the one who screwed it all up. I took you for granted. Loving someone is work. Great work, but work. I neglected you, Dani. When I should have been treasuring you." His gaze raked her face. "I loved you. Even then, when I was stump stupid, I loved you. I should have been thanking you every second of every day. Thanking you for being there. For loving me. You make me a better man, Dani. I still love you. I'll always love you."

"I'll always love you too. And just so you know, we make each *other* better, Jon," Danica said, leaning into him and smiling at the feel of his arms sliding around her. She listened to the staccato beat of his heart and knew they'd found each other again. "We're a great *team*."

"God, Dani." He held her tight. So tight she

wouldn't have been surprised to feel her body sliding right into his, becoming a part of him. "I love you so much. Be sure about this. Be sure that you want me as much as I want you—" He pulled back, stared down into her eyes and grinned. "Because I swear to God, I'll never let you get away from me again."

She kissed him to seal the deal.

USA Today bestselling author Cherry Adair recently saw her first hardcover, *On Thin Ice*, debut to critical acclaim. Her single title, *Hide and Seek*, was chosen as one of Romance Writers of America's top ten books of the year, and her novel *Take Me* has been optioned for an Oxygen Network movie of the week. Cherry and her husband live in the Northwest.

Nothing to Lose

• • •

JILL SHALVIS

To Cherry Adair and Julie Elizabeth Leto,
for graciously sharing their readers with me

Prologue

"Gotcha, you bastard." Ignoring the chill in the room as well as the late hour, Will Malone frowned at his computer as his fingers flew over the keyboard. "Yeah, there you are. *Dead* bastard."

He froze the frame on the museum's security disk. Enlarged and enhanced. Then stared at the picture of the man who'd been born Mario Alvarez but also went by Tomas Manning, Bennie Martin, or any of his other fifteen aliases that Will had unearthed so far. Will memorized every inch of Alvarez, the man who'd killed his sister.

Wendy. Shoving back from his computer, he tunneled his tired fingers through his hair, leaving it standing straight up.

Though Wendy had been dead and buried for

131

three months, he'd just now managed to track down her chameleon-like killer via these miles and miles of tapes from the San Francisco Historical Preservation Society and Museum. Wendy had worked at the museum as a jewel specialist, yet no one else had ever seen Alvarez, the man who'd quickly swept Wendy off her feet before conning her out of two million dollars worth of sixteenth-century gems that she'd been working on. He'd then murdered her and left damning evidence framing her for the loss of the jewels and smearing her name and reputation postmortem.

On the tape, the dark-haired, dark-eyed Mario pretended to enjoy one of the exhibits of assorted historical jewelry. Just a man enjoying a day off. By now he could be anywhere on the planet, working up a new con, stealing someone else's baby sister's innocence and her life.

Will's eyes, shot from long days and nights of surveying the tapes, cut to the picture frame sitting on the desk next to the computer.

Wendy's trusting smile beamed back at him, and he met it with a grim smile of his own. "I've got him now," he promised. "I'll find him." He wouldn't rest until he did.

He was beyond exhaustion, felt it in every bone of his body. He knew he had to pack up and close out Wendy's apartment, but he wasn't ready to face it. Not until Mario was behind bars.

Or in the ground.

His head began to throb from the long hours of sitting. He pushed himself up from the chair and stepped to the window to take in the sweeping hilly view of San Francisco.

As a DEA agent, he'd spent so many years out in the field tracking down the scum of the earth, he'd forgotten what it was like to be a desk jockey.

He didn't like it.

But he had his lead now, and back in the field he'd go. Unofficially this time. He'd given the FBI a chance and they'd blown it. Mario was still out there, getting away with murder, so Will would see this through himself, somehow.

But Wendy would still be gone. His throat tightened. His sister had been the sweetest, kindest person Will knew. She'd added light and love to his life, and she hadn't deserved what had happened to her.

No one did.

The society and its rich patrons had banded together, offering a cool million in reward for their precious gems back. But Will would do this one for free if it meant getting to put Mario away. He stared out the window and told himself to get some sleep.

But how could he rest when he was so sure that Mario was already working a new con, on a new victim?

Mario hadn't played by the rules with Wendy, and

wherever he was now, he still wouldn't be doing so. But, damn it, Will had to. So he would. Come hell or high water, Mario was going to pay.

Will wouldn't rest until he made sure of it.

Chapter 1

Los Angeles

The ingredients for a really bad day were all in place. Nasty breakup with Tomas the night before, her alarm clock failing to go off, and now her lost keys.

Actually, it had been a bad week. And, if she was being honest, an off month.

Okay, truth. It had been a rough year.

But that was all going to change, Jade Barrett told herself as she searched her overflowing junk drawer for her spare set of keys. Sure, the Tomas thing had thrown her off. They'd met at an estate sale. He ran a service that handled high-end probate and estate sales, and she'd been checking out some inventory for Heirlooms, her antique shop. The persuasive, fascinating man had been calling and chasing her ever since. She still marveled at that novelty, having a guy chase her—at least until last night, their two-month anniversary.

He'd looked as tall, dark, and charismatic as ever, and had been making noises about cojoining their businesses, using her stock as collateral to start up a West Coast operation, citing warehouses and numbers that had made her head spin, and her stomach sink. She liked her shop just as it was. Small. She liked the control, liked the coziness.

Then he'd upped her unease by mentioning moving in together. She'd even caught him looking wistfully at the jewelry display in Heirlooms—specifically, the few diamond engagement settings she had.

She'd always figured that when a man got close to asking for her hand in marriage, she'd be over the moon about him. She supposed she'd been too busy trying to keep afloat financially, or wondering what exactly was still missing in her life, why she felt an odd void. She couldn't quite put her finger on it.

Or maybe it came down to one simple fact, that despite her two months with Tomas, she didn't feel like she really *knew* him.

She felt she herself was easy to know, something her bookkeeper, Jody, always disagreed with. *You hold back*, she'd accused Jade time and time again, which she supposed was the reason why, after a year of working together, they weren't yet close.

Jade liked to keep to herself, that's all. She'd lost her father when she'd been eight. He'd been a cop, killed when his cover had been inadvertently blown by her mother, who then sank into a depression and died not long after.

Traumatic as that had been for Jade, the sole witness to her father's murder, she'd been young, and had gone into a warm, kind foster home. She'd recovered. Yes, maybe she still was afraid of the boogeyman in her closet, and had a thing against guns and hated violence in general, and maybe she'd remained a tad bit aloof when it came to commitment, but it worked for her.

In fact, a good part of the attraction to Tomas had been his mysterious, sexy, charming ways, emphasis on the mysterious. If he wasn't the commitment type, then neither would she have to be.

But last night, he'd come over, talking about the future. And she'd known. There wasn't one, at least for them. He'd stood in her bedroom, his long, elegant fingers on the precious antique baby rattle collection on her dresser, including her grandmother's rattle, the one and only sentimental item she owned, and his eyes had filled with cold, hard, calculated interest.

When Jade had called him on it, he hadn't smiled or joked it away. So she'd told him it was over between them, but instead of leaving, he'd let his veneer slip, showing her a heart-stopping fury. He'd picked up her grandma's rattle, fingered it roughly, and when she'd grabbed for it, he'd pushed her.

Shocked, she'd fallen, bumping her head on the brass base of her floor lamp, and had actually blacked out for a moment. When she'd sat up, he was sitting at her side, full of remorse and regret, but she'd been done. Kicking him out of her life had been easier than actually getting him out of her place, but she'd been firm, threatening to call the police. And finally, he'd gone.

And for the first time in two months, she'd slept like a baby.

Now she finally located her spare key in the back of the junk drawer. *Good.* Though it was a Monday, her usual day off, she had some new inventory she needed to catalog and price, and decided getting to it would be the pick-me-up she needed. Slipping her grandma's rattle into her pocket for luck, she left the condo she rented and caught traffic on the 210. By the time she got to Montrose, the small touristy spot where she leased a storefront, the sun was valiantly trying to peek out from the morning's mist. A good sign of things to come, she figured.

Even so, she had to park down the street and around the corner, but parking in Montrose on any day was an exercise in frustration. Walking down the narrow street lined with spring flowers, meandering oaks, and lots of shoppers, Jade got an unwelcome surprise.

Tomas's empty forest-green Jag was parked right out front of her shop. Parked behind him was a black truck, not empty. A man sat behind the wheel. He had a lean, rugged face with light brown hair that looked as if it'd been combed by nothing but frustrated fingers. His eyes locked with hers and held, and the oddest thing happened.

She couldn't look away, and the intensity of the connection confused her because she was certain she'd never seen him before. But then she was jostled by a couple of joggers. Staggering a few steps on her heels, she caught her balance and started walking again, but couldn't stop herself from taking one last look. The sun bore into the truck's windshield now, distorting her view, and distracted by Tomas's empty Jag, she turned away.

Tomas couldn't be waiting inside her shop; he didn't have a set of keys. She unlocked the deadbolt and let herself in the glass door with the pretty wooden welcome sign. With the hanging bells tinkling, she inhaled deeply the scent of cedar and lemon oil, and much of her tension drained away. God, she loved it in here, the one place she'd ever given her heart and soul to.

The front room was filled with furniture she'd found and carefully placed, and all had one thing in common. They were lovingly cared for, fully enjoyed, and old. She was certain a psychologist would have a field day with her need to surround herself with things that had all existed through time, giving comfort and the feeling of roots.

She ran a finger over a chest of drawers, open and filled with lace and linens, but went still when from behind the sales counter, from the large back room where she held all her uninventoried items, came a rhythmic squeaking she couldn't quite place. Setting her purse behind the counter, she moved past the curtain of beads and flipped on the light.

Taking up most of the room was her newly requisitioned Queen Anne bed, and on it was Tomas's bare ass pumping up and down on top of . . . "*Jody?*"

Jade didn't realize she'd staggered backward until she felt the light switch cut into her back. The light flicked off, and then back on as her knees started to give before she locked them. Jody and Tomas. Together. Doing the horizontal tango on her bed.

"You're going to ruin the silk comforter," she said in a shockingly normal voice. "Get off."

And then she walked out. Grabbing her purse off the counter, she headed out of the store and into the morning sunshine, blinking like an owl because there were still flowers blooming, still people walking around, as if everything were normal, perfectly normal.

Her eyes locked on the Jag. She had a sudden and vicious need to break the precious windshield or scratch the paint. Missing keys, her ass. Tomas had stolen her keys! She kicked his tire and then hopped up and down as pain shot through her toe. "Damn it, *damn it.*"

She hobbled all the way back to her car and drove

home on shocked, numbed autopilot. Inside, she tossed her purse down and went to her fridge for an ice pack. She sat right there on the kitchen linoleum, put the ice on her toe, and thunked her head back against the fridge. And then, went still.

It was *her* shop. *Her* stuff. *Her* life. And she shouldn't have left it! Lurching to her feet, she limped out, got into her car, and hit the gas. She made it halfway back to the shop before she caught the blue and red lights flashing in her mirror. "Oh, this is just *perfect*."

She steamed through the thirty minutes it took the officer to write her up. "I'm having a really bad day," she told him, tapping her fingers on the steering wheel.

"Uh-huh. That's what they all say." He kept writing. "I had a flat tire already today. You don't see me whining."

"Is your boyfriend boinking your friend?"

His pen stopped moving. "Okay, you win."

"Gee, thanks." She sighed and put her head down on her steering wheel. By the time she was free to go and got back to her shop, the pain and anger were choking her.

The Jag was gone. So was the black truck, and the man in it. There was, however, a different man outside her shop. Mr. Tyrone, her landlord. When he saw her coming, he gave her a long look as he lifted a . . . padlock? "What's going on?" she asked him.

"As if you don't know." The short, chunky, balding man was out of breath as he placed the padlock on the door and jangled it to be sure it held tight. He shot her a look of remorse. "I liked you, Ms. Barrett. I liked you, a lot."

Clearly she'd entered an alternate universe. "Mr. Tyrone—"

"Your bookkeeper called me, said she wanted to warn me."

"Jody?"

"She was looking out for me, she said. She said that you hadn't authorized her to pay the rent for two months, that you were going under fast."

"*What*?" Jade had thought she'd already experienced the worst she could experience in one short morning.

"I'm locking you out." Mr. Tyrone hitched up the pants that were always sinking south on him because his waist was twice as wide as it should have been, and he had no hips. "I'm sorry, Jade. I have to protect myself."

"No, wait. I—"

"When you come up with the back rent, you know where my office is." With one last tug on his waistband, he walked away, his pants already slipping down.

"But I have the rent money!" she called after him. "You should have been paid! Mr. Tyrone— You *have* to let me in there. My checkbook's in there!" Stunned,

Jade watched him go, then pressed her face to the window, looking in at her entire life, trying to figure out what she wanted to do. Smash something, yes. Cry, most definitely. Instead she pressed harder against the glass, where her eyes caught on her cash register.

Open. Empty.

And beside it? Her checkbook, also open. "Oh no. Oh no, no, no, *no* . . ." She whipped out her cell phone and called Jody. No answer. She tried Tomas next and got another nasty shock, a recording saying the cell number was no longer in service. She didn't have his work number; she'd always reached him via his cell.

Oh God. They were going to wipe her out, if they hadn't already. She ran for her car, fumbling through her purse as she went. In the two months she'd been with Tomas, she'd never been to his place, which should have occurred to her as strange, but it hadn't. He'd said he traveled so much, that his place was too small, and she'd never pushed.

"*Idiot*," she told herself yet again, and raced straight for her bank, knowing she'd be too late. Tomas had gotten her and good, and he was gone, with Jody's help.

That part really bit. Her own personal trust meter had failed her.

The police could help, and she'd call them, but truth was, she'd been had. She knew nothing more than Tomas had been charming and intelligent—and slick. Very slick.

In the bank, things went from bad to worse.

She had three accounts: a personal checking account, which she kept only a couple of hundred dollars in; her business checking account, the balance of which she wasn't exactly sure of because Jody had been handling it, but she guessed to be at least the three thousand she'd just deposited from a particularly large sale the week before; and her savings account, which should have a few grand as well.

It didn't. All three accounts had been wiped out. According to records, it had happened slowly, over the past month.

And she'd not noticed a thing. What kind of a fool did that make her? Her throat tightening, her eyes burning so that she could barely see on the drive home, she let herself into her condo. She needed to call the cops, make a report. . . .

It took a moment for anything else to sink in, but gradually it registered: Her place had been ransacked, carefully and purposefully. Thoroughly. Cabinets open, sofa overturned, drawers on the floor, contents scattered everywhere.

She jumped at the knock on the open door behind her. Turning, she stared into a face she recognized but didn't know.

The man from the black truck.

He wasn't the sort of man one forgot. She just

hoped he wasn't as dangerous as he looked. Up close now, she got a few more details. His tawny hair was on the wrong side of his last haircut. He had a tough, lean jaw and a wide, firm, unsmiling mouth. He stood tall and rangy in her doorway, dressed in casual black, though nothing about the man looked casual. Before she'd wondered what color his eyes were. Now she could see he had the sharpest green eyes she'd ever seen.

At the sight of her condo and its condition behind her, his jaw tightened, and those eyes went flat and cold. "Are you hurt?"

A killer wouldn't ask that question, she reassured herself, and hoped she was right. "No. I'm not hurt."

He angled his head for a better look. "Do you know what they wanted?"

"Who?" she asked.

He pierced her with those extraordinary eyes. "The men after Mario Alvarez."

"I don't know who that is, and I don't know you. Look, I've had a really, *really* bad day." Her voice was beginning to wobble, and horrified, she pushed him back a step, trying not to feel the easy strength of him beneath her fingers. With her other hand, she reached for the door, not about to let a thief, a condo wrecker, a possible murderer inside. "So if you'll excuse me—"

Lifting an arm above her head, he slapped a palm on the wood before she could shut it in his face.

She'd had just enough of a nightmare day for that to really infuriate her. Putting both arms into it this time, she tried to muscle the door closed, but now she couldn't budge it, or him.

He didn't smile or try to put her at ease as he outmuscled her either. He just simply held the door open and leaned in far too close. "Look, however bad you think your day has been," he said in an extremely quiet voice, "you're still breathing. Remember that."

Then, without a care to her wishes, he brushed past her, moving through her condo with easy yet edgy masculine grace. His gaze swept the living room and the mess, and at the sound of glass tinkling in her bedroom off to the left, he whipped out a gun from beneath his shirt so fast her head spun.

"Oh my God." She covered her face, the ultimate hiding her head in the sand. "Not a gun. I can't do this. I really can't."

"*Stay*," he said in the softest, most dangerous voice she'd ever heard, and with his free hand to her belly, pushed her back around the corner, out of sight. "Stay," he said again, and stared at her for a beat.

"Staying," she whispered, wrapping her arms around her middle as she began to shake.

Chapter 2

Will quickly scoped out the small apartment's living room as he moved through, adrenaline pumping through him. Empty. There was no one in the hallway either, and as he burst into the only bedroom, taking in the entire room with one sweeping gaze, he knew he was alone.

He should have nabbed Mario when he'd had the chance this morning at the antique shop, but instead, when he'd realized Mario was being followed, he'd decided to sit back until he knew what was going on. Now he figured Mario had pissed someone off, and that someone thought this woman knew something, which didn't bode well for her.

He toed the pile of shattered porcelain in front of the dresser. Someone had swept everything off the top of it to the floor, and the last little piece falling had been what they'd heard.

"My collection," came a distressed voice behind him, and then she was kneeling at his feet, reaching for the sharp shards.

"I told you to wait out there," he said, and hauled her up before she could cut herself.

Her eyes were wide on his hand, and the gun in it. "I r-really hate guns."

He stuffed the gun in his waistband, and covered it with the hem of his shirt. "What were they looking for?"

When she only stared at him in shock, this little pixie of a woman, maybe five foot two in her shoes, with choppy, shiny dark brown hair to her chin and melting brown eyes that were too large in her face, he gave her a little shake. "Tell me."

"I . . . don't know."

"*Damn it.*" Earlier she'd had a creamy complexion that had reminded him of a china doll. Now it was waxen with shock, her eyes dilating as he swore, punching him in the gut with remorse.

"I'm sorry." She shrank back, away from him. "Please don't hurt me."

Christ. He scrubbed a hand over his face as he struggled for patience. "I'm not going to hurt you." Because that didn't seem to soothe her, he turned away to give her a moment. He'd seen the whole story in her eyes anyway. She knew nothing.

"I don't have any money to take. My ex already did that."

He turned back at that. She seemed to be a contradiction of beauty and stubbornness, and a sexiness he couldn't explain, but he saw no subterfuge. No hint of any lie.

Mario *had* already done her in.

Will squelched the urge to throw something and settled for stalking the length of the small room. All he'd wanted was to get the son of a bitch to a jail cell to rot. He'd been so sighted on that goal, he hadn't thought of who might get in the way.

He turned back. She'd sunk to her knees in front of the pile from the dresser, fingering through the pieces of porcelain like she'd lost her puppy. The thought of her getting hurt because of this, possibly because of him, coiled his gut.

She picked up a single shard and let out an anguished sigh. More remorse sneaked in like a thrifty little bastard, but then he remembered Wendy, and the wave of sorrow and the need for biting revenge beat back any remorse. "You help me and I'll pay you five hundred."

She lifted her head. "Dollars?"

He very nearly smiled, but not with amusement. "Five hundred *thousand* dollars." Half the society's reward, if that's what it took.

"Five hundred *thousand*." She went even paler, and then right before his eyes, hers rolled in her head.

"*Shit.*" In two strides he was at her side, crouching down, shoving her head to her knees. "Breathe. *Breathe.*"

"I'm . . . trying."

"Try harder."

At her sides her fists clenched as she panted for air through the panic attack. She wore a short denim skirt that had risen high on her thighs when she'd dropped to the floor, and an eye-popping yellow halter top that matched her high-heeled sandals. The whole getup should have been silly to his practical mind, but instead was sexy as hell. So was the bared, tanned soft skin of her back, the row of delicate bones lining her spine reminding him how long it'd been since he'd kissed his way down a woman's back.

"I told you, this has been a very bad day." Her breath shuddered in and out. "I couldn't find my keys. I should have known to just pack it in right there and call it a day, but no." She squeezed her eyes shut. "Tomas in bed with Jody. A speeding ticket. And I think I broke my toe when I kicked that rat bastard's tire. And then he stole all my money, and I can't get into my shop, and now my house has been ransacked—" She straightened and leveled him with a tearful, hopeful expression. "I'm dreaming, aren't I? Tell me this whole thing is just a bad dream."

When he slowly shook his head, all hope drained out of her face. She swiped her arm beneath her nose and looked around at the utter destruction of her bedroom. Her short hair danced around her cheeks. "I don't understand."

No, he could see that she didn't, but he was beginning to. "What's your name?"

"Jade."

"You know your boyfriend as Tomas Manning, right?"

"He's not my boyfriend. He's a rat bastard."

"Yeah, well, he's an internationally known rat bastard with more aliases than you have years on you, who has personally fenced close to ten million dollars' worth of antiquities across the country and is now wanted in about twenty states for those crimes, as well as for murder one."

She sat there, and her wide unpainted mouth trembled open, her drenched eyes lifting to his, confused and hurting. "Murder?" she whispered.

"Yeah, murder."

"I don't want to see anyone die. I *can't* see anyone else die."

He had no idea if she was crazy, or just in shock. "Count your lucky stars that you didn't get in his way, or that you weren't here when the goons after him couldn't find what they wanted." He wrapped his fingers around her slim, surprisingly toned arm. "Now get it together. We have to move before they come back here to shake some information out of you."

"Oh my God."

"Where's Mario, Jade?"

"I don't know."

"If those guys find him first . . ." He let that hang in the air.

Her eyes flickered with fear. "There's a woman with him. An ex-employee of mine. She stole from me, but I don't want her to lose her life."

"Then let's hope she's smart."

"She is." Jade put her head to her knees and gulped air. Her short hair fell forward in a shiny curtain, exposing the back of her neck in a way that made her look even more vulnerable. Her small trim body trembled, and when she turned her head to stare at him, she nibbled on her full lower lip, which looked to be made for nibbling, and he couldn't look away. "What is it you want from Tomas—Mario?" she corrected.

He wanted to see him in hell. "He's holding on to a pile of gems that don't belong to him. My guess is that he's looking for a fence."

"Fence?" She looked confused, and adorable in that confusion. "You mean someone to sell the gems to?"

"That's right. Where would he go, Jade?"

"I don't know." She looked around at the mess. She'd had shelves along one wall, which had been flipped. Her closet had been dumped, the chair in the corner slashed. The room had been seriously trashed, with a violence that still shimmered in the air. "I need to call the police."

The cops would only slow the whole process down. If Will didn't get to Mario now, he'd slip under again, using a different alias on his next con, and it might be three more months before Will caught wind of him again.

There'd be another murder, he knew it. Time mattered. Every second mattered. But she reached for her phone.

Will wrestled it out of her hand and held it high above her head. "We can do this better without them."

"There's no 'we.' " Her voice trembled nearly as badly as her body. "I don't know you."

"Will Malone."

"That doesn't tell me much."

"I'm one of the good guys."

She eyed him with fear and suspicion. "How do I know?"

He sighed. Considered. Then flashed his ID.

She looked at his picture, then cut her eyes to his. "You're an agent of the federal government?"

"See? Good guy. Let's go."

"Go where?"

"To find your boyfriend."

"*Ex*," she spat between her teeth, ignoring the hand he held out to help her up. With her chin thrust high enough in the air to give her a nosebleed, she rose by herself and came barely to his shoulder, look-ing young, a little ravaged, and a lot shaken. She crossed her arms over her chest and gave him a stub-born look. "How does an agent of the government come up with half a million dollars to hand out?"

Not about to answer that right now, or any time for that matter, he just lifted a brow.

"Fine." She snatched the phone out of his hand. "Then I'll just call the police."

He waited while she fumbled the phone on. Then he said agreeably, "Fine. Let the cops come and inter-view you, then leave you alone to this mess, which is when you'll most likely be visited by whoever did this in the first place."

She swallowed audibly, and he ruthlessly pushed his advantage. "They'll ask you for information, Jade. Using unsavory means to get it." That much was likely true, and he looked her over. She wouldn't handle it well. She was small and untrained, and in a way he still didn't understand, sexy as hell. Oh yeah, they'd lap her up and spit her out, and maybe, *maybe*, let her live to remember it for the rest of her life. "Do you have a baseball bat?"

"Why?"

"You're going to need it to try to protect yourself."

A small sound of terror escaped her lips, but he ruthlessly kept his voice hard. "Take me where I need to go, Jade, and it won't be an issue. I'm going to pay you, not hurt you. Five hundred grand."

Her soft, dewy eyes met his. "This isn't happening."

"It is and you can't stay here." He grabbed a small denim backpack off the floor and opened it. A tube of lip gloss rolled around the bottom. "Throw a few things in here and let's go. Get ID, too."

She glanced around uneasily. "You really think they'll come back?"

He looked her right in those milk-chocolate eyes and tipped the scales in his favor, without a drop of guilt—something he'd gotten good at. For a DEA agent, nothing was ever black and white, but various shades of gray, which had worn on his conscience, his morals, his very soul. "Oh yeah," he said silkily. "They'll come back for you. You're going to be a tasty morsel for them, too."

She glanced uneasily at her bed.

"Where will Mario go, Jade? Back to your shop maybe?"

"How do you know so much about me?"

"Because I've been tailing Mario for two days." Infuriate her. A woman infuriated would stop at nothing to exact revenge. "I heard him coming on to Jody. That's who is with him, right?"

Her eyes clouded. *Bingo.*

"Where would he go?" He toed some of the mess on the floor at their feet. There was glass everywhere. Also some personal effects: her keys, her wallet, her passport.

"I told you! I don't know where he'd go! Maybe Baja. He told me once his parents retired there, but he was probably lying." She scooped her wallet off the floor.

"Mexico," he muttered, and nabbed her passport as well, tossing it into the backpack.

Jade just stood there, looking a little lost. Will knew she was working on autopilot, locked into her fear. He took the bag from her. "A pair of pants. A shirt or two."

She pulled the items from her closet, and he shoved them in the pack. He moved to the dresser. He pulled open the first drawer, got lucky, and grabbed some underwear, ignoring her shocked choke. "Real shoes," he told her, and moved into her bathroom to grab her toothbrush, toothpaste, and a brush off the counter, dropping them all into the now-bulging small backpack.

When he came back to her, she was wearing flats instead of the heels, and had what looked like a porcelain rattle in her hands. And because he was watching her so carefully, he saw it all over her face when she remembered something. He opened his mouth to push her, to get her to open up and tell him, but another sound shuddered through the house.

A door creaking.

Jade gasped and straightened. Will moved quickly, stepping close, covering her mouth with his hand before she could make a sound and give them away.

Once again he pulled out his gun, and her eyes widened. "Stay," he mouthed, and slipped out of the bedroom.

Jade backed up until the wall was at her back. Her heart thundered in her chest. There was a roaring of sheer terror in her ears.

You're going to be a tasty morsel for them.

No. She stuck her grandma's rattle, the only one left now, back in her pocket and dove to the floor, sticking her hand beneath her bed, frantically reaching for the only weapon she could think of.

There, but just as her fingers closed around it, she heard a whisper of a sound behind her.

Craning her neck, she caught sight of a pair of scuffed athletic shoes, which came to a stop only a foot from her. *Oh God.* Moving as fast as she could, she scooted back out and came to her knees, face to crotch with her intruder as she wound up to swing at him with her umbrella.

Chapter 3

Will easily deflected the blow, tossed the umbrella aside, and hauled her up to her feet. Eyes glittering with temper, he wrapped an arm of steel around her body and yanked her against him, putting a finger to her lips, following through with an expression that had any words jamming in her throat as he gestured with a jerk of his head that they weren't alone.

Oh God, oh God.

She nodded to show him she understood.

He thrust her backpack in her hands and without a word dragged her to her window, letting go of her to reach for the latch. He was taller than Tomas had been, more leanly muscled, too. She doubted he carried an ounce of fat, and yet there was a solidness to him that Tomas had lacked. That most other men lacked. His movements were fluid yet utterly economical as he slipped on her backpack while gesturing that she should get on the ledge. The outside ledge.

The outside ledge that was two stories above the ground.

Stomach in her throat, she turned back to her tossed bedroom, her heart racing at the thought of running from some unknown danger, of running headfirst into another, bigger one.

With Will's eyes hard on her, fathomless and direct in a way that shook her to the core, she stuck her hand in her pocket and fingered her grandma's rattle. The height from the second story had never bothered her before, but then again, she'd never considered crawling out on the ledge and climbing down the oak that grew right outside.

It was crazy. *She* was crazy. This guy, smooth and confident, and quite frankly the most attractive man she'd ever seen, could be no different than Tomas for all she knew.

She should have called the police when she had the chance.

As if he'd read her mind, Will leaned in, and put his mouth to her ear. "One full million if you hurry your sweet ass up, and don't get us killed right now. One million, Jade, to help me find Mario. See justice served."

Justice. She believed in justice, and Tomas should pay for his crimes.

And one million dollars . . . She could buy a place.

Get her shop opened again. Be comfortable without counting pennies as she'd done all her life. All these silly, frivolous thoughts bounced through her head so that she couldn't dwell on the other, more pressing thought.

She might not live to spend it.

She swung her legs over, balancing on the ledge, then made the fatal mistake of looking down. At the sight of the narrow planter with flowers and the tree base, lined on both sides with hard concrete, all of which looked *very* far down, her stomach pitched.

"Stop." Will hooked an arm around her waist. "Keep your eyes straight ahead," he commanded in that barely there whisper as he joined her on the ledge. "Reach out for the branch."

He had one arm braced behind her now, and the other still around her. Her eyes locked on his forearm, tanned and corded with hard strength. He smelled good, came the inane thought. He smelled really good.

"Do it."

His silky demand was underlaid with warning, reminding her that while he might smell good and look even better, he was a perfect stranger forcing her out a second-story window.

Her vision wavered as the dizzying height danced spots in her eyes. "I hope Tomas rots in hell."

"We're going to make him pay right here on earth, Jade. Go."

"Going." Holding her breath, she reached out for the branch.

"Swing down. Hand over hand until you get closer to the trunk, then set your feet on the branch beneath you. Grab on to it, and drop. Don't scream, don't make a sound."

Bark dug into her palms as she followed the directions to the letter. Tree climbing hadn't been something she'd done as a child, and now she knew why. It was a dirty business, and hurt as the bark bit into the tender flesh on the insides of her legs and her arms as she crawled, holding her breath. But she kept moving, flattening herself back against the trunk when Will shimmied down after her onto that last branch. Then she fell to the ground in a graceless heap.

Above her, Will swung down with confident ease, arms and legs outstretched before he dropped without a sound and straightened.

"Who's up there?" she whispered.

"Well, it wasn't the Girl Scouts, trying to sell cookies."

Right. Okay, then.

One million dollars.

More than she'd ever dreamed of, and a chance for justice. She wouldn't be a victim, not ever again, but in order to get to that point, she had to help Mr. Tall, Gorgeous, and Surly here find Tomas.

Then a funny popping noise interrupted her thoughts, and the bark exploded above her head.

Will grabbed her, and protecting her with his body, shoved her in front of him and around the corner of the building. "Move," he said, but he didn't need to shove her again because there came a series of popping noises now.

Gunshots, she thought slightly hysterically.

They were being shot at.

And she was running for her life.

Another pop, and this one whizzed by her ear. She tripped over the sidewalk and would have fallen on her face, but Will slid an arm around her and yanked her upright. "Go. *Go, go, go.*"

"I am," she panted.

"Faster," he suggested, not panting even a little. "*Way* faster."

Will could have moved more quickly on his own, but he was towing Jade, whose legs were far shorter than his. Spurred on by the thought of a bullet tearing through their flesh, he tugged her hand, propelling her down the row of condos.

Unfortunately, they were moving in the opposite direction of his truck.

"Where to?" Jade gasped.

At the end of the row now, he glanced back. No more chunky man in black hanging out Jade's window with his Glock and silencer.

Which meant he was tearing through the condo and down the stairs to get out here.

That gave them only a few seconds at most.

They needed to get to his truck, but that was out of the question for the moment because it meant backtracking, and possibly running into another trigger-happy intruder. "Here," he said, and pulled her around the corner.

There was a garden, thankfully lush from spring rains. Against the building grew a long line of some sort of tall bush, perfect for camouflage. Flattening Jade against the wall, he looked into her eyes. Glassy and dilated, and she was breathing like a misused racehorse. "Are you hurt?"

"S-someone was shooting at us."

Cupping her face, he tilted it up. "Are you hurt?" he repeated.

"Not as much as I'd be, if any of those bullets had hit their target."

His lips twitched into a rare smile, or at least half of one. It'd been a long time since he'd felt like smiling at all. "We have to keep moving."

"We passed my car."

"Yes, with the four slashed tires."

She gulped hard. "Slashed?"

"When the coast is clear, we make a run for my truck."

"And then what?"

Her body was trembling, and he pressed just a little closer to try to help. "You know what then."

"We find Tomas."

"Bingo."

Her eyes narrowed. "Are you sure you're the good guy?"

"I swear it."

"Just tell me how you have a million dollars to offer as a reward."

"A patron-rich San Francisco historical society put up the money to recover what Mario stole. And trust me, if they're willing to pay that much, imagine how little your life is worth to the guys chasing you."

"Very little."

"Double bingo."

She gulped again, and despite the fact that her skin sheened with perspiration, she shivered. "A really bad day," she whispered.

Looking into her terrified face, he felt his heart soften. Not good. Ruthless was his middle name. Fact was, Jade should have been smarter about her life, and the men in it.

And what about Wendy? Should she have been smarter, too?

With a sigh, his thumb swept a path over Jade's cheek. She had a scratch there from climbing down the tree, and he suddenly wanted to put his lips to the spot. "This whole thing might get worse before it gets better."

She nodded. "I know."

"He doesn't deserve to be out there, Jade."

"I know that, too."

"Then say it."

"I'll help you find Tomas."

"Mario."

"I'll help you find whoever the hell he is. And you'll make him pay for ruining my life." Her voice caught. "Right?"

"I'll make him pay," he vowed. "Count on it."

Chapter 4

I'll make him pay. Jade absorbed Will's words, just as she absorbed the heat and strength of him as he pressed her into the wall.

She was hurting, inside and out, and yet none of it could rise above the sensation of his touch. His palm was warm on her cheek, his fingers callused. His thighs and chest brushed hers. He felt like one solid muscle.

Then that solid muscle tensed. He lifted his head and narrowed his eyes, clearly sensing something she couldn't hear or see. "Wait here," he breathed.

"Getting tired of that." But he was already gone.

The sun was bright overhead. At her feet, a lone ant wandered in circles. The bushes pressed into her, aggravating the cuts and scrapes she'd earned climbing down the tree.

Better than a bullet, she reminded herself.

Then, from around the corner, she heard footsteps approaching. Heavy footsteps.

But . . . Will didn't make a sound when he moved.

Oh God. *Where is Will?* She hesitated, but the footsteps kept coming, and picturing a nameless figure in black, holding a big gun pointed right at her, she decided she'd just lost the option of waiting.

Whirling, she took off. The long line of thick bushes hampered her. She counted how far she had to go before she could turn the back corner of the building. Four bushes. Then three, two. One. There was a wide-open gap between the last bush and the corner. She didn't dare slow down enough to glance back, but she had an itch there between her shoulder blades . . .

She already knew she was going to run into trouble in the back of the building. Each bottom-floor unit had a back deck, contained by low fences. She could have hopped any one of them and entered a sliding glass door, losing herself inside an individual condo—assuming first, that the glass door was unlocked, and second, that the person inside wouldn't freak at the wild woman breaking in with a bad guy on her tail and packing heat.

But she caught a break. She'd forgotten about the common-area patio, with the four barbecues, community hot tub, and picnic tables. She ran toward it, breath sawing in and out of her lungs. She hopped the fence, completely forgetting that anything athletic was beyond her.

Her skirt snagged on the low fencing and twisted around her hips as her foot got caught between two slats of wood, whipping her upside down, where she hung for one brief heartbeat, her face an inch from the concrete.

Then her skirt ripped, and she hit the ground.

Because she imagined her pursuer pointing his gun at her, she was up and running again without so much as brushing the gravel out of the scrapes in the palms of her hands and knees, running past the benches and the hot tub, heading directly for the door that read: MAINTENANCE, NO ENTRANCE.

It must have been some sort of divine luck that the thing wasn't locked, but she didn't stop to consider that when she burst through it, and then shut it behind her.

The room was a small maintenance room, maybe four feet by four, with a metal shelving unit loaded with supplies for the hot tub, and a few tools. A single lightbulb swung overhead. Chest heaving, her hands pressing palms down on the door at her back, Jade blinked into the surprised eyes of Ed Bahn, the man who maintained the property.

"No one's allowed in here." He stood there holding a bottle of chlorine in his big, bony hands, a tall, reed-thin sourpuss of a man in his fifties who made it a sport to snipe at everyone he came in contact with. He was mean as sin, but infinitely more appealing than whoever had been shooting at her and Will.

And where is Will? If she let herself wonder, she'd lose it. "Ed." She gulped for air. "I need to hang in here a minute, okay?"

"Not okay." Ed shook his head. "I'm leaving. I have to lock up." He pointed to the door. "Get out."

"Oh no, you can't leave, not yet." Nasty as a pit bull he might be, but she still didn't want him to run into a bullet.

"Look, missy, I'm leaving now. If you want to stay in here by yourself, fine, but don't keep that bulb working. Electricity costs money, you know. Lock up after yourself, you hear me?"

"Ed—"

Too late, he was opening the door, grumbling to himself as he always did, turning off the light, and she had to slap a hand over her mouth to keep her terrified scream still in her throat.

He'd shut her in.

In the dark.

The age-old fear reached up and grabbed her by the throat. She stared at the door, at the handle, the only sound in the room being her own panicked breathing through her fingers. *Relax, Jade. Breathe.* At least it wasn't completely black, she told herself. Light came in around the badly hung hinges. She stared at that light, concentrating on putting air into her lungs.

Strain as she might, she didn't hear any gunfire, didn't hear anything.

It was so dark. *Too* dark. Her hand slid into her pocket and curled around the baby rattle, as if it could offer comfort in a world gone mad. But she knew she couldn't just stay in here forever. What she really needed was a weapon, something to protect herself with if it came to that. She spared a moment to wish she'd taken those self-protection classes Jody had urged her to take with her at the community center last fall.

At the thought of Jody, something panged deep inside her. She didn't understand half of what happened today, but knew that Jody had to be in even more danger than herself if she was still with Tomas somewhere, running from God knew whom.

She told herself it didn't matter, that Jody would get whatever she had coming to her for betraying Jade, not to mention aiding and abetting, but Jade just couldn't quite maintain her anger.

The handle turned.

Her life flashed before her eyes as she pressed back against the metal shelving unit, shoving a fist against her mouth to keep in her scream. Silence was key, she knew this, and tried her damnedest to disappear into her own skin.

171

The door creaked as it opened. Her heart all but stopped as a solidly built shoulder and a long, rangy arm slid in through the crack, blocking the sunlight, a mere shadow as the intruder wrapped his long fingers around her wrist.

She opened her mouth to scream, but before she could, he slipped all the way inside, and a now-familiar hand covered her mouth. "Shh," Will said. "They're still looking for us, searching the place."

Before she could react, he yanked her to him, bumping her body into his hard, immovable one. Though she didn't know him from Adam, she bit back the urge to put her head on his shoulder and cry.

"You blocked yourself in with no escape route," he breathed in her ear, his lips tickling the sensitive skin there. "Not the smartest plan."

"You ditched me."

"I've kept you safe this far. You could show a little trust."

"Trust? *Trust?*" She nearly laughed, but she was afraid she wouldn't be able to stop. She settled for poking him in the pec with her finger. "I want to know what's going on. Do you hear me?"

"Shh."

"No, I won't shh, I—"

Hauling her up against him, he slammed his mouth over hers.

Shock held her immobile, but he didn't ravish,

didn't plunder. Instead, he kept the connection soft, warm. His body shuddered once, as if the control cost him greatly, and when he opened his mouth in an intimate and erotic invitation, stroking his tongue along hers, she dug her fingers into the hard muscles of his shoulders and met him halfway.

She'd already known his mouth to be wide and firm, rarely smiling, but she didn't know he'd taste like forgotten dreams and have lips as giving as a spring rain. She didn't know his kiss would eradicate the horrific fear that had been driving her, replacing it with a heat and a need such as she'd never known. God, he felt good, so good, and she lost her mad, lost her fear, lost everything but the desire for more, while in the back of her heart a very small voice wondered . . . how could a guy who carried a gun for a living be so . . . extraordinarily sensual?

He rocked against her, a subtle, quiet movement that threatened to melt all her bones away, threatened to leave her a quivering heap on the floor of the maintenance closet. But then he pressed her back, taking her weight between his gloriously hard body and the harder wall at her back, one arm banded around her hip, the other holding her head in the palm of his big hand as he kissed her again. And again.

Finally he dragged his mouth from hers, staring down at her, blinking slowly, as if coming off a drug. Or a potent kiss.

She opened her mouth, and he set two fingers against her still-wet lips with one shake of his head. Then he took his fingers away and came at her again. This time he both plundered and ravished, and she practically crawled up his body to get even closer, loving the feel of his hard chest—squashing into her breasts, teasing the sensitized tips of her nipples— needing, needing so much it shocked her to the core, but it didn't matter, he gave it.

None of it made any sense, but then nothing about the day had made any sense, and when he pulled back this time, her legs would have given out on her if he hadn't been holding her up. Her hands, still fisted on him, loosened. Beneath her palms she could feel his heart, steady and sure, pumping fast but still rock solid.

She had a feeling the world could be coming apart and he'd still be rock solid.

"We need to get out of here." He glided his thumb over her lower lip until it trembled open. He had calluses on his fingers, she thought inanely, assuring her this man was no desk jockey. He probably used his gun on a daily basis without blinking, terrifying women for a hobby, and she'd been a fool to trust him, but she'd had no choice.

Still didn't.

Before she could dwell on that, he tugged her out of the maintenance closet and back into the open, which nearly gave her a coronary. Her entire body twitched, and she felt more vulnerable than she'd ever been.

"There." Pointing to the first condo, he stayed at her back, practically hunching over her, protecting her body with his.

She'd been imagining the damage a bullet could do, the way it would tear into her, but she didn't like imagining it tearing into him either. Clearly he wanted to go through a condo to the front of the street rather than all the way around the long line of the building.

But where then? To her car, whose tires had been slashed? To where some unknown guy waited with a gun?

"Go," he said in a rough whisper as he rushed her over the low fence—she didn't fall this time; she couldn't have, not with his hands guiding her, slipping around her waist to help her—and into the tiny backyard of the first condo, which she happened to know belonged to Mrs. Tokimoto, a seventy-year-old woman with a tendency to mind everyone's business but her own.

But that worked in their favor, because the older woman had left her sliding glass door slightly ajar. By the time they slipped inside, Jade was practically hyperventilating with fear and panic. *Please don't be home*, she prayed silently, not wanting another innocent person to enter the nightmare that was her life. *Please.*

One quick look into the living room, neat as a pin with furniture that looked as if maybe it'd been around since the early seventies, and she took a breath of relief. No sign of the innately curious Mrs. Tokimoto.

Grabbing her hand, Will pulled her silently through the living room, past the pristine plastic-covered green and orange velour couches and glass coffee table, past the pear and peach wallpaper. They were heading past the open staircase with the light green walls, making their way toward the front door, when a noise came from above.

"Hello?"

Mrs. Tokimoto. Before Jade could register that fact and up her stress—already at a Prozac level—Will grabbed her, propelled her beneath the staircase and against the wall, and held her out of view with his body.

She didn't need the caution in his gaze to know she should swallow her scream. She didn't need anything but the knowledge that if she brought attention to herself, or Mrs. Tokimoto, she might get them all killed.

Chapter 5

"Is someone there?" Mrs. Tokimoto's voice trembled with age as she leaned down over the stairs. "Hello?"

Jade's nerves were shot. She trembled, and her teeth rattled in her head. Delayed shock, she was certain, but she couldn't catch her breath to save her life.

Will's hands squeezed her waist in warning, his broad shoulders blocking the view of anything but him, and his intense, see-all eyes. Locked onto those, she held herself absolutely rigid, her mouth clamped down hard on the scream building deep inside of her from the tension, from the fear that any second the men chasing them would come crashing through that slider, guns blazing.

Will's eyes told her not to move, not to breathe.

Not a problem. But she craned her neck, trying

to see the glass door, needing to know when the end came.

"I locked the slider," Will breathed in her ear. "It's going to be okay."

Okay? How in the world was anything going to be okay ever again? She just shook her head. It didn't matter if he locked the door; this hell wasn't over.

"Hello?" Mrs. Tokimoto said again. "Anyone there?"

Oh God. *Don't come down here, Mrs. Tokimoto, please don't.* Panic twisted inside her like an insidious beast. She realized she'd set her forehead to Will's chest, fisting her hands in his shirt to hold him close so that she couldn't see. She only wished she couldn't hear, couldn't feel. Hell, she wished she wasn't here at all.

Then Will's finger lifted her chin, making her look at him, into his deep, unwavering eyes. His jaw was tight, with sympathy or regret, she wasn't sure. Probably annoyance. But he kept his hand on her, held her gaze prisoner with his, and mouthed her name in a way that told her she wasn't alone. She wasn't alone and he wasn't going to let anything happen to her.

Again she shook her head. She couldn't do this. She wasn't an adventurous woman. Scary movies and books were too much for her—she read only romance. And the not-breathing thing? Bad idea.

Spots began to dance in front of her eyes, but she only tightened her mouth, afraid to open it.

Will's gaze dropped to her lips. "Breathe," he mouthed, and ran his thumb over her lower lip in a slow caress, and when it became apparent she couldn't, he dipped his head. His mouth was only a fraction of an inch from hers. He looked into her eyes, and in his she didn't see temper, or even annoyance, but a shocking patience and understanding.

It was almost too much, and she opened her mouth to suck in some desperately needed air, letting out a squeak in the process.

With a grimace for the sound, Will slid his hands down the length of her arms, entangling her fingers in his, moving both of their hands to the base of her spine. Pressing her forward, nudging her into his body, he covered her mouth with his, swallowing her next squeak.

Will told himself he had no choice but to kiss her, no choice at all. Her breasts were still pressing into his chest, as well as her quivering belly and thighs, and his physical response to her heat and angst and body didn't so much surprise him as nearly annihilate him.

The kiss itself felt more like leaping into a circle of flames, instantly hot, licking at him in spots he hadn't expected her to reach. Deep, wet, messy . . .

Finally, she tore free, staring up at him with those wide, huge eyes, her breath coming in short little shocky pants, her mouth still wet from his. Her face was the palest porcelain, her chest rising and falling too fast.

Twisting her hands free of his hold, she once again grabbed on to his shirt. His hands went to her hips, holding her still so she wouldn't do something stupid like run. Her hot little bod still quivered against his, and her heart, *Christ*, it was pounding so hard and fast he knew she was only seconds from meltdown.

A meltdown he had to avoid at all costs. He stroked his hands down her back, meaning only to soothe, needing to soothe in a way that was alien to him really, but she just shook her head again. He knew she wanted to be brave, wanted to do so on her own.

"*Hello*?" the old woman above them called out.

Jade jerked.

Ah, damn, she was going to lose it. Will could see it coming, so he gave up on the soothing and went back to the kissing, kissing her hard and long, kissing her like he was a starving man and she was some kind of twelve-course meal.

More like his last supper.

And still it wasn't enough—he couldn't get enough. The next thing he knew, he'd pressed her up against the wall and dug in with a shocking gusto. Her mouth opened to his in a soft, tentative movement, tasting sweet and hot and so damned good he didn't think he'd be done for a good long time.

Given how she'd wrapped her arms around his neck and clung, she felt the same way. His fingers slid up and down the warm back that her halter top bared for him, stroking heated skin. She was the softest thing, so damn soft, and as he slid his hand down to cup and squeeze her extremely squeezable ass, he added perfect to the list.

"I'm losing my mind," the woman above them said to herself.

Join the club, Will thought, sinking into the kiss. *Join the club.*

Jade thought the same thing, because surely this buzzing in her ears, the heat flooding her skin, the way her every pulse point pounded, meant she was losing her mind as well.

From above them now came nothing but silence, then the sound of a door shutting softly.

"She went into a bedroom or bathroom," Will whispered against her ear in that way he had, drawing chills down to her toes.

Not trusting her voice, she nodded.

"We need a place to hide until dark."

She put her mouth to his ear this time. "Downstairs."

He went utterly still, and his eyes flared with heat.

181

From her mouth, she realized, and the knowledge made her want to talk in his ear again.

Clearly she *had* lost her mind to be thinking in such a manner with her life on the line.

"There's a basement in these units?"

She nodded. "Mrs. Tokimoto doesn't do stairs well. I don't think she'll go down there without good reason."

"Well, let's not give her one."

The stairs were dark and just a little musty, and as they tiptoed their way down, she could feel his hand low on her spine, guiding her, keeping track of her in the growing dark as they hit the bottom.

If she licked her lips, she could still taste him. In fact, she was having a hard time, vacillating between terror and arousal, and her poor body was confused as hell. Her nipples were hard, but her heart still raced. Her legs felt like jelly, but between them she was damp.

Worse, she had no idea which emotion she expected him to appease, the fear or the desire.

She didn't understand how she could trust him like this. There hadn't been many men in her life, but they'd all been calm, quiet types. Beta. Until Tomas, that is, and given how that had turned out, she should be running from this hard, edgy alpha man.

Instead, she'd put her life into his hands. She'd *kissed* him.

Adrenaline, she assured herself. That's all it was.

At the bottom of the stairs, the room was dark and smelled . . . old. Normally she liked the smell of old, but not this kind of dusty, icky, creepy old.

And the dark brought back her terror. A sudden beam of light startled her. It was Will, holding a pen flashlight that he'd pulled out of somewhere. *Thank God.*

There was one long strip of a window only inches from the ceiling, facing the street nearly at ground level, but protected with a shade that didn't let in any sunlight. Will studied all of it, silently taking it in. There were two large sofas and a chair, all of which were draped with plastic, and then piles and piles of boxes of files and papers, overflowing onto the floor and covering every square inch of the place.

And then he looked at her. She had a feeling nothing escaped his notice—not the cut on her cheek, not her ripped skirt—and though his jaw tightened, he didn't say a word. He flicked off the light. The darkness was all-consuming, and closed in on her in a familiar, terrifying tightness. "Will."

"Hang on."

She heard just the faintest of noise for a moment, but with the light gone, she couldn't see a thing, not even a hand in front of her face, and it messed with her head—which had been messed up enough today, in her opinion.

Another slight sound.

But after a moment she couldn't decide if she'd really heard anything or if her brain was playing tricks on her. Her nerves were strung so tautly she could hardly stand it. She just wanted to sit and think, wanted to process all that had happened since she'd made the unfortunate decision to get out of bed that morning.

And she really, really, *really* wanted the light on. Yet another soft sound, just a whisper really, this time so close it raised goose bumps on her skin. "Will—"

Fingers reached out and entwined with hers, causing her to nearly leap out of her skin.

"Jumpy," he said, and though a moment ago she'd been pliant in his arms, nearly mewling with pleasure, now she wanted to smack him.

"I can't see!"

"Yeah. That works both ways." He was nothing but a disembodied, low husky voice in the dark. "I barricaded the door with a stack of boxes. Not that they'll find us here," he added at her sharp intake of breath.

Much as she'd thought she'd grown up, her childhood fear of the dark was not only still with her, but fully intact. God, she hated this, hated it with a fearful passion, but she happened to be on fearful overload at the moment, so she said nothing, but resisted when Will reached for her. "No."

"You're cold. Come on, come here." Again he tried to draw her close but she dug in her heels.

"I can't." She swallowed hard and shook her head, then realized he couldn't see any better than she could. "I can't," she said again.

"Jade?"

Every time she blinked, she was back, a child, in the dark, alone with her dead father. "Put the flashlight back on."

"There's nothing down here. I checked. We're okay."

Her throat felt like she'd swallowed glass. "The light. Please." Her voice wobbled on the "please," and she hated herself. But she said it again. "*Please*, Will."

"Jade. We're okay." Gently but inexorably he tugged, sliding an arm around her, half pulling her, half carrying her, until suddenly her feet left the ground entirely, and then she sank onto what had to be one of the couches.

He'd moved everything off of it, including the plastic. She felt him sink next to her, at her hip. "Thought I'd keep us comfortable, seeing as we're going to be here for a while."

"We can't just stay here."

"No choice at the moment. We've been made."

"Made?"

"Three of them, all armed, searching the perimeters as we speak. I don't think they've got me though, or my truck. But you . . . you they clearly want."

Oh God. She couldn't do this. She couldn't. "How will you get out of here?"

"We. How will *we* get out of here. You don't really think I'd leave you alone in this?"

"No."

"Good, because I'm not going anywhere—" He broke off when something from in her pocket beeped.

"My cell," she whispered in horror.

"See who it is. Quickly, Jade."

She stared at the lit display. "Jody."

"Answer. Find out where Mario is."

She clicked on the phone but didn't say hello. She couldn't—it was stuck in her throat.

"Jade." Jody's voice dissolved into tears. "Oh God, is that you?"

"Yes."

"Jade, listen. I know you don't want to, but I have to tell you how sorry I am. How stupid I am. It's my mom, you know that, right? She's got cancer, and no insurance. Tomas promised me he'd give me everything I could ever want, and I was stupid enough to fall for it." She began to sob. "He just dumped me off on the side of the road. Like yesterday's trash." Her voice faded a bit, as if she was looking around her. "I think I'm somewhere off the 5 South, somewhere just past San Diego. I was thinking . . . maybe you'd come get me. Jade?"

So she was safe enough, certainly safer than Jade. Knowing that, Jade simply turned off the phone. "Mario didn't kill her." There was real relief in that. It left her free to feel as angry as she wanted. "I need some light."

"Soon."

"No, you don't understand. I *need* the light." She closed her eyes, pretending to herself that all she had to do to see was open them.

It didn't work.

"You know I'm right here." He put his hands on her arms, drew her close. "You're safe."

For now. But how long could that last?

Helluva day. She'd fallen for the wrong guy, had been betrayed by a friend, and now found herself in the middle of two different sides she didn't understand anything about except that her safety hadn't been predetermined.

"Jade. Talk to me."

She licked her dry lips but kept her eyes closed. "I'd rather see."

"I know." As if he knew she was a breath from freaking out again, he stroked his hands up and down her arms. "Soon, I promise. Talk to me instead."

"Why?"

"It'll pass the time."

It might. She could ask him questions, too. Find out about him, his life. Get a better picture of the man who'd kissed her so passionately. Maybe they could have a real conversation, one that went both ways for a change, and she'd find herself opening up . . .

"Tell me about Mario."

Jade bit back her disparaging laugh at that, and had to shake her head at herself. When would she get it? In this nightmare she'd found herself in, she didn't matter. She wasn't even a person.

She was the pawn.

Chapter 6

"We should call the police," Jade said.

"Yes," Will agreed. "As soon as we can tell them where Mario is." He kept his hands on her. It seemed to help her beat back the fear of the dark she had, the one that was trying to swallow her whole. "Come on," he said softly. "Talk to me."

"There's nothing much to tell." Her voice was low, and still a little trembly. "Tomas and I met at an antique function two months ago, and he asked me out. He was persistent when I said no."

He tensed at that. Wendy had said the same thing, and yet she'd opened up to Mario shockingly fast, scaring Will, scaring the rest of their family and friends.

Wendy had brushed off their concerns, and a month later, Will had gotten that panicked late-night call he'd never forget, with Wendy in fearful tears, saying Mario had done a bad thing and she was scared.

With murder on his mind, Will had raced to her place, only to find her gone. She'd shown up in the Los Angeles River the next day, dead, about the same time the gems had been discovered missing.

But the answers had died along with her. It was believed that she'd acted as an accomplice to the crime, then been deemed unnecessary.

Unnecessary. Christ, that slayed him. "Persistent," he said slowly to Jade. "As in . . . physically aggressive?"

She said nothing and his heart sank. "Did he hurt you, Jade?"

"At first he was a perfect gentleman," she said very quietly. As if ashamed. *Goddamn it.*

"But after a while," she went on, "it seemed off to me. He knew everything about me, and I got to know nothing in return. I questioned him."

"What happened?"

"He brushed off my questions, saying he only wanted to know more about my business to help me, that he thought he could buy and sell out of my shop, and make it profitable for both of us. But it made me uncomfortable because he didn't want to tell me where he'd get his inventory."

"Probably because the inventory was hot."

"He suggested a couple of times that the gems I had were more valuable than the settings they were in. That I should strip them, let him sell them for me."

"Where he could swap them out with some of his."

"Sort of like laundering them."

"So to speak. Why did you say no?"

She didn't answer.

"Jade."

"Because he was starting to scare me."

Ah, hell. He reached for her, pulling her against him, stroking a hand up and down her slim back in the dark. "Didn't you have anyone to call? Family?"

"No. I have no family left."

"I'm sorry."

"I know. But you're going to get him."

"No doubt," he promised. "Can you tell me anything else? You mentioned Mexico."

"His parents live in Baja. They bought a bar in the name of a fish, or something like that."

"Baja." There were a dizzying number of bars there.

"I have an old world map in my office, and once I caught him tracing Cabo San Lucas, looking sad—" She broke off. "I hugged him for it," she said, angry. "Can you believe that?"

"Yes, I can. He's slick, Jade. And now, back to my original question. Did he ever hurt you?"

"No. Not until last night."

His stomach clenched. "Tell me."

191

"I broke it off with him, and asked him to leave. He pushed me, and I lost my balance. I fell, hit my head."

Will was grateful for the dark so he didn't have to try to wipe the rage off his face. He slid his hands up her body, cupping the back of her head, his fingers lightly sinking into her hair to feel the bump there. "Here?"

"I'm okay."

"Yeah, you are." Leaning in, he kissed her once, softly. "And you're going to stay okay."

"You don't know that."

"Yes, I do." He'd failed Wendy. He wouldn't fail Jade, too.

She shuddered, and he gathered her in. She surprised him by pressing her face to his throat. "I'd thank you," she said very quietly. "But I'm still mad that I'm here, and at the moment I blame you for that."

In the dark, he smiled bleakly. "Whatever keeps you mad, baby. Because mad'll get you through." He realized he was still stroking his fingers up and down her body. Something about her was softening him, and he couldn't afford that. Neither of them could. Only hours ago he'd been willing to take down Mario at any cost, even if it meant destroying one Jade Barrett's life.

But now that he realized she'd done nothing to deserve any of this, same as Wendy, he couldn't do anything but protect her through it. She was soft and sweet, everything his life wasn't, and though he hadn't known he was missing anything, he knew now.

"I'm tired of being a coward," she whispered into his throat, winding her arms up and around his neck with a trust that destroyed him.

"You're not a coward, Jade."

She went still, then turned her head, slowly, letting her lips and nose and cheek graze the side of his jaw as she tipped her face up in the dark. He couldn't see her, but he could feel, and knew her mouth was a breath from his. "You're not," he said again, softly, and kissed her.

He kept it quiet and tender rather than the hot ball of fire it'd been before, or he'd intended to, but the taste of her took over his senses, and he slid his hands over the torn denim skirt barely covering her hips now, pulling her onto his lap for better access.

She let out a sound, a hum of pleasure and desire mixed, and it undid him. So did the weight of her small breast filling his palm. He rasped his thumb over her nipple, which ripped that sound from her throat again, but she covered his hand with hers, stilling his movements. "This is a bad idea."

Her nipple was still hard beneath his fingers, a velvety pulsing point that had his body hard and achy. He wanted to say that this thing between them had a mind of its own, that they were in close proximity, with no end in sight, that they should take every spare second for themselves that they could, but he had no right to say any of it. He was here, with her, to get to Mario.

Not for this.

But, damn it, she'd already gotten to him. In a matter of only one day she'd gotten to him, and deep. "A bad idea?"

"That's right."

Even with her fingers over his hand, he managed to glide his thumb over her again. Her body jerked, and she couldn't quite bite back her soft sigh. It floated on the air between them, erotic in its neediness.

"Your body is telling me something different, Jade."

His other hand skimmed down her skirt to her bare thighs. He wondered if between them she was wet. Wet for him. Wanting to know, he spread his fingers wide, his thumb glancing over the soft, creamy skin of one inner thigh.

Again that little murmur escaped her, sexy as hell, and made even more so by the sound of frustration in it. His thumb took another lazy stroke, higher this time, and just barely brushed against the material of her panties.

Oh yeah, she was wet.

And at the knowledge, he went painfully hard.

Belying her words, her arms tightened around him, as if she was afraid he'd let go before she wanted him to.

He had his own fears as well, such as not wanting to let her go at all.

But she stood, and now the only sound in the dark, grim room was her heavy breathing. "I don't know you," she said. "Not really."

And after Mario, that would matter to her, very much. He stood, too, and reached out for her, getting her on the first time because she hadn't gone far. Wouldn't, not in the dark that so petrified her.

"I want out of here, Will."

"Soon," he promised.

"I need out *now*."

Her hand was cold, too cold, and he rubbed it between his. "Sit a sec. Let me go see if they're gone."

He moved to the high, narrow window, straining up, barely shifting the shades to look out. The afternoon sun glinted off the sidewalk, and off the hood of an unmarked luxury sedan that slowly cruised by.

Too slowly.

"Not yet," he whispered, watching for a long moment before moving back to the couch in the dark. "Stretch out, Jade. Relax, if you can."

She didn't move, and he sat, pulling her back

against him, setting her head on his shoulder, wrapping his arms around her to keep her warm. "Just close your eyes."

"When I do, I see my shop, locked off to me."

"We'll get it back. You don't want him to win, Jade."

"No." After a moment, she let out a shuddering sigh and relaxed against him. "No, I don't."

Chapter 7

Alone in the dark, she knew. He was dead, and the men who'd killed him were waiting for her to come out so they could kill her, too.

The blackness closed in on her. She could see and hear nothing.

But she could feel. She could feel his lifeless body at her side, the sticky wetness that was his blood leaking out the gunshot wound on his chest, past her fingers as she held pressure on it.

And yet, even at age eight she knew it was too late, but she couldn't stop. If she stopped, she'd have to face it.

Her father was dead.

God, she hated the dark. Hated listening to her own unsteady breathing, hated the utter silence around her.

"Jade."

She jerked. Her time had come. She was going to die now, too. "No. Don't. Please don't."

"Jade, wake up," a low voice whispered in her ear.

Real, not from her dream. Big warm hands, also real, capable of both calmly using a gun and also giving mind-numbing pleasure, tightened on her. "You're dreaming, Jade. Badly. Come on, wake up now."

Her eyes flew open but the dark remained, and she gasped.

"It's okay." Will rubbed his jaw against hers, and she realized she lay over the top of him, nestled in his lap. "It's me. It's Will."

"I can't see."

"It's dark. You had a dream."

"It's over."

"It is." But he held her for another long moment, running his hands up and down her chilled arms. "You always dream like that?"

She could have told him it hadn't been just a dream, that what she'd been facing in her nightmares had really happened, but she shrugged.

"Jade."

"It's nothing."

"Does it have anything to do with your fear of the dark?"

She hesitated, too long, and though she couldn't see him, he tilted her face to his. "Does it?"

"Yes," she whispered, and for balance in her crazy world, slid her arms around him. "But it's old stuff."

"It was about your father."

"Yeah." She drew in a shuddering breath. "He was a cop. A homicide detective. He was killed when his cover was blown."

His hands tightened on her. "I knew it was bad."

"I saw it happen. I was eight."

"Ah, Jade." His lips brushed her temple. "Baby, that's not fair."

"I recovered. I was fine. I *am* fine. I just sometimes . . . the dark . . . I don't like the dark."

"And twice now you've been stuck in it. No more, Jade." He pulled her to her feet and led her to the window. "It's time to go." He pulled the shade on the high, long, narrow glass, which didn't change the lighting in the room because it had grown dark outside as well.

"There are boxes here," he said. "You'll climb up on them and follow me out."

Right. Climb up. Climb out. Check.

Will didn't use the boxes; he didn't have to. He pulled himself up with sheer strength. His head disappeared first, then his broad shoulders.

And she was alone.

Eager to follow, she climbed the boxes and reached for the window, but it wasn't as easy as he'd made it look. Her hair got caught on the latch, and she bashed her shoulder on the ledge, but from the outside, hands pulled her through, and then she was lying on the ground, in the dirt planter, surrounded by the myriad of annual spring flowers that had so recently bloomed.

Will pulled her to her feet. "Come on."

They passed her car. She eyed the way it sat low to the ground, on four slashed tires, and automatically slowed. "Oh my God."

"Keep moving." He pulled on her hand, but before they went two more steps, a telltale ping buzzed past her ear and shattered her passenger window. In slow motion she watched it splinter. "Oh my God—"

"*Shit.*" Will forced her into a dead-out sprint, while pulling out his gun. "My truck. See it?"

Another ping. She waited for the searing tearing of her flesh, but it didn't happen. Three cars down was his truck. "Yes. I see it."

"Get in. Fast, Jade. And get low."

In. Fast. Low. That was all she could repeat to herself before he shoved her toward the passenger side, and kept her body in the protective custody of his until she reached it; then he rounded the back of the truck at a sprint before hopping through the driver's door just as the back window shattered.

Swearing again, Will thrust the truck in gear and hit the gas. "Down," he demanded, and added a rough hand to the back of her neck to make sure she got down enough. As they whipped through the streets, Jade caught slivers of glimpses of the city from her low perch as shock hit.

Or maybe it was the old shock.

She had no idea. She'd been running on adrenaline and fear for too long now. "It's a miracle, you know."

Will didn't respond, and she glanced over at him. He was driving fast but calmly, his gaze divided between the road in front of them and the rearview mirror. His hair was whipping around, as was hers, in the wind through the blown-out window, but he might have been driving them toward a moonlit walk on the beach, he looked so casual.

Then she took a deeper look. His eyes were ice. His jaw might have been carved from granite.

Not so casual at all.

And still he drove with a cool precision, taking them through neighborhoods she'd never seen before, until she was good and turned around.

"It's a miracle," she said again over the wind whipping through the vehicle, "that neither of us was hit."

He still didn't answer.

"Where are we going?"

"Cabo. By way of LAX," he said tersely, and she didn't try talking to him again until thirty-five minutes later, when they parked in a short-term parking lot. He turned off the engine, and let out a slow breath. "Okay, I need you to listen carefully." He didn't look at her, just kept eyeing the mirrors and all the cars around them. It was early evening yet, and there was plenty of activity—cars coming and going, people walking. He looked less than thrilled with all of it.

"Were we followed?"

"Tailed for a bit, yes." His voice was still clipped, with none of the earlier warmth in it. "We lost them."

She let out a slow, relieved breath.

"For now."

And the breath backed up in her lungs.

"We're going to go inside," he said. "Scope out the flights to Cabo leaving tonight. We're married. Newlyweds. Spending the cash we just got from our wedding for the honeymoon."

"Will—"

"We'll buy our tickets with this." He reached beneath his seat and pulled out an envelope busting at the seams. When he lifted the flap, Jade saw that it was filled with cash, which he separated into two fistfuls. "We'll buy fully refundable tickets because we're not sure how long we want to stay. We just want to hang out on the beach and make love to each other all day long. In fact, we can't keep our eyes off each other, or our hands. Got it?"

Not trusting her voice, she nodded.

He thrust out one handful of the cash. "Keep this in case we're separated."

She took the money and gulped.

He looked at her for a long moment, saying nothing. There were lights in the parking lot, sending slants of yellow beams through the Jeep. His eyes glittered. Not with a barely controlled anger, as she'd thought at first, but with pain. "Will?"

He shook his head and reached into the back, coming up with a small white first-aid kit, which he tossed into her lap. She looked down at it, and then up at him.

"How are you with blood?" he asked.

"Blood?"

A car drove past them, the bright white headlights flashing through the front of the truck, and for a moment she could see quite clearly.

Will was gritting his teeth. A line of sweat ran down his temple.

And then she saw why. His arm was covered in blood. Her heart stopped. "You were shot."

Chapter 8

"Yeah, I was shot." With a grimace, Will ripped the left sleeve of his shirt away. "Jesus, I'd forgotten how much it hurts."

"Ohmigod." Jade came up on her knees in the passenger seat to lean over him for a look. "*Ohmigod.* We need to get you to a hospital."

"It's okay, just scratched me good," he said, peering at the ripped flesh of his bicep where the bullet had grazed him. He felt a line of sweat run down his spine, and he shuddered as the fire sang down his entire body. "Just have to stop the bleeding and wrap it up." He struggled to get the rest of his shirt off.

She tried to help him with shaking fingers. When his torso was bared, she stared at the wound in horror. "Oh, Will. This is bad."

"No. Bad would have been a few inches to the

inside." He tried a smile, but she didn't return it, and he sighed. "I think the airport frowns on letting bloody passengers on the planes."

"I imagine so." Fingers shaking, she opened the first-aid kit, pulled out a few gauzes and then looked at him. "Ready?" She looked green.

"Open the door and get some air," he instructed.

She shook her head. "I'm okay." She opened the gauze. "It's you who's not." Leaning over him, bracing herself with a hand to his chest, she pressed the gauze to the wound.

He sucked in his breath through his teeth and said every foul word he could think of.

She bit her lower lip, her eyes huge on his. "Oh, Will."

"It's fine," he grated out.

"It's not." She pulled back and gingerly lifted one corner of the gauze. "This isn't going to work. We need to go to the hosp—"

"We're not stopping now." Sucking in air at the movement, he turned to face her. She was straddling the stick shift in her torn denim skirt, which had risen high enough on her thighs that if it'd been daylight, he could have seen those panties he'd so briefly touched earlier. That he could even think it, now, in the midst of this, told him he was going to make it. "I've been tracking Mario for two goddamn months. I can taste him. We're going to Cabo to find him."

"And what then?" She checked on the bleeding

again, which was finally slowing down. Pale as moonlight, she rifled through the first-aid kit, grabbing a tube of antiseptic cream, a roll of two-inch gauze, and some tape. She glanced at him, waiting for an answer.

Not exactly the wallflower he'd thought.

"Will? What then?"

I'll make him pay for Wendy's murder.

She opened the tube of antiseptic, squeezed it on a fresh pad of gauze, and pressed it to his wound, making him see stars.

"Will?" She touched him, the first time she'd done so without him touching her first. She cupped his face, turning it toward her. "You're hurt. It doesn't make sense for you to go now. Surely if Mario is so wanted, you have others working with you who can take it from here."

She believed that Mario was his own personal caseload. She thought that because he'd let her, even though Mario was the FBI's concern, nothing at all to do with his job as a DEA agent. He didn't intend to do anything stupid, he would never risk his oath as an agent, or his own morals, but he did intend to do whatever it took to get Mario behind bars.

Her fingers were cool heaven on his face, and he had the oddest urge to set his head on her breast and close his eyes. "I want to do this personally."

"Why?"

"Because—" He jerked when she began wrapping

207

his arm in the clean gauze, bending to her task so that her hair tingled over his bare chest.

"I'm sorry," she whispered, casting him a regretful glance. She took more gauze and began to wipe at the drying blood, cleaning it off his arm, chest and side. Towering over him, concentrating on her work, she let out low, soft sounds of sympathy as her fingers danced over his bare skin. She'd braced herself up with her free hand on his good side, and oddly enough, that was all he could feel, her hand on him. He wanted her to put her lips on him as well, and he stared up at her, thinking all it would take was one little nudge at the small of her back and she'd tumble down over him. She'd snuggle close and—

"Will?" With a frown, she slid a hand to his forehead. "You're hot."

He wrapped his fingers around her wrist. "Yeah."

"It's bad if you're fevered already."

"I'm hot because you've got your hands all over me."

He couldn't see her blush in the darkness, but he could feel the heat of it as she pulled back and sat on her heels. "I have some aspirin."

He let out one short, mirthless laugh and scrubbed his good hand over his face. "Yeah. A whole bottle should do it." He reached for a clean shirt from his backpack, and gritting his teeth began to pull it on. "You have to change your skirt."

"I know." Jade's hands joined his, smoothing his

new shirt down over his chest and his good arm. Then she grabbed her spare pair of pants from her backpack. "Close your eyes."

"Why?"

"I'm going to change now."

"Right." He squelched the urge to smile, because it was absurd that it amused him that she was modest. So he obeyed. He closed his eyes, then felt her shift, heard her low, murmured curse, and suddenly it didn't matter that his eyes were closed, because he could picture her shimmying out of her skirt. For one blessed moment the image in his mind erased the pain in his arm.

"Okay." She sounded breathless.

He opened his eyes. She smiled into his. "Thanks." She squeezed his hand, playing with his brain some more, then looked over the job she'd done on his arm before she glanced back up. Her smile faded at whatever he had on his face. "What?"

He touched her jaw. "You're nothing like I thought you were going to be in that first moment I saw you."

"And what did you think I was going to be?"

A pain in his ass. "Not the strong, courageous, beautiful woman looking at me right now."

"Really?" She let out a small smile. "You're not who I thought you were either."

"And who's that?"

"The bad guy," she said simply, getting out of the

car before he could call her back, before he could tell her not to put her trust in him, that he was a bad bet.

A really bad bet.

Crossing the street toward the terminal, Jade felt Will squeeze her hand with his good one as he led the way. His transformation from gunshot victim to "doting new husband" was a bit unnerving, and she glanced at him.

He smiled down at her. *Smiled*. She hadn't seen much of that, and whoa, baby, she had to say that was probably a good thing. Slow and lazy, full and warm, all with a dash of wickedness thrown in, and staring up at him, she stumbled over her own two feet.

"Careful, baby." He pulled her tighter to him, to his good side. "Can't have my new wife breaking her ankle before the honeymoon even starts." His sinful smile went downright naughty, and her body temperature, along with her pulse, shot off the chart.

Then he upped the ante even more when he leaned down and playfully bit her jaw. "I have plans for you, you know."

Oh God. Goose bumps rose along every inch of her body, even as she knew he was pretending for anyone watching them. She opened her mouth to tell him that he didn't have to pretend yet, no one was paying them the slightest bit of attention, but still smiling, he tightened his grip on her.

Play along, his eyes said while the heat of him burned her skin, making her recognize he was still in unthinkable pain.

If he could do this while so badly injured, she sure as hell could. She'd pretend he was her new husband, who had intentions of ravishing her the moment they got alone. It wouldn't be difficult, seeing as apparently her entire body was wishing for that very thing.

He kept his stride even, walking along with a sure, easy confidence, and if she hadn't seen the bullet trail in his flesh herself, she'd never guess.

Except she did know, and when someone jostled into them at the curb, she felt his flinch reverberate through her body. Worry for him filled her, adding to the mix of fear and angst.

As they entered the terminal, he nibbled at her ear, his breath sending a shiver of heat down her spine. "Two men at six o'clock— No, don't look. They're searching for us. Keep moving."

Oh God, oh God. Keep moving. They headed toward the ticket counter of Mexi Air. The line was wrapped around and around, twisting in a series of S-turns like her stomach.

Appearing unperturbed, Will settled into the line and pulled Jade tightly to his chest, running his hands down her spine and cupping her butt. His expression seared every nerve-ending in her body. "Happy fourth-hour anniversary," he murmured in a seductive voice.

The couple in front of them, looking to be in their late thirties, had a small infant sleeping in a stroller between them. The woman smiled. "You're just married? So sweet. Honey, isn't that sweet?"

Her husband shook his head at Will. "My condolences."

His wife smacked him upside the head, making him laugh and rub the spot. "I was just kidding! I remember being a newlywed: I got lucky three times a week."

Will laughed softly, as if three nights a week weren't going to be enough, and the sound put even more butterflies in Jade's abdomen.

But Will just hugged her closer. "They just passed us," he whispered in her ear.

And she realized he'd turned her away from the men's view, once again protecting her with his body.

She didn't want that to move her. After all, he was simply doing his job, going after Mario. Her tagging along was a necessity for him, and whether he melted her bones or not, she needed to remember that.

Finally, it was their turn in line. They bought their tickets, and then Will nudged her aside while he spoke quietly to the woman behind the ticket counter.

Afterward, he murmured in her ear, "I have to go through a different kind of security because of my gun. Don't be alarmed when we're separated."

They made their way through security, were indeed separated while Will dealt with his weapon, then finally headed toward their gate, stopping at the restrooms, where Will had them change their clothes again.

When Jade came out, she found him in soft, faded Levi's and a plain, light-blue T-shirt. Average Joe. Except nothing about his long, rangy, solidly built body seemed average Joe.

He looked over her low-rider khaki cargo capris and white blouse, and nodded. Apparently she suited as Mrs. Average Joe, and they continued to the gate.

"But this is the wrong one," she pointed out when he stopped six gates short.

"You're mistaken," he said lightly. She looked into his eyes and understood. He didn't want to go to the right gate, not this early, and possibly have the men after them figuring out which flight they were taking. She forced a smile. "You're right. You're distracting me."

"I plan to do a lot more of that."

She didn't know how to take such statements from him. Was he still pretending?

They had two and a half hours to pass before they could board, and she didn't know if she could handle the idle time after the wild suspense of the day. She had Will take a seat, startled when he pulled her onto his lap and began nuzzling at her neck.

"What are you doing?"

He inhaled her in. "Loving my new wife."

Despite herself, Jade's bones melted. From a few seats away she heard a woman's voice. "Oh, Fred, look. Newlyweds."

Jade forced herself to relax, but with Will's hands possessively on her, his warm breath tickling her neck, his teeth—oh, God—his teeth taking hot little bites out of her, it was impossible. "I can't think," she whispered desperately. Her hands clutched his shirt at his chest. "Please, Will."

"They're walking by."

They were walking by. She sank into him, into the public display of affection that she'd never engaged in before, her eyes crossing when Will dragged her lower lip between his teeth and nipped. She opened her mouth and dove into the kiss, blinking when she grasped the fact that Will had pulled back and was looking at her.

"Jade." In his voice she heard both amusement and arousal, and she could only stare at him. "They're gone."

"Did they look over here?"

"No." He looked alert now, and far from the man who'd just kissed her. A chameleon, she knew now.

When she'd first set eyes on him, he'd scared her to death with his dark, edgy, dangerous air. But in the hours since then she'd seen depths to him, pieces of the man, a sharp intelligence, a surprising wit. A fathomless warmth and compassion. "Who are you?" she whispered, shaking her head. "Who are you really?"

His hands slid down her sides to her hips, which he squeezed. "Your husband. The man who promised to cherish you and keep you safe forever." His hands were gentle on her, terrifyingly tender, as if he was trying to tell her it was all going to be okay. But she didn't know how to believe it, and she put her forehead to his. "Are we going to make it?"

With his good hand, he lifted her chin. Kissed her softly. "Oh yes, we're going to make it. Trust me on this."

She wanted to. With everything she had, she wanted to.

Chapter 9

They boarded the airplane. Will watched everyone embark, carefully taking stock of each face, and who they were with. He had an aisle seat, with Jade next to him in the middle seat. She looked tense, ready to shatter from nerves by the time the plane took off. She had opened her backpack and was holding the rattle she'd told him was her grandmother's, running her fingers over the porcelain.

His arm was killing him, and all he wanted was a few solid hours of sleep, but he stroked a hand over her hair. "You holding up?"

She put the rattle away and zipped up the pack. "Don't worry, you won't be disappointed on your first night of marriage." She grinned at him, though the smile didn't reach her eyes.

He stared at her, so strong, so utterly amazing. But for a twist of fate it might have been her who'd been shot, and he didn't think he'd have been able to live with that. Selfish. Bringing her here with him to find Mario had to be the single most selfish thing he'd ever done. He should have left her in the States, safe—

Jade cuddled into him. To anyone watching, they were two honeymooners unable to stop from hugging each other at every corner. She put her face into the crook of his neck. "Stop it."

"Stop what?"

She lifted her face. "You couldn't have left me there. It was too dangerous."

He stared at her. "You reading my mind now?"

"Isn't that a wifely duty?" She put her hand on his chest, palm to his heart, and kissed his ear. "Tell me the truth. Are you really okay?"

Tell me the truth. . . . He hadn't done that yet, and he'd probably rot in hell for this one.

"Will."

He looked at her again.

"Are you?"

"Yeah. I'm really okay." If one didn't count the intense throbbing where he'd been shot. But Jade looked so tense beneath the surface, so exhausted, he made his smile real as he touched her face. "Sleep," he urged softly. "Just for a little while."

"What if you need me?"

He could have told her he hadn't needed anyone, not for a very long time. He'd have sworn his life on the fact that he didn't need anyone now, and yet as he stared into her warm, dark eyes, he found himself wondering what it would be like for this to be real, for him to have someone watching his back, or just to be at his side, whether he needed her or not. "I'll wake you."

She yawned. Smiled a little embarrassedly. " 'Kay."

But she didn't move.

"Close 'em, Jade."

Almost as if against her will, they drifted shut as she fell into slumber, her face turned toward him, her hand still open on his chest. He stared down at it, at that gesture of trust, and felt his throat tighten. Chances were if his arm hadn't been on fire, he'd have tugged her closer. Chances were it wouldn't have been any husband act either.

Chances.

He'd taken a lot of them today, and certainly had more in front of him. But he'd gone into this situation willingly, knowing what he was getting into.

Jade had not.

And at the thought, he gritted his teeth and pulled her closer anyway, a movement that had nothing to do with staying in character, and everything to do with the fact that the rules had changed yet again. It wasn't about just Wendy anymore, or his revenge, but about this woman, and keeping her safe.

That he was falling for her just added to the complications.

*   *   *

They got off the plane at the Los Cabos airport, and waited in the luggage area for Will's bag. They hadn't been able to carry it on because of his gun.

Will wasn't sure what time it was, and his arm blazed with fiery pain so that he decided against even lifting his wrist to check his watch, but he guessed it was somewhere in the neighborhood of two in the morning. He'd finally given in and had taken a fistful of Jade's aspirin, which might as well have been candy.

Jade kept looking at him, and he knew she was worried.

It was sick of him, he knew, but he liked her worried about him. Liked it a lot. She stayed close to his side, looking sleepy and rumpled and extremely sexy.

The airport was practically deserted. Only a few stragglers moving through, all with the staggering look of the drunk or weary.

The wide-open spaces of the terminal were a concern. Sitting ducks. He had no idea if they'd been followed this far, but they had to get out of here. "We'll find an inn or something," he said, still scanning the area for anyone who looked as if they'd like to take another shot at them.

"Hold on," Jade said.

He expected her to head toward the restroom. Instead she went to a rack of pay telephones and pulled out the phone book, flipping through the yellow pages.

"What are you doing?" He wanted to get her tucked away somewhere, where his revenge wouldn't get her hurt.

"Since I messed up our honeymoon reservations, I'm looking for a place to stay." She smiled; then when he moved close, she whispered, "I'm looking for a bar with a fishy name." Her short, choppy hair fell into her face as she scanned the list of bars, running her finger down the page.

Her fingernail was a pale, glittery pink, and chewed short. For some reason, that very human little habit tugged at him.

So did the look on her face when she lifted it and shook her head. Defeat. She rose wearily, but managed another smile. "Let's just go wing it."

A shower, a meal, and a bed, he thought, and not necessarily in that order. He touched her face. "Yeah. Let's wing it. After a few hours of sleep, we'll start fresh."

A fresh start. After all Jade had been through, she held on to that like a lifeline. She walked through the airport on Will's good side, holding his hand in hers, which he lifted to his mouth to occasionally nibble on her knuckles, looking for all the world like a man completely and totally absorbed in his new wife.

221

But she knew him now, or she was beginning to. He wasn't at ease or casual at all, but carefully and surreptitiously keeping an eye on all around them.

No one paid them the slightest bit of attention, but that didn't stop the tingle of awareness down her spine, or her wondering if they were going to be shot at again.

They discovered there were no rental cars available at this hour, no bus service unless they went to a separate terminal, which Will didn't want to do. From here there was nothing but a lone taxi, a car that looked as if it'd been to hell and back. They slid into the backseat together, Will holding her close to his good side. Beneath his shirt he still felt too hot, and when he moved too quickly, she could feel his muscles tremble. Sick with worry, she kept looking at him.

He smiled at her, though it lacked the brain-cell-destroying power of his usual smile.

Because it was dark, they couldn't see much, but could smell the ocean and the warm Baja night air. After twenty minutes, the taxi driver stopped in front of a small hotel done in Spanish tiles and a myriad of wild, lush plants nearly overtaking it.

Inside was small but neat, with more green plants, hanging from the ceiling and the walls. There was a fountain in the middle of the dimly lit lobby, with fish living in the catch pond. Behind the counter sat a teenage boy. His head was slumped in his hands, his eyes at half-mast as he stared at a small-screen TV from which came what looked like a Spanish game show.

Will spoke to him in Spanish, and then handed over some cash. In return he received a card key, and then took Jade's arm, leading her across the tiled floor, making her realize she'd practically fallen asleep on her feet. "Sorry," she murmured.

"Don't be." He didn't say anything else until they'd walked down a hallway and around the corner. There were four rooms at this end, and he opened the last one on the right. The room was tiny with rose-colored paint on the stucco walls, and an eye-dazzling wall hanging in such brilliant colors that it made her wish for sunglasses. There was a postage-size bathroom, a single dresser, and one bed, all neat and equally eye-popping in bright, primary colors.

It made Jade blink. A lot.

"They didn't have two beds in a room," he said quietly, watching her. "And I didn't want you alone. Is this going to be a problem?"

She thought about the one bed, and all they could do on it together. Not trusting her voice, she shook her head.

"Okay, then." He pulled off his shirt and moved into the bathroom as his hands went to the button on his pants.

Galvanized by what the sight of his bare, smoothly

223

muscled physique did to her, she jerked when she heard the shower turn on. Then he poked his head out. "Do you want to go first?"

"Um . . ." She closed her eyes. "No. You go ahead." She spent the next few moments listening to the water, picturing him long and lean and nude, soaping himself up—

Oh boy. She busied herself pulling the first-aid kit from her pack. She'd have to help him get his wound freshly bandaged—

"Your turn." He stood propping up the doorway, wearing only a towel wrapped around his hips. Hard, lean, chiseled strength, damp and smelling like hotel soap.

For a moment, she just stared at him, and then embarrassed at that, went to move past him, but he reached out and stopped her, tucking a strand of hair behind her ears.

Her entire body reacted.

"Jade? You okay?"

"Yep." With a glance back at the single bed, knowing they were both going to be crawling into it, together, she swallowed hard. "I'm okay." She shut the bathroom door.

Ten minutes later she opened it, wrapped in the three remaining towels. Her own personal armor.

His lips curved at the sight of her, but then he frowned and moved toward her. He wore no shoes, no socks, no shirt. . . only a pair of khaki cargo pants, which were unfastened, and she couldn't take her eyes off him. And because she couldn't, she saw the pain and exhaustion in his eyes. "You're hurting," she accused.

"A little."

Her heart broke. Meeting him halfway, she put her hands on his chest, bending in to kiss him just above his wound. "I'm so sorry."

"Jade." His voice was low, rough, as his hand came up and stroked her hair. "You're killing me."

"Me?"

"I made you come here. I made you leave your safe life to do this."

"No. Mario did that. And you're going to put him in jail for it."

"Yeah." With what looked like a bitter grimace, he turned away.

She eyed his long, sleek back, saw the new and terrible tension, and went still. "Right?"

He sank to the bed, combed his wet hair with the fingers of his good hand, his expression tight with misery.

"Will?" She moved closer, until her knees bumped the mattress. "That's why we're here. To put Mario in jail."

He nodded.

Not relieved, she grabbed a new wrap from the first-aid kit on the bed, but he pulled her down beside him. Then slowly shook his head. "But you should know, I wish I were here for something else entirely."

She stared into his eyes, her heart racing. "And what would that be?"

"I wish I could just kill him."

Chapter 10

Jade stared at Will, the wrap forgotten in her hand. "What?"

"You heard me."

"But . . . killing Mario, in cold blood . . . that's murder." At the affirmation swimming in his eyes, she swallowed, hard. "You're a DEA agent. Our government agencies don't just kill. They put the bad guys in prison."

He laughed harshly and scrubbed his good hand over his face. "Yeah. Look, it's just what's in my gut. I won't. I can't, not without risking everything, my job, who I am . . . I'm just telling you what I wish I could do."

Shaken, she put her hands in her lap. "That seems harsh for a thief."

"In San Francisco, there's a historical society that funds a traveling museum for antiquities, all historic, and all priceless. My sister, Wendy, worked there, as a gem specialist. She was . . . sweet and giving. She'd give a perfect stranger the shirt off her back."

A very bad feeling grew within Jade. "You're talking about her in the past tense, Will."

"About four months ago, a new exhibit came in, a priceless exhibit of gems, and she was in charge of cataloging and restoration. At about the same time, she was being charmed senseless by a man."

"Mario."

"He called himself Bennie Martin. But yes, it was Mario. Using her own security against her, he stole the gems, and when she caught him with them, he killed her."

"Oh my God. Oh, Will, I'm so sorry."

"He vanished. This was two months ago. In that time, my sister's name had been dragged through the mud."

"The museum thinks *she* stole them?"

"Yes. Because she had to have given him her security codes."

"Maybe she didn't do that willingly."

"I know she didn't."

She shivered, thinking of the dangerous temper she'd seen in Tomas's eyes on their last night. It'd scared her, badly, but she hadn't paid with her life. Wendy had. Oh God. She couldn't get past the hollow look in Will's eyes, the utter devastation in his voice, and scooted closer to slide her arms around his waist. He was as rigid as stone, but at her touch, a sigh shuddered out of him, and he set his cheek on her head. "I've been going crazy, Jade. No one can catch him, not the FBI, the cops, no one." He fisted his hands on her back as impotent rage shimmered through him. "I figured if *I* find him, I find the gems. And when I do, I can clear her name."

"But instead you found me. Whining over my messed-up condo." She choked back a sob. "I'm sorry."

He touched her face, lifted it up. "Jade," he whispered, just that, just her name, and then kissed her. "You might have been next. I thought you might be when I got hit." Remembered fear filled his eyes. "*God.*"

"But I wasn't hurt," she whispered, and not thinking, only reacting to him, his closeness, she leaned in and kissed the corner of his mouth to show him.

He hugged her tight. "Inside me. I didn't think anything or anyone could be, but there you are."

She got a glimpse of his eyes, deep and intense and full of things, things that caught her breath, but then his mouth was back on hers, soft and coaxing now. Not gentle, nothing that made her heart trip into her throat like this could be gentle, but she didn't need that. And neither did he. What they needed was to feel alive, needed to feel their hearts thumping, the blood pumping through their veins. Sinking her hands into his wet hair, she murmured his name, her pulse kicking into gear when his hands hauled her onto his lap. "Your arm," she gasped when he pulled off the towel around her wet hair, and then the one around her shoulders.

"You watch my arm." His fingers danced over the edge of the third and last towel, right where it was tucked in between her breasts. "I'll watch you." He tugged and the terry cloth fell away from her body. He let out a rough groan at the sight of her. "Look at you. So small and delicate. Soft." He ran his fingers over her shoulder, her collarbone. "And yet the strongest, bravest woman I've ever met." Bending his head, he bit her jaw, urging her back on the bed as his mouth worked its way down her throat, then to a bared, aching breast. He drew her in, teasing with his teeth, then sucking her in between the roof of his mouth and his tongue, which lashed at her nipple. Long before his hand slid down, past her belly, into her short curls, slowly outlining her, then sinking into her, she was panting his name with every breath.

"You're wet, Jade. Are you wet for me?" He blew a breath over her wet nipple, then nibbled at her other one before kissing a path the way his fingers had gone. Urging her legs wide enough for his shoulders, he lightly bit her inner thigh.

"Will—"

"That's me." Then he kissed her. *There.*

Her hands gripped the bedding beneath her, seeking purchase in a world gone madly spinning. "Will— God!" She cried out when he sucked her into his mouth, using his tongue, his teeth, his fingers. The trembling began from deep, deep within her, nothing like the usual mild pleasure she obtained from sex. This involved much more than a single sexual organ. It also involved her brain, her heart. Her soul.

"Come," he whispered against her wet flesh. "Come for me, Jade."

And just like that, she did. She let go with a shameless ease, spinning dizzily out of control, into a new and terrifying chasm, a prisoner of his hands, of his mouth, of her own need for him.

Before she could catch her breath, he crawled up her body and kissed her. "Again," he murmured.

Yes, again. More. In fact, she was going to die if he didn't sink into her, now. She ran her hands down his back to squeeze his butt, then back up his damp muscles to grip handfuls of his hair, trying to tug his mouth back to hers.

"Not yet, Jade." Gathering her hands in one of his, he pulled them over her head, his eyes tracing a hot trail over her bared, vulnerable body.

"*Will*." She arched her hips to his, watched his eyes flame.

"Again," he repeated, and slid his hand over her torso, scraping his thumb over her nipple, dipping

231

into her belly button, his fingers cupping between her thighs, stroking her to a point of madness, then easily tipping her over the edge.

While she lay shocked and gasping, staring up at him, he let her hands go, claiming her mouth with his as he levered her hips and finally, *finally*, drove himself into her. Their twin groans melded in the air while her body closed around him like a tight, greedy fist.

Pleasure simply swamped her, along with an onslaught of emotions she'd have sworn she wasn't ready to face, and certainly not with a man she'd known less than twenty-four hours. It built so quickly she could hardly believe it, but when he began to move, she felt the tremors begin from so deep she could no more have stopped them than a barreling freight train. Lost in it, lost in him, her eyes drifted shut.

"Don't," he said roughly. "Don't close them."

Her eyes flew open to meet his, watching as everything he felt, everything he was, reflected in his eyes. "Watch me." He groaned. "Let me watch you . . ."

She struggled with that, and tried to hold back. Engaging her heart here, with him, was not smart. Always in her life, she followed a plan. Knew the way to that plan. But this, with him . . . there was no plan. There never had been. *He* was in control, filling her to bursting, taking her to a new place, to new heights, something she hadn't even believed possible.

But he wasn't totally in control either. His breath came faster, his skin gleaming as he looked down at her. "Do you feel this?" Holding her head between his hands, he slowly thrust into her. "Do you feel me?"

"I feel you." She held onto his slick shoulders, digging her fingers in as she arched to meet him stroke for stroke, and gave him the rest. "I feel nothing but you."

A low groan rumbled from deep in his throat as he linked their fingers on either side of her head. She held on to him tight, letting him take her where he wanted to, her own helpless cries bouncing off the wall as she sank into the shocking, wild passion he offered. When his body tightened, shuddering as he buried his face in her throat, emptying himself into her, it triggered her own leap, and as she fell, she held on to one thought: She hadn't meant to engage her heart, not ever again, but it was engaged now.

Engaged and locked.

She awoke just before dawn, violently aroused, entangled with another body. Legs, arms, mouths. *Will.* He pushed her back, towering over her. She couldn't see him in the dark, but felt every inch, crying out when he sank two fingers into her. And when he lowered his head, suckling at a breast while he lightly brushed his thumb over the core of her, she cried out again, exploding on impact.

He gripped her hips. Her entire body quivered, still locked in the throes of an orgasm that wouldn't end, and she hovered there, arching, writhing, needing him to plunge into her.

But he went utterly still.

"Will?"

"Shh." Then he flattened himself over her, wrapping his arms around her body as he rolled with her off the bed to the floor. They hit hard, with Will on the bottom, breaking her fall with his body. He grunted in pain, and she gasped his name, but that was all she got out before he cupped his hand over her mouth in the darkness.

That's when she saw it, the spear of a flashlight from outside the window, stabbing into the room, over the wall and the colorful wall hanging.

"I doubt that's the Easter Bunny." Will pushed off her, staying low to grab her backpack, which he tossed her way. "Get dressed." On his knees, he tossed her the clothes she'd taken off before her shower the night before. "Quickly, Jade."

He didn't have to tell her—she was already working her buttons closed as fast as her shaking fingers could go.

She could hear him doing the same, and when she

blinked through the dark, he was in jeans, barefoot and with his shirt unbuttoned, checking his gun.

Then he jammed the gun into his waistband, shoved his feet into his athletic shoes, and grabbed her hand. "Let's go."

She might have asked where, but the truth was it didn't matter.

In that moment of time, with him standing there— hair mussed from her fingers, holding his arm in a way that reminded her he might have been killed yesterday, his good hand on her possessively, protectively—she'd have followed him anywhere.

Anywhere at all.

Chapter 11

Jade had to press her lips together to keep from hyperventilating from the stress. With dawn barely broken, the hallway outside their room was still dark.

"This way," Will whispered, and taking her hand, ran with her down the hallway until they came to a side door. "Stick close."

"Like glue," she promised, and clung for one moment when he hugged her tight, then reeled when he kissed her hard.

It was different now. They'd . . . been together. There were complicated, messy feelings sinking in the pit of her belly, and she wondered if he felt the same. Wondered if the situation had been different, would they stand a chance?

Far before she was ready, he pulled her into the breaking dawn, into the back lot, which had a few rows of cars. Will tossed his backpack into an open Jeep that didn't have a top. "Hop in," he said.

"Whose is it?"

"We'll figure that out later."

"But . . . that's illegal."

"Jade. Do it."

She looked horrified. "Will—"

"*Now.*"

Will hot-wired the vehicle, and then glanced back at the hotel, and the room in which they'd stayed. Clearly the men after them believed Jade could lead them right to Mario's door. The hotel rooms on the bottom floor were still dark except for the last room—their room. From inside it a flashlight beam bounced around.

"*Will.*"

He looked over at Jade's pale, pale face as the Jeep coughed to life. She'd seen, too. Everything he felt for her burst from his heart to his throat. He hadn't expected to feel something like this, now, for her, but there it was. Emotions so deep and real, he didn't know how he'd lived without them. "I know," he said. "I see them." Ignoring the pain in his arm, he hit the gas and took them out of the lot and down the road, the wind whipping at them, along with the knowledge that if they'd been any slower . . .

Jade kept her head turned away from him, taking

in the landscape that had been too dark to see last night. The elevated plateaus and dry lowlands in the distance conflicted with the lush green tropical feel to the beaches they drove past. The resorts lined every square inch of beach, from high-end fancy hotels to the more economical dwellings.

She reached down and opened her backpack, pulling out the tourist pamphlet she'd picked up in the lobby the night before. "How do you say fish in Spanish?" she asked.

"*Pescados.*"

"Yeah, that sounds familiar. . . . Hey!" She turned a triumphant face toward his. "Dos Pescados Cantina. Two fish. His father named it that because he only ever catches two fish, in the ocean right outside the back door of the bar."

Damn, if her smile wasn't the sexiest thing he'd ever seen. "Is there a map in that thing?"

With her brow furrowed in concentration, her head bent to her task, she navigated, and fifteen minutes later they pulled into another parking lot. The Dos Pescados indeed sat right on the beach, next to a marina, both appearing to be past their heyday. A decade past. The building itself was pseudo-Colonial, and probably would have been named a historical monument in the States. Or bulldozed for property value. A flashing sign in the window read: ABIERTO.

They sat in the idling Jeep in the pale gray dawn light and looked at it. "Why would a bar be open at six in the morning?" Will wondered out loud.

Jade lifted a shoulder. "Maybe it never closed."

"Exactly." He eyed the place for another moment. Too still. Too quiet. "Jade—"

"I'm not staying here. Don't ask me to. After all this, and how far we've come, I want to see it to the end."

He looked into her eyes. Beyond the exhaustion and fear, there was determination. She'd been through so much, and he didn't mean just with Mario. Her childhood hadn't been a walk in the park, and yet she'd made herself. She'd grown up and done what she'd wanted to do. Now Mario had taken something from her, and she deserved to get it back. Personally. Not thrilled with what that meant, and the danger she could face, he blew out a breath. "Let's go, then."

Together they walked the dirt driveway toward the building, with Will keeping a hand on Jade's back. There were no other cars around. The only sounds came from the obnoxiously loud bird in the bushes lining the walk and from the ocean pounding the surf across the street. The air felt thick and warm, and when they opened the door to the bar and looked inside, the air inside came thick and warm, too.

And smelled of death.

Through the windows the early sunlight slanted in, showing tables covered with empty bottles and glasses. Beneath their feet the floor felt sticky, and was littered with peanut shells.

But for the lack of a crowd, the place might have been frozen in time during peak business hours— except for the one person lying on the bar itself, arms and legs spread, mouth and eyes open.

Mario Alvarez, dead as a doornail.

"Oh God." Jade put a shaky hand to her mouth. "Is he . . ."

"Oh yeah." Will eyed the mess around them. "I'm thinking it's time to call this in." He searched Mario's pockets, and was shocked to come up with a wallet and a Palm Pilot.

"Why would they leave that on him?"

Will glanced at her. "Why do people do half the stuff they do?" He realized she was shaking like a leaf, and just as green as one. "You holding up?"

"Better than he is."

A grim smile crossed his face. *Atta girl.* "I'd say a lot better." He flipped open the little palm-held unit and started accessing the data.

"Looks to me like they did this in the height of the evening's festivities," she said, looking around, anywhere other than at Mario's body. "Maybe with a full house all around, thinking that in the cha they wouldn't be seen."

"And maybe they were wrong, and they *were*

241

"And everyone cleared out in a hurry."

"Yeah. Look at that. *Payday.*" Will lowered the unit so she could read the screen. "His daily log. From the day before yesterday."

" 'Sell gems to Jade,' " she read. " 'Pay off Frank before he breaks my kneecaps.' " She stared at the words and frowned. "He was going to sell me the stolen gems. But . . . I couldn't have afforded to buy them."

"Probably only one or two. He needed quick cash."

"And I broke up with him before he could get it."

Will glanced at the body on the bar. Mario's slacks were torn at the knees, revealing two bloody masses beneath the material. "He was right. They broke his kneecaps."

Jade eyed the gaping hole in Mario's linen shirt on his chest and shivered in horror. This could have been her fate, too, if not for Will. "They added that fatal bullet. Why would they do that if Mario still owed them?"

Will fiddled with the palm-held and then showed her another entry, this one dated yesterday.

Get gems back from Jade.

Jade stared at the words, her stomach jittery. "But . . . he never gave me any gems."

"My guess is that several people believe he did."

They both looked at Mario.

"And because they believe it," she said slowly, "he became dispensable. And now . . ."

"They're after you," Will said. "Now we call this in, because until this Frank guy is nailed, you need some serious protection."

"If it hadn't been for you, it'd already be too late for me. *Will*—"

At the sound of tires on gravel outside the windows, he swore softly, pocketed the Palm Pilot and grabbed her hand. They ran past Mario, with Will pulling out his cell phone as they went. He tried to turn it on as they ran through the bar into an extremely small kitchen and storage area, and then out the back door, across the already warm sand toward the marina.

"No battery," he said, then swore and stuffed the phone into his pocket and tugged her along even faster.

The sun had made an appearance, sitting low on the hills in the east, casting the ocean in mauves and purples. The rhythmic sound of the water smashing onto the beach drowned out the slapping of their shoes on the wet sand as they kept running, far past the time Jade wanted to collapse in an exhausted heap.

"Hurry." Will leapt onto the wooden dock bordering the marina, reaching back to pull her up.

Lungs burning from the run, Jade didn't look back

but took his hand and climbed up, following him as he ran along the docks. She had no idea what they were looking for, and didn't have the breath to ask, nor the breath to mention she had her cell phone, somewhere in the bottom of her backpack.

At the end of the second dock they came across a small powerboat, and a tall, lanky man standing in front of it.

"A *panguero*," Will said quietly to Jade. "A boat-man."

The *panguero* was dressed in dark trousers and a light T-shirt with a large floppy hat to protect him from what would surely be a brutal sun in a few hours. He was setting up a sign, which Will read to her. "He rents himself and his boat out to tourists to see the *ballenas*. The whales." He pulled out some cash. "*Una hora?*"

The man counted the money, stuck it in his pocket. "*Sí, sí.*" He handed Will a key.

Will tossed his backpack onto the deck of the boat. Straddling the dock and the gunwale of the boat, he reached out a hand to Jade. "I paid him extra to get the boat without a guide."

"But do you know how to drive this thing?"

As she climbed in, he made his way to the front of the boat. "Does it matter?"

"Not much," she admitted, glancing anxiously behind them. "Whatever you do, go fast."

"Already on it."

*   *   *

Jade shoved the hair out of her eyes and tried to see, but Will had them at full throttle. The wind whipped at her, and the sun glinted off the choppy water and into her eyes, completely blinding her. She hugged her backpack to her chest and kept a lookout the best she could from the seat next to where Will stood behind the wheel, driving the boat.

"Do you see them?" he shouted over the roar of the engine and the wind.

"No." She sat backward on the bench, her gaze glued to the water.

"Keep looking. They're not going to give up."

"But I don't have the gems!"

He cut her a glance, and as he did, his cold, flat eyes warmed. "I know. It's going to be okay, Jade."

Looking up at him, hugging her legs to her chest for warmth, tired and cold and hungry, she believed him. It was crazy. It made no sense. They were somewhere in the Pacific off the coast of Baja, running from guys with guns who hadn't hesitated to kill two people that she knew of so far, and yet she really did believe him.

He stood with his legs braced wide apart, one hand on the wheel, one hand on the level that was apparently the gas. His shirt was plastered to his body, arms bare—except for the left one with the bandage—and corded with strength, his shoulders broad enough to take on this whole mess in order to see justice served for his sister's senseless murder. "I can't believe Mario's dead."

He glanced over at her, his jaw tight and bunched. "I'm glad." He blew out a breath and shook his head. "I'm glad."

"I know." Everything within her ached for him. Fighting the wind, she stood up, holding onto the dash, setting her hand on his arm. Beneath her fingers, his muscles leapt. "But, Will, I'm glad it wasn't you."

He closed his eyes for a beat, then met hers. "I've killed before, Jade. And I'll do it again. My job—"

"I know. I can deal with that. I can deal with all of this."

He lifted a shoulder, as if wanting to believe that, but not quite sure. "Any sight of them?"

"No—" She broke off with a startled scream when the windshield in front of them shattered.

"Found them," he said harshly. "Duck." When she just stood there, paralyzed, he pushed her down to the floor by his feet.

Which left only Will's back for a target. "Get down!" she screamed at him.

"I need both hands on the boat."

Oh God. She argued with herself even as she slung her backpack over one shoulder and reached up and under the hem of his shirt to pull the gun out of his waistband. "*Oh my God.*"

"Jade." His eyes met hers for one tortured beat,

246

and in them she saw that he knew what it cost her to do this. "Flick off the safety," he said hoarsely.

Shaking violently, she followed his directions, then came up on her knees and pointed the gun at the boat gaining on them. It was larger than the one they were in, some kind of offshore speedboat with two engines off the back that even she could see would easily overtake them in another minute.

"Take aim. I love you, Jade."

Her fingers jerked on the trigger, and the gun went off. She whipped her head toward Will. "You . . . *what*?"

"I love you. Careful, don't blow a hole in our boat." Using the toe of his foot, he nudged the tip of the gun up.

"You love—" She broke off with another scream when they were hit again, directly in the engine compartment. Smoke began to rise, and swearing, Will swerved the boat.

The boat behind them swerved, too.

Will swerved the other way.

Again, they were followed.

"Stay low, Jade, and hold on."

She stayed low and held on, staring up at him in shock. He'd just tossed that I-love-you at her as casually as he'd directed her on how to use the gun. "What are you going to do?"

"I'm going to do a one-eighty at a high speed. The boat behind us is going to do the same in order to

247

catch us. They're bigger, top-heavier. They're going to flip."

She swallowed hard. "Are we going to flip, too?"

"No. No, we're not. But you have got to hold on. Hold on and remember what I just told you."

"You l-love me."

"That's right." And he jammed the gas down and yanked on the wheel.

Chapter 12

They spun like a child's toy top, skidding in a circle over the water at a dizzying speed. Jade held on, but she wasn't prepared for the velocity, and went flying into the side of the hull. Pain exploded in her head and ribs, making her see stars, but she had a hold on the passenger seat, and dug her fingers into the cushion.

And still they spun.

She managed to hold on, the backpack she'd been hugging squished between her and the floor. Seawater poured over the side in a large wave as the ocean pummeled them, and though they pitched high for one sickening moment, the boat held in the spin and didn't tip.

The driver of the other boat, upon seeing them take such a short turn, tried to do the same, but Will had been right. It couldn't hold. In front of their eyes, the boat flipped, and upside down it skipped over the water like a pebble, once, twice. Three times.

And then exploded into a ball of flames.

Jade held on to the base of the passenger seat as Will steered them out of their spin. She stared in horror as the flames from the other boat leapt high into the air.

Hands grabbed her shoulders, then her face. She looked into Will's eyes. On his knees in front of her, he looked hollow and beat and terrified. "Jade? Are you all right?"

The other boat vanished beneath the orange and red flames and smoke. The nightmare was over. *Over*. "Yes, I'm okay."

He picked up her cell phone. "Maybe now we can call for help."

"Yes." Because there might be more bad guys with guns. Maybe that Frank guy who liked to break knee-caps. She shivered.

And when Will finished with his call, suddenly there were two of him, wavering in and out of her vision. Two sets of sharp eyes as green as the sea, two square, strong jaws, two hard, warm bodies that she didn't think she'd ever get tired of.

She wondered if she could keep them both, and the thought made her laugh, because she realized she didn't regret a single thing that had happened. She couldn't, not when the whole experience had given her so much. Confidence. A sense of being. The knowledge that she could do anything she set her mind to. And Will. It'd given her Will.

He touched her head. His fingers came away red with her blood. "*Christ*. You *are* hurt."

Yes. Yes, she was. In fact, now she thought she might throw up. The pain in her ribs was making itself known, making it difficult to breathe. But she *could* breathe, which meant she was still alive, and alive was good. Alive meant she could tell Will what she'd just discovered about herself. About him. About them. "Will—"

"Don't move." He grabbed her backpack from her fingers and ripped it open, pulling out a shirt, ripping a strip off it. Then he was pressing the cloth to her head.

"Ouch. Will—"

"Shh, baby. You're bleeding everywhere." He kept looking around them, which put her on edge because they weren't completely safe yet.

She put her hand on his wrist. Actually, she put both hands on his wrist because she was still dizzy, and it took two hands to find his. "I want to tell you something. It's important."

"What else hurts?" he demanded.

"My ribs— No, stop it," she said when he ran his hands down her body, his face tight and grim and terrified. *For her*. "Will, listen. Both of you."

He stared at her. "There's a Coast Guard cutter in the area. They'll be here in minutes. We're going straight to the hospital—"

"I love you back."

"They'll stitch you up, and then we'll—" He stopped cold and stared at her, emotion swamping all four of his eyes as turbulent as the sea around them. "What? What did you just say?"

"I said I love you."

His mouth tightened. "That's your concussion talking."

"No." She reached for one of his jaws, missed, and instead gripped his shirt, right over his heart. "I knew I loved you before the concussion. I think I loved you the moment I opened my door to you." She tried to lift her other hand to him as well, but it was caught in the backpack, which tipped and spilled across the deck. Everything tumbled out; her spare pair of pants, her toothbrush and toothpaste, her grandmother's rattle—

"Oh no." Time stopped as she stared at the cracked porcelain. "Oh no," she breathed, her throat closing. "I must have landed on it—" She broke off in shock and grief when the rattle divided into two pieces, spilling gems into her hand. Beneath the harsh Baja sun they glinted red, blue, green, yellow . . . blinding them.

Will ran a finger over the pile in her palm, the stones reflecting the light around them, pulsing as if alive. "So Mario wasn't that stupid after all. Fairly innovative hiding spot." His gaze lifted to hers, and softened as he stroked a strand of hair from her face. "Full circle, Jade. Do you see it?"

"I had them all along . . ." She marveled over that as Will pulled her onto his lap, careful with her aching ribs, holding pressure to her head wound. "And now I have you."

"And now you have me," he agreed huskily, pressing his lips to her temple.

She grinned foolishly. God, he was so pretty. And he was hers. But then she sobered a bit as the next thought sneaked in. "For how long?"

He looked into her eyes, making her realize she'd spoken out loud. "You should know, I've never felt like this about another woman. *Never.*"

Her breath caught at the way he looked at her. Held her. "I've never felt like this either. But we started so fast . . ."

"We're not going to burn out," he said fiercely. "It started out strong—it'll stay strong." With sweet care, he cupped her face. "Which means I'm all yours." He kissed her as a Coast Guard cutter glided through the choppy water toward them. "For as long as you want me."

For a good long time, she thought with a sigh. A good long time . . .

Epilogue

Three months later

Will set the bouquet of flowers down on Wendy's grave, ran his fingers over the letters of her name, and felt the familiar pang stab at him. When he straightened, two arms came around him.

And lessened that pain. Hugging Jade back, he set his cheek on her head and felt his world right itself simply because she was standing next to him.

"She'd be so proud of you," Jade said. "Finding out what happened to her, clearing her name."

"I think she'd be happier knowing something good came out of this. Something good and strong and lasting."

Jade tipped up her head and looked at him with a question in her eyes.

Leaning in, he kissed her. "You and me," he said,

and pulled out a small velvet box, about five inches by two.

Jade stared down at the beautiful velvet box. "It's not my birthday."

"I know."

"It's not anything."

"It's three months to the day since you walked into my world and gave me my life back."

With a soft laugh, she shook her head. "I didn't give you your life back, you—"

"Open the box, Jade."

"Okay." She laughed again, a little nervously, and it tugged hard at his heart. There hadn't been many people in her life to give her things. It made him want to give her the moon.

"I told you I didn't want the monetary reward," she said softly, running her finger over the box. "And I meant it. I hope you didn't do anything foolish—" She lifted the lid as if afraid he had a snake in there waiting to bite her, then stared into the box. "Oh, Will." Her eyes went brilliantly shiny. "My grandma's rattle. You had it repaired."

"I did. But because of the way it cracked, a change had to be made."

She ran a finger over the brass hinge on one side, and then the hook on the other. "It's like a little storage box."

"Yes. Open it, Jade."

Her eyes flew to his, and for one long shimmery

moment everything she felt for him, everything he felt for her, danced between them. Then she flicked the hook and opened the rattle.

And gasped.

Inside sat another antique. A diamond ring, made from a vintage gold setting, and . . . "You set one of the gems we rescued."

"They gave it to me. To us. Say you will, Jade." Because she hadn't, he took the ring out of the box and reached for her hand. "Say you'll wear the gem that brought us together, and be mine. For the rest of our lives." He shot her a melt-her-heart smile.

"Oh, I'll say it." Her hand shook but she still held it out for him. The ring slipped right on. "I'm yours. Which means you're mine, too." She smiled, her whole heart and soul in it. "For better or worse, Will. Here we go."

Jill Shalvis is the bestselling, award-winning author of over a dozen romances, and has won numerous awards. She lives near Lake Tahoe with her family and is at work on *Seeing Red*, a May 2005 release. You can visit her Web site at www.jillshalvis.com.

Dare to Desire

• • •

JULIE ELIZABETH LETO

To Cherry Adair and Jill Shalvis . . . always a pleasure, ladies!

And to Laura Cifelli, for giving me this amazing opportunity to blend a really sexy story with high-stakes romantic suspense. What a rush!

Chapter 1

"The house is perfect. I'll take it."

The real estate agent uncrossed his arms at Macy Rush's definitive declaration. He opened his mouth to speak, but another voice from the foyer beat him to the punch.

"Well, you see, Ms. Rush, that's going to be a problem, since I already own this pleasure palace."

Macy didn't have to turn around to know who had spoken. Only one man wore that particular custom blend, based with an essential oil whose name she'd forgotten. And yet the woodsy, spiced aroma, tinged with the sweet smokiness of tobacco, retained the power to cause a warm prickle of gooseflesh over her skin. Even if she hadn't heard the dulcet tone of his voice from just across the room, the scent of his cologne gave him away, nearly drowning her in a wave of memory.

"Dante Burke," she announced, steeling herself before she turned around. Seeing him again could knock her off guard—if she let it. But she'd die before she allowed the man to so much as make her breath catch. He'd done his damage. She'd recovered, and now she had no intention of suffering a relapse. "Why am I not surprised?"

The agent beat a quick path to the back door, making his true profession clear. Real estate agent, no. Secret agent, yes. With her eyes, Macy followed the retreat and then locked gazes with Dante Burke, the man who had, not so long ago, ripped her reputation, her career and her heart to shreds.

He was still gorgeous, damn him. Slick, dark hair pulled back into a queue. Rich, tanned skin that glowed from the Saint-Tropez sun. A lithe, muscled body accentuated by a suit that probably cost as much as the asking price of the house. Still breathtaking and still lethal—and still so full of himself, she wondered how there was room for both of them in the entrance hall.

He gestured into the living room, but when she didn't instantly comply, he strolled down the stairs with the same grace and style as James Bond and Fred Astaire combined. She rolled her eyes. Only Dante Burke could manage to be insufferable when he'd done nothing more than walk into a room.

"Not surprised by my initiative? You shouldn't be. Stands to reason that the Arm would beat T-45 to the most important property in New Orleans. Especially with world peace at stake. I bought the place two weeks ago."

"And yet the house is still listed on the market," she said, suspicious, her hands inching into the pockets of her jacket. Beneath the slick leather, she caressed the cool steel of her backup firearm, a sleek 9mm Smith & Wesson LadySmith. With her main weapon tucked in her shoulder holster and several alternative weapons strapped to various parts of her body, she should have felt entirely secure, even in Dante's presence. But she had a good idea of why he'd beaten her here, and consequently, she possessed no confidence that he wasn't about to seriously screw up her case. "Why didn't you remove the listing?"

"Friendly neighbors delivering casseroles of jambalaya can be such a nuisance."

He wandered toward the window and with a quick flick of his penetrating gray eyes, likely spotted the T-45 agents positioned across the street who'd been ordered to watch her back. Lot of help they'd do her now. The enemy was within.

"You're the first showing I've allowed," he said, turning, his self-assured grin confirming her supposition.

Clearly, he knew why she was here. He'd likely come for the exact same reason. And yet, Macy had to continue a verbal dance and make sure her suspicions were correct before she acted. He might be simply on a fishing expedition, with no real evidence of why the house on Prytania Street in the Garden District of New Orleans could end up being worth more than the listing price . . . about one billion times over.

"How gentlemanly of you," she lied, "allowing me to see something you have no intention of letting me have."

"I'm just that kind of guy."

The slight European lilt in his voice fueled her ire and she had to force her breathing to steady. He hadn't been overseas in years. Since birth, practically. And yet he still possessed that distinctly urbane air that had once attracted her all-American girl hormones. Luckily for her, she remembered his past transgressions well enough to keep his allure at bay. "Don't get me started on the kind of guy you are, Dante. You won't like my assessment."

"I'll just enjoy the sound of your voice then."

"Enjoy this then," she snapped, starting toward the door. "You're a son of a bitch who can't be trusted. And now that I know you're here, I'll return to Paris and throw one hell of a party. With you in charge, I'm certain the world will soon be coming to an end."

With the lightning-fast reflexes that had propelled him to the top of his class in the spy business, Dante grabbed her arm. With equally fast instincts, Macy spun, ducked and rolled, ending her move with Dante's arm pressed tightly against his back. He'd let her have the upper hand, but she wasn't about to refuse such a gift if he was stupid enough to give it.

"Don't touch me," she warned through clenched teeth. Her emotions raged, a lethal combination of anger, spite and fear. He wouldn't control her again. Not ever again. If she allowed him even the slightest element of domination, he'd find ways to rule her entirely. She'd never allow him to command her again.

He answered her with a whisper that was both smooth and hypnotic. "I plan to touch you extensively and intimately over the next few days, love. And you'll let me. In fact, you're going to beg me."

She could break his arm. She knew she could. He had hardly tensed his muscles against her counterattack, so certain he was that she didn't mean business. She should crack a bone, just to prove a point.

But that wasn't her mission. She couldn't allow her emotions to interfere. She needed the house. Short of brute force—and she was certain the three-story cottage was crawling with agents from the Arm who would relish the chance to take her down—she had to go the cerebral route.

She released him, pushed him away roughly, though he barely stumbled. He turned and, with utter coolness, straightened the cuffs of his tailored shirt.

"You're full of yourself, Dante."

"That's part of what you loved about me once."

267

"I don't make the same mistakes twice."

He arched a dark brow, which only made his light gray eyes more piercing, more mesmerizing. "Don't make such declarations so quickly. I haven't offered you my deal yet."

"I didn't come here to deal," she countered.

"No, you came here to buy this house so you could find the hidden code that might—might—avert a nuclear attack on the United States from unnamed terrorists who, at this moment, are threatening to hijack an abandoned missile silo somewhere in the vast Russian wilderness and use the forgotten warhead to start World War Three."

So he did know her mission. Top to bottom, with every detail dispensed in his signature iced vodka voice.

Damn, damn, damn.

"They don't have the silo yet," she pointed out. "Chances are, the Russian army will stop them before they get that far."

Dante laughed and Macy admitted, silently, that her words sounded utterly ridiculous when spoken aloud. The Russian army was no longer a cold-war powerhouse. The military in the former Soviet Union was in horrible disarray. When T-45, her agency, received intelligence alerting the independent, mercenary spy organization that a terrorist group was working to secure one of the abandoned silos for use against the United States, they hadn't been too worried. The silos had all been disarmed, or so T-45 had been told. Soon after, her organization had been contacted by a consortium of Russian industrialists who sheepishly admitted that while they'd pocketed the money paid to them by the struggling Russian government to disarm the silos, they'd left approximately one hundred live nuclear weapons in the most remote regions of the country. Too expensive and too hard to reach, they'd claimed by way of excuse. And now, too hard to effectively protect from an unnamed threat.

So the Russian consortium had hired T-45 to find the countercode created by a leading Soviet scientist that would render all the previously determined launch codes useless. Without the mathematical fail-safe in their possession, the terrorists would be powerless.

Macy had been assigned the case and her investigation had led her here, to the scientist's winter home in New Orleans—and back into the scope and sights of Dante Burke.

Once she took the house from him, she would have had plenty of time to sort through the rooms and find the code. But things must be more dire than she expected if the Arm was involved. The covert branch of the CIA didn't engage unless all other avenues had been explored.

"What do you know about the code?" she asked, dropping all pretense.

"I know that it's likely hidden somewhere in this house. I also know that I've had a crack team searching for two weeks and . . . nothing."

"So give up," she suggested coolly. "Turn the house over to T-45 and get the hell out of my way."

"No can do, Macy. We know that when the terrorists finally take a silo and break the launch code, they plan to point that intercontinental ballistic missile at a U.S. target. This is a national security issue. T-45 needs to butt out."

Macy watched Dante survey the room as he waited for her reply, his eyes assessing the vintage furnishings with cool familiarity, never lingering on one thing, other than the mirror, for more than a split second. Typical. And to think she'd once found his arrogance exciting.

"A consortium of Russian industrialists has hired T-45 to find the code," she told him. "That's what we intend to do."

He mulled her admission for a moment, then grinned cryptically. "The same consortium that should have disarmed the missiles over a decade ago? We were wondering how they'd try to cover their asses."

"Now you know."

"Makes no difference. I have the house, but no code. You have nothing."

Macy ran her hand through her hair, somewhat surprised to catch Dante's eyes softening as she did so. What was he up to? "You're wrong. I have me. I'm the best finder in the business. You supervised my training, remember? How long did I take to excel beyond the Arm's rudimentary procedures? Weeks? Months? I'll find the code."

"But you need access to the house."

Macy knew she'd regret her next move, but she had no choice. She had a mission to complete. She couldn't allow her pent-up feelings toward Dante to keep her from achieving her objective.

"So let's deal," she offered.

He leaned back into a Georgian antique library chair, the winged back surrounding him like the high neck of a vampire's cape. She should have been immune to his mysterious allure by now, but obviously she wasn't. Not that his charisma mattered—so long as she had the spirit of a good fight in her bones, she'd remain safe from his magnetic pull.

"I'd hoped you'd want to bargain," he said. "In fact, I have a proposal in mind that I believe you'll find quite tempting."

God, she was going to regret this. "Let's hear it."

He folded his hands together and steepled his long fingers. She couldn't fight the tiny chill chasing up her spine.

"I'll allow you access to any and all rooms in the house, one at a time, over the course of the next week. I'll clear all Arm agents from the premises. Your work will be entirely secure. Once you have the code, you can take the sequence back to the consortium, though I will insist that the Arm receive a duplicate code in case the industrialists do not work in the best interest of the United States."

Macy was a lot of things, but gullible wasn't one of them.

"What's the catch?"

He grinned and his eyes slanted into a stare that was nothing short of predatory. "I want you."

"Excuse me?"

He stood and crossed the room in three smooth steps. On instinct, Macy drew her gun, just in time to press the barrel against the taut muscles of his stomach. The force of the steel against his vulnerable flesh didn't seem to faze him one iota.

In fact, he looked down at her with amusement dancing in his gray eyes. "Need I say it twice, love? I want you, and if you wish to search my house, I intend to have you. In any and all ways possible."

Chapter 2

If he'd had any sense at all, he would have worn his Kevlar this morning. As the luridness of his offer slowly seeped into Macy's brain, the jab of the gun against his gut increased. If she was any other woman and he'd made the same sexual offer, he wouldn't have entertained even an inkling of fear that he'd be turned down, much less that he'd be shot for his audacity. But he wasn't dealing with *any* other woman. Macy Rush not only had motive, and now opportunity, to kill him, she had enough justification to warrant an immediate acquittal from any court in the land.

"Offer denied," she said, her words seething through her teeth. "Try again."

He shifted his position, but Macy simply shoved the gun farther into his stomach. He'd ordered his men to leave him and Macy alone and knew they wouldn't disobey unless shots were fired. Too late for him at that point, but at least the house wouldn't fall into the hands of T-45. Not that he was worried. Odds remained that the terrorists who'd made the threat would not have the manpower to bring their plan to fruition. Still, Dante had learned long ago that most international anarchists did not reveal their intentions to their enemies unless they were confident of their ultimate success.

And yet, time was on his side. With Macy looking for the code, he figured he'd have the crucial combination in a matter of days. He could afford to hitch the mission on his own personal agenda. He couldn't change the past, but the future was ripe for the taking.

Just like Macy.

Boldly, he pressed closer so that her breasts crushed against his chest. The old fire they'd once shared instantly sparked. He could see the attraction in her crystal blue eyes. He could feel the lust in the stiffening of his sex.

"My offer stands, Macy. I want you back. Truth be told, I never wanted you to leave."

"Then you shouldn't have betrayed me."

"I can explain that."

He didn't bother to try, though. Even before her eyes narrowed with keen disbelief, he knew Macy wasn't ready to listen. Any explanation he offered now would fall on ears deafened by anger and righ-

teous indignation—reactions he'd expected, anticipated, even planned for. If he had to choose from
the full range of Macy's fiery emotions, anger
wouldn't have been his first choice to deal with—but
it sure as hell beat indifference.

"You've had ten years to create an elaborate explanation for your actions, Dante. I can only imagine
what spin you've come up with. But I don't want to
hear excuses. Not now. Not ever. I'm only interested
in finding the code."

He leaned slightly forward, so that his breath
teased her wispy red bangs. "I'm offering you the
chance to find the code with virtually no interference
from the Arm. All you have to do is let me make
love to you."

Without warning, Macy pocketed her gun and
stepped away. She shrugged her jacket closed, but
not before he noticed the telltale peaks of her nipples
through her smoky blue silk blouse. The sight evoked
a surge through his blood that heightened his confidence and libido. Yes, he wanted her. That much
he'd known. But she wanted him, too—whether she
liked it or not.

Chemistry was a powerful thing.

"You're becoming sloppy in your old age, Dante,
allowing personal desires to interfere with a mission."

Dante shrugged nonchalantly, but his eyes remained trained on Macy as she stalked around the
room. She'd already begun her search.

He crossed his arms, bracing himself against the powerful effect she had over him. Yes, he wanted her, but he wasn't about to tip his hand, not when the prize was so worth the danger of the game. "I'm merely attempting to accomplish two crucial goals at one time. In fact, the economy of my plan is quite impressive. It's win-win."

Macy speared him with a spiteful glare. "This is the best you can do to seduce me? Hinge the success of my mission on my having sex with you?"

He grinned. "Brilliant, isn't it? Flowers and poetry don't move you, my love. They never have. But dangle the carrot of another successful mission in front of you and you can't resist."

Macy pressed her lips tightly together and he could see her fists flex inside the pockets of her jacket, straining against the leather. Like him, Macy was a professional liar. She could fool the best that the world's intelligence agencies offered. But so could he. Even from the beginning, they'd learned that lying to each other was a complete waste of time. He'd managed to feed her a mistruth only once since he'd known her and that decision had cost him her love.

Love he was determined to get back.

"Macy, you must admit," he continued, "that I've taken good care of myself over the years. I'm not unattractive. I can't imagine you'd consider sleeping with me such a huge sacrifice."

She arched a dark red brow. "Are you so hard up?"

"No, just hard."

He didn't bother glancing at his crotch to drive his point home.

"That's crass," she sniped.

"No, that's honest."

Without response, she stepped into the foyer, moving around the partitioning wall so she could see fully into the house—and escape his close scrutiny. From the street, the cottage appeared relatively small, though he had no doubt she'd studied the blueprints during her mission prep. But now that she was finally inside, she would recognize the impressive scope of the layout. The nooks and crannies built into the walls—the overflow of antiques that filled nearly every space.

On his orders, nothing had been removed from the house and every piece of bric-a-brac had been x-rayed, examined, catalogued and then returned to its original space. Even the precise arrangements of the knickknacks, chairs, settees and claw-footed tables had been studied for patterns that could lead them to the code.

But so far, the Arm agents had come up empty. The code, likely a collection of letters, numbers and symbols, could literally be anywhere in the house.

He followed Macy as she assessed the scope of her mission, stopping when his groin nearly brushed against her backside. He took a moment to close his eyes and inhale the subtle scent of her perfume, a cool aroma tinged with sharp lemon, refreshing mint and soothing chamomile. When he opened his eyes, he realized how close he'd leaned in. His nose was less than an inch from her hair.

He wanted her beyond reason. At one time he'd questioned the depth of his need, even railed against the connection that floated only a step below obsession. But now he accepted that his love simply ran deep and a man like him could stop at nothing until he won back the woman who owned his heart.

"I refuse your offer," she said coolly.

"You have no alternative."

"I could kill you."

"Then my men would kill you. Neither the Arm nor T-45 would have the code, all because you don't want to face what we once had together."

"What we once had died the day you betrayed me." To her credit, her voice remained steady and strong.

"Maybe. Are you courageous enough to find out for sure?"

Macy glanced over her shoulder, her eyes narrow slits of blue. "I know for sure, the same way that I know I'll find the code."

She stepped away again and tapped her large stud earring, then extracted a hair-thin wire that stretched from her ear to her mouth. The fiber-optic communicator glowed green at the tip.

"This is Rush, reporting in."

As the agent monitoring her message replied, she brushed beyond him to the front window.

"Patch me directly to Marshall. We've got a little problem."

The burn of his stare scorched the back of her neck, but Macy refused to turn around. She'd once thought Dante Burke couldn't be any more arrogant and confident than he had been ten years ago when they'd first met—he the master agent and she the rookie spy. How wrong she'd been. Now she was one of the most sought-after "finders" in the covert operations business, the next in line to helm T-45, the quintessential elite spy organization envied by everyone from the CIA to MI5 and Mossad. And yet, Dante Burke wanted to bargain for her body.

Well, he could have her goddamned body. It was her heart he truly wanted—and that he'd never possess. Never again.

"Marshall, here. Do you have the house?"

"Negative," Macy answered. "The Arm owns the property. Has for two weeks."

"Why didn't we know?" Marshall asked.

Macy winced. "Sometimes, the Arm covers their tracks fairly well."

Abe showed his annoyance with a series of unintelligible grumblings. None of the agents who worked for Abercrombie Marshall ever admitted to understanding when their boss's voice lowered to a gruff mumble—likely because no one wanted to know what the man was saying. He was probably firing them all, and if they asked him to speak up, the dismissal would become permanent.

"How many agents on-site?" he finally asked with clarity.

"Unknown. Burke is here. He's doing the bargaining."

"The Arm doesn't negotiate with T-45."

Macy pushed aside the sheers blocking the light from the window. Through the low-hanging branches from the century-old oak outside, she spied her fellow T-45 agents, glad they'd been sent to watch her back. Unfortunately, just a few steps away, disguised quite effectively as a man painting a garden fence and another as a carpenter repairing a broken shutter, were two Arm operatives. A standoff between the two organizations would clearly get them nowhere.

"Apparently, the Arm will negotiate today. He's offering me full access to the house. His agents have failed to find anything of use after two weeks of searching."

"Maybe there is nothing to find," Abe offered.

Macy shook her head, her chest tightening. For as

long as she'd been working with Abercrombie Marshall, he'd always shown the utmost confidence in her instincts and her deductive skills. She'd left the Arm—and Dante—because neither the top dogs in the organization nor her lover trusted her as implicitly as Abe. And she'd never proved him wrong. So why, after all this time, did the sharp sting of even a logical question still remain?

"No," she insisted, determined to shake the topsy-turvy reaction to having Dante back in her presence, much less her life. "I studied Bogdanov's journal and letters. I've interviewed him myself. The code is here. I'm positive."

"Bogdanov is insane, Macy."

This much was true. Grigoriy Bogdanov, once the golden boy of Soviet computer science, had been examined by T-45's elite neurologists from New York, London and Tokyo. They all agreed that the man who had designed and implemented the newest computer system to operate the nuclear silos for the Russian government suffered from an extremely aggressive form of dementia. His moments of clarity were few and far between, and no combination of medication or therapy had been able to reverse the damage to his brain cells or coax the healthy pathways of his mind to reveal the information only he possessed—the countercode that would render all attempts to launch the nuclear warheads useless.

Macy had spent a rigorous week with Bogdanov

after T-45 pulled him into protective custody from the bucolic mental institution where his wife had stashed him—the very wife who'd turned up dead just one day after the terrorists transmitted their first threat to the Russian government. Macy knew that further attempts to extract the code from Bogdanov's memory were impossible, but she also believed the man too intelligent and too meticulous to store the crucial combination only in a vulnerable human brain. She knew the code existed; she'd tracked it to New Orleans. Now, she simply had to find it.

And to do that, she had to sleep with the man who'd once broken her heart.

"Insanity seems to be running rampant around here," she answered.

Her boss chuckled, his deep bass voice rumbling through the state-of-the-art connection with thunderous clarity. Abercrombie Marshall had been with T-45 for as long as anyone in the business could remember. Like her, he was an American ex-patriot spy denied a chance to rise through the ranks of the intelligence community in the United States—he because of his race, she on account of her tarnished reputation, courtesy of Dante Burke.

"What does he want in exchange for his unexpected cooperation?" Abe asked.

Macy glanced over her shoulder. Dante remained standing near the threshold to the parlor, his incredible body framed by the archway, his silver eyes locked on her with pure, unadulterated lust.

"He wants a copy of the countercode in case our clients don't use the combination to benefit the United States."

Abe paused. Macy turned back toward the window and pressed her eyelids closed, waiting for the question that was sure to come.

"That's not all he wants. Damn it, Macy, he wants you, doesn't he?"

"Affirmative."

"I should order you out of there," Abe said, his deep voice brimming with anger.

"Why? There are worse things a woman could do to save the world, right?"

With a smirk, she disconnected the call and turned back to Dante, straightening her spine and tilting her chin upward so he knew he hadn't beaten her. Despite the traitorous thrill that snaked through her bloodstream at the thought of his hands on her flesh again, pleasuring her in ways only he ever had, she knew one thing with perfect clarity—he could have her body, but he'd never, ever, sneak back into her soul.

Chapter 3

Exhaustion pressed Macy onto the bed around one o'clock in the morning, her body jostling the secured laptop computer lying on the mattress so that a strobe of metallic blue light flashed across the darkened room. Even after she closed her eyes, her vision swam with schematics, code markers and patterns. The key points from the dozens of Arm reports she'd read before daybreak repeated in her brain like mantras to failure, all spoken to her in the melodious baritone voice of Dante Burke. The sensual timbre of his voice so invaded her mind that she didn't hear him when he actually called her name from the doorway.

She grunted in response.

"Have a hard day?" he asked.

With annoyance giving a shot of spitfire to her spent energy, she turned her head to see him leaning against the threshold to her room. In a white shirt rolled up at the sleeves and expertly tailored slacks in cool slate gray, he was the epitome of casual style. He'd loosened his hair so that his rakish dark locks nearly touched his strong, square shoulders. He'd pulled out all the stops in ensuring that, at least physically, he was perfect.

She, on the other hand, undoubtedly resembled a dishrag that had been used to wipe down a filthy kitchen. Working through the puzzles that were Bogdanov's kitchen and parlor from dawn until long after dusk wiped the sparkle off a woman. If he didn't find her irresistible tonight, so much the better.

"What do you want?" she asked, knowing full well what the wide range of his desires might include. She'd finished her search for the day. The time had come for her to pay the price for his cooperation.

"Find anything?" he asked.

"Nothing beyond all the hidden cameras you've had installed throughout the house. You were watching me the whole time."

He shrugged. "Voyeuristic tendencies are prevalent in our profession."

She rolled her eyes and shifted to lean up on her elbows. Her arms ached, but she spared him a wry smile. "It's more prevalent in some than in others."

"Depends on who is being watched. Some people are innately . . . impossible to ignore."

He stepped toward the threshold, but she had her

gun drawn and sighted before his foot crossed from the carpet in the hall to the wood in her room.

"We had an agreement, remember? This room is mine."

And hers alone. After assuring her boss that she was prepared to take Dante's offer in exchange for full access to the Prytania Street house, she'd created a private haven within the walls of this small bedroom just off the hallway to the kitchen. He'd agreed that she could search the tiny maid's quarters to her heart's content and Dante would refrain from invading her personal space for the duration of her stay.

Unlike all the other rooms in the house. Those rooms came with a price.

When she'd agreed to his challenge last night with a stiff and cold handshake, she'd never expected the twist he'd introduce to the deal. She should have anticipated he'd up the stakes at some point, but for the briefest instant, she'd actually thought he cared about saving some unnamed American city from destruction more than he cared about his sex life.

How wrong she'd been.

In order to gain full access to each room, she'd agreed to his erotic demand. Once she'd searched a room top to bottom—once they knew that the code would not be found there—he would disengage the hidden cameras and she would make love to him in that room. She'd have no right of refusal, no voice in how he reintroduced her to the delights of their lovemaking. She'd have to submit entirely to his amorous intentions, no questions asked.

Since she'd already agreed to his clearly desperate plan to win her back, she didn't balk at his added terms. Maybe this interplay would be good—for both of them. Clearly, the man needed to understand that the relationship they'd shared years ago was over. For her part, she was looking forward to some hot, sweaty, mindless sex, especially since in the end, Dante would learn that while he might still possess the power to excite her body, he'd never again hold any influence over her heart.

He stepped away from her weapon, his eyebrow quirked in amusement.

"You shouldn't pull a weapon if you don't intend to use it," he warned.

She slid the 9mm beneath her pillow. "Who said I don't intend to use it?"

"You're not a killer."

"You have no idea how I've changed," she insisted, despite the fact that he was essentially right. Macy had the skills and training to take care of herself, but she preferred using her wit to work her way out of dangerous spots. "Since I left you, Dante, I've been living a very different life. Working for T-45 is light years from my experience with the Arm. You have rules. A government to answer to."

"And you have Abercrombie Marshall. He's not exactly a wild-eyed rogue."

She nodded, unable to argue with such a widely known fact.

"He's the most ethical man I've met in this world of traitors, liars and thieves."

"What does he think of our little deal?"

Macy rolled to the edge of the bed, sitting upright as she stretched her shoulders to loosen the tightness settling between her joints. "He doesn't know the particulars, and what he doesn't know won't hurt him."

She glanced up at Dante. God, how could he look so utterly smug and superior when he'd had to resort to blackmail to get her into his bed again? Did nothing shake this man's limitless confidence?

"What he doesn't know won't hurt you either, Macy. I hope you're prepared to enjoy yourself."

"I could enjoy myself just fine here alone in my room."

He straightened, a sarcastic slant to his quirked grin of a mouth. "I can hardly believe what I'm witnessing. You're not afraid of me."

She stood and marched to the door, knowing full well he was attempting to manipulate her. She responded all the same, preferring to deal straight up rather than expend her energy in some fruitless game of cat and mouse.

"Stuff it, Dante. You want to screw around, that's fine. I agreed to your offer. But know this—you're wasting your time if you think I'll ever come back to you."

She'd come too close. When the tip of his finger skimmed her chin and cheek, igniting a warm sensation before she had a chance to move away or object, she had no choice but stand firm. Once engaged, she couldn't pull back. She couldn't show him the least indication of weakness or he'd surely use her vulnerability against her.

He pressed his full palm against her skin, reminding her with a simple touch of the intimacy they'd once shared. Score one for him, except Macy hadn't needed reminding. In nine long years, she'd never once forgotten the intensity of his sweet caresses, their all-night-long chats about everything and nothing, or the lovemaking that lasted until both their bodies grew numb from sensual overload.

In fact, the night before he'd betrayed her to her superiors, he'd lured her to a favorite hideaway, a cabin deep in the Virginia forest where they could escape the world of covert operations that had come to rule both their lives. In the seclusion of their private escape, he'd seduced her with all her favorite indulgences, from a scalding shower with multiple streams of water beating down on them as they made love against the glass to a wild game of hide-and-seek in the woods outside that ended with a session under the stars that had left her satiated for hours.

Then she'd awoken the next morning alone in bed, laughing innocently as she picked twigs and leaves from various places on her body, never for one minute suspecting that while she languished in the sweet soreness of incredible sex, Dante had returned to headquarters to file a crucial piece of intel that ended up saving several agents from detection and, ultimately, death. Intelligence she'd gathered—and had shared with him.

Now, she was about to charge headlong into the same brand of hot, mind-altering sex. Only this time, the outcome wouldn't be nearly the same. He couldn't break her heart, not after she'd worked so hard to make sure the brittle, delicate pieces never formed again. Not with him. Not with anyone.

Dante released her, breaking the tentative spell that had lured her into the past. He stepped back and gestured to the hallway. He was ready for his payment and she had no choice but to comply. "You are back with me, Macy, at least in body. For now, I'm willing to work with what I have."

"I need a shower," she snapped.

"No time. I've calculated this evening down to the minute. You'll simply have to enjoy my plan for you as best you can."

He led her across the hall to the kitchen and Macy

was forced to admit to herself that even after picking through every cabinet and examining every plate, cup and saucer in the entire twenty-by-twenty room, she wasn't as grimy as she expected. Bogdanov's wife had employed a meticulous housekeeper, one whom the Arm had no doubt debriefed and likely had in custody since T-45 had been unable to locate her. Macy tried to throw her mind into working out the odds that the woman was worth the effort of finding, but she couldn't resist the distraction of red-pepper scents drifting off the stove, mingling with the incredible aroma of garlic that had been cooked to perfection in a slathering of extra-virgin olive oil.

She spun in his direction. "You cooked?"

"You're hungry, yes?"

Her stomach growled loudly, effectively answering the question.

He grinned. "I hope you like the native food. I've been here two weeks, more than long enough to develop an addiction to Cajun and Creole cuisine."

She attempted to fight a grin, then decided that she had to save her energy for more crucial battles.

"You've never cooked for me before," she commented, walking fully into the kitchen and attempting to leave her wariness at the door. She hadn't expected this pampering, damn him, but she was pleased nonetheless. When he'd informed her that he wanted their first tryst to take place in the kitchen, she'd imagined they'd recreate a hot and heavy scene from their past—the night she'd attempted her first home-cooked meal and they'd ended up fucking on the butcher-block table surrounded by the scent of charred game hen and overcooked asparagus.

But this table, a delicate cherrywood covered in lace and set with the fine bone china and sparkling lead crystal she'd examined only a few hours ago, would surely collapse under the weight of two humping bodies.

He strolled to the stove, lifted a heavy pot lid and inhaled the fragrant steam that wafted from inside. "I've broadened my interests since taking over the Arm. I'm not in the field as much anymore. Waiting for operatives to report in can be very tedious."

She wandered to the table and flicked a soft linen napkin, displacing the carefully set silverware a millimeter from perfection.

"Do you regret your move?" she asked, then pressed her lips together, feeling her own wave of regret from posing the question in the first place. Damn it, she didn't want to know anything about who he was now—not beyond the monthly reports T-45 provided on the leadership of the intelligence organizations around the globe. How could she retain her distance if she delved into his personal life?

"Never mind," she said, holding up her hand before he had a chance to respond. "Forget I asked."

He slid the chair out for her. "As you wish."

But she'd done the damage, despite his gracious response. She'd shown her hand, even briefly, implying that her interest in him hadn't ended when she'd walked out his door. He'd use that knowledge against her. He'd be a fool not to—and Dante Burke was anything but a fool.

Chapter 4

Watching her eat became Dante's immediate and tor-
turous reward. The way she slid the food into her
mouth, the way her lips pressed together tightly as
she chewed, the way her eyes drifted closed when
the flavors exploded lusciously on her tongue nearly
drove him insane. At first, she'd tried to shovel the
oysters Bienville into her mouth as if she were
wolfing down a fast-food hamburger, but her finely
honed appreciation for sensual pleasures quickly
won out over her dire need to rush through the meal.
With utter fascination, he watched her delight as she
licked a dab of the creamy Parmesan and garlic sauce
from the corner of her mouth. He silently thanked
the chef at Arnaud's for teaching him the secret to
the delectable dish.

Encouraged, he refilled her wineglass halfway,
wondering if she had any idea what he had in store

for her next—or that his carefully planned seduction was already well under way.

She reached for her wine. "You're not planning on getting me drunk, are you? If you are, I should warn you. I've developed a much stronger constitution against the effects of alcohol while living in France."

He topped off his own glass, then returned the crisp Chardonnay to the table. "I'm keeping up with you. Either we'll both be drunk, or neither. Isn't it bad enough that I've had to force you to share a meal with me? My obsession with you only goes so far."

She snorted gently with laughter, holding the glass carefully by the stem, swirling the golden liquid just beneath her nose so she could inhale the exquisite aromas from the fine French wine. "Still, you must be fairly beyond help if you'd jeopardize a mission just to lure me into bed."

"I'm jeopardizing nothing. You conducted your searches today without interference, didn't you? Completed two rooms with intense precision, by my estimation. And you do have to eat, whether I'm here or not."

She tore a piece of rustic French bread from the loaf in the center of the table and dipped a corner in the remaining Bienville sauce. "I also have to sleep."

He sipped his wine and chuckled. "You forget how well I know you, Macy. When you're on a mission, you rarely sleep more than an hour or two at a time.

You caught a catnap between rooms today. I watched you."

With an intense gaze, he leaned forward, catching the momentary pinkening in the apples of her cheeks. "Are you aware that you snore?"

She slid the glass into place, not the least bit ruffled by his comment. Okay, so he was exaggerating. She didn't snore . . . exactly. But she did make tiny little noises while dreaming, the kind that enticed a man to consider all the sweet possibilities of what might be going on in her resting subconscious. He could only hope that she was reliving some liaison of theirs from their past, though he knew she'd never admit something so revealing—or so intimate.

She popped the last of the bread into her mouth, chewed, swallowed and pierced him with an unshakable ice-blue stare. "What's next?"

"A salad with tasso ham—"

"That's not what I meant."

Her gaze skewered him, but not without a hint of humor. Nine years had changed Macy, something he hadn't wanted to acknowledge before now. She wasn't the same bright-eyed, excitable agent she'd been before, beating everyone to the briefing room in the mornings, volunteering for extra assignments so she could amass more experience in various aspects of the business. She wasn't so intense, so focused on proving herself that she couldn't laugh with her colleagues or take the natural ribbing offered by operatives who'd spent more time in the trenches than she had. No, this Macy took her time, savored her wine and her food, only raised her hand for assignments that appealed to her expertise. This Macy had the ability to laugh at herself, not take every situation with the utmost seriousness, even when gravity might have been warranted. This Macy provided a whole new challenge—one entirely more suited for the man that nine years without her had forced him to become.

"What do you want to happen next?" he asked.

She lifted her napkin from her lap, tossed it on the table, took one last swig from her wine and stood. Sensing an attack, Dante scooted his chair back. He had a clear agenda for tonight, but figured a moment's deviation wouldn't affect the final outcome— not when she seemed so intent on proving some point.

As he expected, she swung a leg over him and landed on his lap, her sweet center instantly pressing against his sex. She speared her fingers through his hair and smashed her mouth down on his for a hard, hungry, explosive kiss.

The flavors nearly knocked the sense right out of him. Garlic and spice from the appetizer, woodsy undertones of oak from the wine and the innately sweet and addictive flavor that belonged to Macy and Macy alone. Despite his plans for a slow, drawn-out and carefully orchestrated seduction, he couldn't help but surrender to her assault, if only for a moment.

He slid his hands around her back. Her muscles, tense and bunched, did not loosen beneath his touch. Even her tongue seemed intent on winning a war rather than participating in a fair exchange of thrust and parry. The realization forced him to tear her off him and curse his moment of pure male weakness.

She kicked her leg over him again and stood up straight, her eyes blazing. She swiped her wrist over her lips before she spoke.

"What's wrong, Burke? Too hot for you?"

He straightened his shirt and retrieved his fallen napkin from the floor. "Just the opposite. Too cold."

She stepped back, her balance tentative and her eyes glazed with an emotion that could have been either anger or lust. With Macy, it was sometimes hard to tell.

"You didn't specify how I was supposed to react to you," she said. "I just assumed you wanted your sex hot and heavy and fast. That's how we've always been, you and me."

She slowly reached out and touched his shoulder, and he had to exert all his self-control not to recoil. He'd underestimated her. She could weave the web of mind games just as well as he—except that his motivation would keep him on top. She might try to turn the tables on him, but he wasn't about to allow her enough room to completely spin.

He snatched her hand in one quick grab, then turned her wrist and placed a soft kiss on the sensitive skin near her pulse. Then, standing, he led her back around to her chair, seated her again and then cleared the plates away.

"Things have changed, Macy. I've changed. Nothing will be as it was before, if I have my way. Which I will, of course."

He retrieved the second course, complete with a new bottle of wine to complement the lightly dressed salad. He had five courses planned, each more delicious than the last, each paired with a fine wine that he'd pour with elegance and patience and attention to sensual detail. She'd tried to take over the seduction and she'd failed. He wouldn't allow her the upper hand.

Without a word, she picked up her fork and sampled the salad, and just as he expected, the piquant combination of ingredients knocked her anger away. He uncorked the wine and, after placing new glasses in front of them, poured the Pinot Grigio he'd discovered last year in Venice. By the end of the meal, Macy's senses would be so primed, the idea of jumping him in order to do the deed and be done for the night would be the farthest thing from her mind.

* * *

Macy watched Dante carefully stack the dishes in the sink while she finished off the last of the brandy he'd served to complement the delicious crème brûlée. She'd had many five-star meals in her world-wide explorations and this one definitely landed in the top ten—not so much for the quality of the food, which had been superb, but because never in her life had she expected such attention and personal service from a man like Dante Burke.

She knew what he was up to. Didn't take a rocket scientist to figure out his modus operandi. But at the moment, sated with exquisite food and even more delectable wines and spirits, she hardly cared. If that meant surrender, so be it. At this point, she had nothing to lose but another hour's sleep.

He dried his hands on a dishtowel and gestured toward the parlor. "Anything else you'd like from the kitchen?"

She stood, noting the extra pull around the button and zipper area of her jeans. "Maybe my sweats?"

His grin was pure sin. "No sweats, but I did arrange a change of wardrobe for you."

Eyebrow quirked, she followed him into the parlor, which glowed with a wide array of candles. She had no idea when he'd lit them—they'd hardly melted—then guessed he'd simply put in a request to one of the half-dozen or so agents she'd seen stationed around the grounds. Though he'd banished all Arm agents from the premises while she worked, the house

301

was his to do with as he wished, including rearranging the furniture to execute a sweet seduction.

He'd cleared the space of all coffee tables and end tables. The marvelous antique mirrors, kaleidoscopic Tiffany lamp shades and cut-crystal vases caught and reflected the firelight so that the room nearly buzzed with flickers of flame. The aroma of beeswax permeated the room with a honeyed perfume that became heady, thanks to the wine. He strolled to the opposite corner of the room and flicked a switch, piping music into the space. She didn't recognize the artist, but the sultry sounds of saxophone jazz slipped into her consciousness and washed away the last of her resistance.

"This is quite the atmosphere you've created," she said.

His smile barely curved his generous lips, but made his gray eyes sparkle like polished obsidian, dark and glossy. "You deserve the best."

She glanced over at a delicate oriental screen in the corner, one she knew hadn't been in the room when she'd searched earlier. "Nice addition."

"Glad you like it. If you slip behind, you'll find the more comfortable clothing I've arranged."

She bit her tongue in making fun of the whole "why don't you slip into something more comfortable" cliché and decided just to go with the flow. The truth was, Dante had sufficiently enticed her. His seduction had worked. She couldn't help but wonder if the spark that had once burned them with its intensity still existed between them. But even if the fire remained, she knew the heat couldn't scorch her again. For that to happen, she'd have to care about their future like she once had—and that simply wasn't the case.

Behind the screen, she found a lovely pitcher filled with rose-scented water, a porcelain basin, a delicate towel and, draped on a padded, satin hanger, an exquisite gown in breathtaking sapphire blue. With long sleeves and no ornamentation beyond a simple diamond broach that would likely sit just between her breasts, the dress was nearly demure in style. Nearly, but not quite.

With a grin, Macy whipped her T-shirt over her head and shed her jeans, which she kicked out of the way. She was game. If the man wanted to torture himself with what he could never truly have, who was she to argue? In fact, if torture was what he wanted, she'd happily oblige.

She washed and dressed quickly, loving how the fabric fell in soft waves over her body while the rose-water enhanced the femininity as it absorbed into her skin. When she emerged from behind the screen, Dante's eyes widened in unhampered appreciation. When he licked his lips, even with the subtlety that was ingrained into his style, she couldn't help but feel a buzz of awareness that persisted long after he spoke.

"You're beautiful."

"You knew that," she shot back.

"I don't recall us taking much time in the past for the aesthetics."

She squared her shoulders. "I wore sexy nighties for you all the time," she insisted.

"Which I removed in three seconds flat."

Macy fingered the diamond broach nestled low between her breasts. Surprisingly, the pin held the entire ensemble together. Once he removed the jewelry, the entire robe would fall away. "This won't take you half as long."

He crossed the room slowly, his hand extended toward hers, his eyes dark with such a combination of desire and restraint that Macy felt certain the man might soon explode. Instead, he pulled her gently into his arms and began to sway to the lazy, luxurious rhythm of the music.

"I don't intend to undress you tonight."

"You said we would make love here. That was the deal." She dismissed the disappointed sound she thought she'd heard in her voice. She'd pushed herself to the limit. So had he. Clearly, she was nearly on the brink of exhaustion.

He tugged her closer, wrapping her hand in his and giving her little choice but join him in the dance. "We are making love. In ways we never have before."

Chapter 5

"Aren't there any good games on?"

Dante glanced over his shoulder, not the least surprised that Sean Devlin had bypassed all of Dante's security and entered the office unannounced, dressed in sweats that looked like they might not have been washed—ever—with a cutoff T-shirt and a Chicago White Sox baseball cap, worn backward. For all his horrid fashion sense, Devlin had once been the best all-around agent the Arm had ever employed, even if he'd only been in the service of U.S. Intelligence for just over two years. Better than Macy. Better than Dante. Had he stuck around, Sean likely would have surpassed his mentor and taken over as chief. Luckily for Dante's career, Sean hadn't been programmed with a stick-to-anything strand in his genetic code. But while the two men no longer worked together, they had remained good friends. Cheating death together had created a lifelong bond.

"The game I'm watching is fascinating," Dante answered, gesturing his old friend inside.

Situated above Bogdanov's garage in a room built by the Arm, the surveillance center allowed Dante an unhampered view of Macy as she searched the arboretum. For over three hours, he'd observed how cleverly she'd ignored the plants, knowing their ever-changeable nature would likely provide no clues to the countercode. She'd used ultrasound and radar technology to explore the soil, and when the technical search didn't satisfy her, she dug in the dirt herself.

She'd counted and looked for patterns in the hand-painted floor tiles and with attention to detail that would have made his eyes cross. She'd examined every weave in the antique wicker furniture, every shadow or beam of light cast by the dim bulbs. Nothing in the room, from the light fixtures to the crevices in the wall, went unnoticed or untouched. When she'd finally stood, dusted off her hands, glared straight into the so-called hidden camera and announced the room was clear, he hadn't known whether to grin or frown. Now that she'd completed the room, they were one step closer to a second night of sensual delights, but as agents, they were also no nearer to finding the code they'd both been sent to discover.

Sean scooted onto the desk behind Dante and peered over his shoulder. "Is that who I think it is?"

Dante flipped off the screen. "Why are you here?"

Though his eyes narrowed, Sean dropped the topic of Macy and her unorthodox presence in the operation. Though he trusted his good friend with the secrets of his personal life, Dante had never been one to kiss and tell. Particularly when he'd hardly even kissed Macy yet.

"Heard you were in New Orleans," Sean said casually, as if his appearance in the middle of a top-secret operation were completely ordinary. "Wanted to check out the action."

Dante grunted. Sean had no more interest in intelligence-related action than Dante did in the current National Football League standings, which Sean undoubtedly knew by heart.

"You're checking up on me," Dante decided.

"Isn't that what friends do?"

Sean poked around Dante's desk, chuckling triumphantly when he found the small humidor tucked beneath a status report from an operation in St. Louis. Never mind that the document was marked CONFIDENTIAL and had the name of a celebrity and several political dignitaries scribbled on the outer flap. Sean didn't spare the file a second glance when he tossed it aside.

"Friends who have phones can call," Dante reminded him.

"Not when the other friend is in New Orleans. Have you checked out that club near Tchoupitoulas and Canal? I hear it rocks."

"I have no time for clubbing."

"Man, you gotta make time." Sean selected a premier Romeo y Julieta cigar, bit off the end, spit out the tip and then shuffled around for a match.

Dante extracted his Colibri lighter from his jacket pocket.

Sean grinned in thanks, ignited a steady flame and then rolled the cigar in the bluest part of the fire. "That's what's missing from your life," he said between puffs. "Time for fun . . . and a good woman."

"One in particular or will any do?"

Sean wiggled his eyebrows and rolled off the desk, suddenly interested in the technology around him rather than answering the question Dante had posed. Dante didn't need Sean to point out that his life had been missing much more than time for relaxation and a good woman. He'd been missing Macy, who probably wouldn't fall into anyone's definition of "good" except his own. She was cunning, cool and aloof. If ordered to, she could lie without conscience and kill without regret.

She also loved her family, considered loyalty the most important virtue and would gladly take a bullet to keep an innocent alive.

So much like him. How could he resist her?

Unfortunately, he'd needed a gunshot wound and

a brush with cold death to bring the depth of his feelings for her back to the surface after their nine years apart. Ever since Sean had orchestrated Dante's rescue from a drug lord's den, Dante hadn't been as content with the status quo as he'd been since Macy had left. Back then, he'd accepted that his betrayal could not be forgiven, could not be undone—even if his motives had been pure. Then after dying twice on the operating table, he realized that anything was possible.

That's why he'd sought her out when the first report of the terrorists in Russia hit his desk. That's why he'd made sure the Arm bought the Garden District house before T-45 could get its hands on the valuable property. He'd known the agency would send Macy.

His change in attitude was also why he'd made Macy agree to this seduction. He'd decided to prove to her that the love they'd once shared shouldn't have been thrown away—even if he'd royally screwed up. But he certainly didn't need Sean to remind him of the importance of his success.

"Why are you really here, Sean?"

Sean stopped fiddling with a prototype nightscope and turned to Dante. His expression was benign, his stance relaxed, but his eyes flamed with ominous gravity.

"Word on the street is that you're in collusion with T-45."

Dante chuckled. He'd thought he'd been so careful about keeping this operation under wraps, but he couldn't control the other side. And Sean had contacts everywhere, even though he insisted to everyone who would listen that he was out of the spy business for good.

"T-45 and the Arm are working on a cooperative mission, yes."

"You can't trust those guys, Dante. They work for no one but themselves. They're mercenaries."

He thought about Macy, imagined her slipping into her shower right about now to wash the rich, black soil off her skin. She'd grab a quick protein bar from her backpack, then indulge in a power nap until she searched the next room on her agenda—the master suite.

"So you came here to warn me," Dante concluded, pushing the erotic possibilities of tonight's activities from his mind. He'd primed Macy's senses last night with the delicious food and exquisite wines, then slow, sensual dancing that forced their bodies close. But in her eyes, he'd seen the spark of curiosity, interest, even desire. He had successfully whet her appetite for another, more intimate interlude. So tonight, he'd test the true limits of her resistance.

"I only came to check out that club," Sean said, "but thought a friendly warning about our counterparts at T-45 might go a long way. Abercrombie Marshall is a good man, but he can't control all his agents all the time. They work with agendas of their own."

Dante grinned, leaned across the desk and retrieved a cigar for himself. He could only hope Sean's contention was true. Only once Macy realized what she really wanted—and what she was willing to do to get it—would he truly win back her heart.

Macy returned to her bedroom around eight thirty, her vision blurry after her search of the master suite. She'd finally thought she was onto something when she found an odd mathematical pattern embroidered into the fabric of Bogdanov's custom-designed duvet cover. Unfortunately, once she had the numbers identified and sequenced, she realized she recognized the pattern as the combination to his safe, which was no help since the Arm had already unlocked the thing and had rifled through all the contents, none of which proved useful.

What had surprised her about the search was the way the luxurious master suite had grabbed her personal attention. Usually, when she worked a room or even an entire house, she completely disassociated herself with the things inside. She loved fine art and furnishings, but when she was on the job, she rarely noticed much beyond the relevant details. But in the master bedroom today, she'd had a hell of a lot of trouble ignoring the fact that in just a few hours,

Dante would have her at his mercy on that huge, fluffy bed.

Macy locked her bedroom door, knowing Dante could pick the antique device with something as common as a kitchen knife, then stripped down to her lingerie and threw on a robe. She didn't know when he'd call for her, but he had been nice enough this time to send up a meal of cold cheese, fruits and wine to sustain her until he invited her to the next interlude of their seduction. She still couldn't believe he'd done nothing more in the parlor last night than dance her around the room. They'd shared slow, sensuous dances, yes, with amazingly provocative music, but except for smoothing his warm palm down her back or across her shoulder, he'd barely touched her. His chest, however, had been pressed intimately against hers. His subtle, spicy cologne had played havoc with her susceptible senses and the natural heat sizzling off his body had nearly driven her insane. By the end of the hour, the sound of his voice had become enough to entice her thirsty libido.

He'd then kissed the top of her hand so gently before informing her that the night was over, she'd almost thought he was teasing. Which he was—in the most powerful way she'd ever experienced.

Just what did he have in store for her tonight?

When a soft knock sounded on her door, her nipples automatically peaked in an erotic Pavlovian response, followed by a warm thrill simmering through her body. She had no idea what she'd experience tonight or what, if anything, he would demand of her. But unlike last night, she was actually eager to find out.

She opened the door, but no one was there. On the door, he'd tacked a flower, a lavender hothouse rose tied with a filmy, iridescent ribbon that curled down to the floor. She couldn't help but detach his invitation to the arboretum and draw the petals to her nose, where she inhaled a powerful scent that nearly weakened her knees.

She found him in the center of the tiny but overflowing room. She shut the French doors behind her, keeping the natural warmth of the atmosphere contained. In her robe, barefoot and holding the rose, she cleared her throat to announce her presence.

He turned around slowly, an inscrutable grin toying with his lips.

"How was your dinner?" he asked.

"Filling," she answered simply.

Through the overflowing ferns and nearly ceiling-high crotons in an array of wild color from gold to green to pink and burgundy, Macy watched Dante grab a towel and innocently dry off his hands. She should have been accustomed to the concentrated smell of the rich and fertile earth all around them, but the assault on her senses once again enticed her.

What did he have in store for her tonight? And more importantly, why was she looking forward to his seduction with such eager interest?

He held out his hand to her. "Last night, I attempted to appeal to your sense of taste and hearing. The delicious food, fine wine, incredible music. Tonight, I'd like to concentrate on your other senses."

A thrill tripped through her bloodstream. As far as Macy was concerned, Dante had hit every sense last night with full force. But if he wanted to work hard at this seduction, who was she to argue? "Like?"

He glanced around the arboretum and inhaled deeply. "Scent, for starters."

Then, they'd head for the bedroom. "And then?"

His smile revealed nothing. "You'll have to wait and see. Anticipation is a powerful aphrodisiac, don't you agree?"

He stretched his palm farther toward her and she couldn't resist stepping closer and laying her fingers gently in his hand. He tugged her forward, then stopped—forcing her to walk through a curtain of foliage of her own volition. Clever, clever man. She had to want this seduction. She had to walk in willingly. Little by little, he was altering the atmosphere, changing the rules without really changing a thing. Intrigued, she couldn't stop her curiosity, not even after she spotted the large, claw-footed porcelain tub sitting in the middle of the arboretum, just to the left of the impressive marble fountain.

Steam slithered off the top of the water, adding to the thick humidity of the room. The dim lights, enhanced by two or three strategically placed candles that reminded her of the glittering tapers he'd filled the parlor with the night before, added a romantic ambience that even the coolest woman on earth couldn't ignore. Two days ago, Macy might have considered herself in the running for that designation, but not anymore. Like it or not, Dante had melted through her icy exterior, exposing the woman within.

And judging by the way he filled the tub with a fragrant powder that turned the bath water a milky, opaque pink, he intended for her to expose quite a bit more. And soon.

Chapter 6

"What have you here?" she asked.

"An indulgence," he replied.

He exchanged the bottle of bath salts for a silver wicker basket overflowing with pink and lavender rose petals, which he scattered over the surface of the water. Macy couldn't help but watch the incongruous scene with boundless curiosity. Even with the light muted and the scents of a hundred flowers buzzing in her head like the bees normally kept outdoors by the floor-to-ceiling glass walls, she couldn't put together the image of Dante drawing a bath for her and the man she'd once known and loved.

He knew she never took baths. She hadn't even liked the whirlpool he'd installed on the balcony outside the Georgetown condominium they'd shared. She'd never been one for a long soak, much preferring the scalding blast of a shower that practically burned the sweat and dirt of a day's work off her skin. Growing up in a household with four brothers—two on either side of the age scale—and parents who thought one bathroom was sufficient for their progeny, she imagined she hadn't had a bath since she'd been a baby. And Dante wanted her in one now?

"What do you really want from me?" she asked, suspicious and suddenly angry. She'd worked damned hard all day, and while she couldn't deny that she'd slept soundly after indulging Dante's requests last night, sated with amazing food and lulled into relaxation while dancing, she suddenly felt wired and antsy, likely because in order to take a bath, she'd have to get naked.

And yet, she suspected he still didn't want to have sex. His game was both transparent and, unfortunately, effective. He wanted her to drop her guard. With her senses and libido primed to the point where she'd forget how he betrayed her and remember only how much he pleasured her, how much they'd once meant to each other, he'd have her right where he wanted her.

He was setting himself up for a huge disappointment, though judging by the confident gleam in his fathomless gray eyes, he had no idea how his plan would fail.

"I want you to relax."

"I don't want to relax," she insisted, wondering what compelled her to argue when the inevitable was as clear as the water had been before he'd tossed in the bath salts. She'd have to give in—at least to a point. Now that she understood his plan, however, she'd find a defense. Hopefully soon. Because little by little, she realized a nine-year-old past hurt simply wasn't enough.

Dante turned the basket over the tub so that the last of the rose petals floated into the water. "You'd probably enjoy relaxing, if you had any idea how to do it."

She ran her hands through her hair. "Let's not play games, Dante. We've been apart for a long time. You have no idea how I spend my free time."

Dante grinned indulgently. "Do you really need me to send for your dossier?"

She huffed impatiently. No, she didn't. Because the truth was, except for sharing an occasional glass of wine with a fellow agent in the bistro two blocks away from T-45's headquarters in Paris, she rarely allowed her mind to shut down long enough to evoke the true benefits of relaxation. Not in the shower. Not when she swam laps in the pool or when she worked out on the technically advanced elliptical trainer she committed to for an hour every day. Even in her dreams, she conducted intense but methodical searches for objects that were both un-named and undefined, never allowing her complete rest from either her psyche or her conscious life.

And now, he wanted her to chuck all that and step

into a steamy, fragrant tub of water and soak while he watched?

She untied her robe. "Turn around," she instructed.

Surprisingly, he did as he was told. She opened her mouth to question his obedience, but then decided not to challenge good fortune. Instead, she stripped and stepped boldly into the milky water.

Only after she caught the glimmer of his smile in the reflective glass of two antique mirrors—one hung just a few feet away from her and one behind—did she realize her gullibility.

"You have become quite the voyeur in my absence," she challenged, refusing to drop instantly down into the water just to avoid his gaze. He'd seen her naked before. She'd seen him. Despite the flush simmering through her skin, she wouldn't surrender to her discomfort, not when such a move would mean more than she wanted to admit to him about his effect on her.

"How can a man resist when the view is so compelling?"

He didn't turn around, but continued to watch her through the cross reflection of the two mirrors. Slowly, the rush of warmth from her blush dissipated. Standing in the hot water, the air above suddenly chilled. When her nipples started to peak, she eased into the hot water.

He clucked his tongue in disappointment.

Immersed to just below her shoulders, Macy couldn't help but feel completely exposed when Dante neared, then stopped. He lingered just a foot or so away, his boot perched on the edge of the fountain, which she realized was tinkling with a soft cool music that invited her to close her eyes and breathe deeply. In the steaming hot water, the sweet rose scents swirling around her weakened her. Her head swam, so she braced her hands on the sides of the tub to keep from losing her balance.

"What did you do?" she asked.

"Nothing, yet."

"I feel light-headed," she admitted. If she'd been dealing with a T-45 operative instead of the head of the Arm, she would suspect he'd drugged the water or perhaps even the perfume. But the Arm generally didn't operate with such chemical slyness. It tended to barge in, take what it wanted and then clean up the mess afterward—much like the man who ran the organization.

Though he didn't seem to be working in bulldozer mode tonight, did he? Even his voice contained a soft, lazy drawl unlike any she'd ever heard from him, even while undercover.

He picked up a large seashell from the edge of the fountain beside her. "Light-headed? That's called relaxation, Macy. I told you last night I wouldn't get you drunk. I also won't drug you. When you return to me, you'll do so of your own volition."

She snorted, but without half the derision she'd intended. With the seashell, he scooped and poured the hot, scented water over her shoulders. The sensation was smooth and milky, as if he'd doused her in a melted emollient.

She released her hands from the sides of the tub.

"I won't return to you," she said, her voice soft with drowsiness.

"Hmm," he replied, pouring another shell full of water across her shoulders.

Arguing further would make no difference. She was in no position to convince him of anything. At this moment, she couldn't convince herself that the sky was blue in the daytime. Slowly but surely, her mind grew too befuddled to form a single coherent thought. When she forced herself to think, her focus fell to the bed in the master suite—their next destination. She found herself anticipating the moment when she crawled into those cool, high-thread-count Egyptian cotton sheets.

"What are you thinking about?"

She shook her head. "Wouldn't you like to know?"

"Very much."

"Sorry," she said with a sigh, leaning back against the porcelain. "My body is yours to command, not my mind."

This time, he poured the water across her neck, so that the flow teased the tips of her breasts.

"Does that mean if I tell you to touch yourself, you'll comply?"

Her eyes flashed open. She'd walked right into this one, hadn't she?

"Is that what it'll take to get you off?" she asked.

He chuckled. "I'm not interested in my own pleasure tonight, Macy. Though I'll admit that watching anything you do affects me." He poured another stream of warm water across her collarbone. "How does the water feel? Hot enough for you?"

At least he'd gotten that part right. The temperature would likely scald anyone else, but the heat felt both familiar and new to her at the same time. "Perfect."

"And the scent? I added an essential oil to the bath, which will account for the perfume and slick feel of the water as it sluices over your skin."

She moved ever so slightly, so that the flow of water fulfilled his sensual promise, but she focused on the truth to keep her antagonism going. She couldn't give in to him—not mentally. Not emotionally.

Well, she could, but would she hate herself in the morning?

"I've never been one for roses," she said.

"Really? I could have sworn the scent would evoke some sweet memories for you. Perhaps I miscalculated."

Hell. Dante never miscalculated, and the moment

he mentioned sweet memories, her mind spun back to the past, long before they'd met, to a summer she'd spent with her grandmother at her home in Savannah, to the rose garden she tended with constant and loving care. Macy had been no more than ten years old, allowed for the first time to visit her father's parents without her four raucous brothers to muck up the landscape. For two solid months, she'd helped her grandmother tend her prized flowers, listened to her stories, spent hours wandering the landscapes beside the creek that ran through the property her father's family had owned for over a century. She didn't remember telling Dante about that summer, but she knew she must have. And he'd evoked that innocent, faraway time with a not-so-innocent bath in a luscious arboretum.

Damn him.

She shifted in the tub, prepared to fight her Benedict Arnold muscles and get out, but he placed his hand on her shoulder and gently eased her back into the water. He leaned forward so that his words teased the tendrils that formed at the nape of her neck.

"Relax, Macy. Let the silkiness of the water awaken you. I'd forfeit my entire holdings to be in the water right now, surrounding you, penetrating you, experiencing every sweet curve and crevice of your body."

She attempted to resist the power of his suggestion, but couldn't. His desire was too evident, too overwhelming, too delicious to ignore. In the past, Dante had always made her feel desirable, but never to this extreme. Never to the point where he'd expose his own weakness for romantic nostalgia in order to prove the depth of his passion. Never to the point where he'd ask her to expose her own weaknesses, too many to count.

She couldn't resist running her hands over her legs beneath the water, up her thighs to the flat plane of her belly or the round curves of her breasts. Despite her arousal, her nipples couldn't fight the intense heat of the water to remain erect. But one brush from her fingertips and they tightened with intense, but lazy, tightness.

She hummed as the sweet sensation eased through her body like slow molasses poured over hotcakes, sugary and thick with anticipation.

Dante knelt beside the tub.

"How smooth is your skin?"

"Like silk," she replied, continuing to run her hands over her body, awakening nerve endings unaccustomed to such delightful decadence.

"What about your muscles? If I touched you now, would you jump out of your skin?"

She shook her head languidly. "Impossible. I'm not sure all my muscles even work anymore. You won't let me drown, will you?" she asked, slipping farther into the water so that only her head and chin were exposed to the air.

"Never, love. I wish I could see you, but the ripples in the water are enough to make me hard. You're touching your breasts now, aren't you?"

She'd hardly realized how hypnotic the sensations could be, her thumbs drawing lazy circles around her areolae, her fingers toying with the buoyant flesh of her breasts, creating a warm cocoon of sweet sensation.

She hummed her response.

"I can't imagine your nipples hardening with all that wet heat surrounding you. They must be so pliable, so sensitive to the slightest touch."

Willingly, she accepted his suggestion. He was right. She had to pluck hard to bring her nipples to full extension, but the sizzling sensations that shot through her blood as a result made the nips of pain entirely worthwhile. Between her legs, her feminine lips pulsed with need, beckoning her attention.

She shifted in the water, exposing a breast long enough for a silky rose petal to adhere to her skin. Her sharp intake of breath matched Dante's. He was watching from so close—and yet, he didn't touch.

She should have opened her eyes to look into his and gauge the level of his reaction, but she didn't dare. She knew what she'd see—and she didn't want to face such intense need. Not when she was feeling the same power on her own. If she looked and saw the kind of desire she imagined he felt, she'd likely pull him into the tub with her. A girl could take only so much teasing without some release.

The minute her fingers slipped between her folds of flesh, she found her clit and boldly stroked herself to madness. Only when she gasped for that final, life-sustaining breath did she realize that Dante's lips were on hers, giving her more than she bargained for, more than she thought she'd ever need.

And yet, not enough.

With a splash, she wrapped her arms around him and drew him near, cooing as he intoxicated her with the long, languid kiss. She wanted hot and heavy—and again, he denied her. He kissed her softly, toying with her tongue with only enough energy to bring her back to earth with gentle persuasion.

When he pulled away, she looked into his eyes. What she saw there made her gasp. How could he hold back, when his gaze betrayed the depth of his need?

"Make love to me," she said, knowing his game could go no farther.

"No," he said, standing and stepping back, creating a chasm of space.

She attempted to stand. Her muscles wavered, but Dante jumped forward and braced her with hands on her elbows. She thanked his quick reflexes with a hungry smile. "You want to make love to me," she said.

"Clearly. But we're not ready."

"Because I didn't come to you? Drop the game, Dante. We're both here. We're both incredibly aroused. Imagine how hot and slick I am right now. Imagine how easy your sex will slip into mine."

She'd gone too far. She recognized the moment his control nearly snapped, when instead of yanking her out of the tub and flinging her on the soft grass of the arboretum to finish what he'd started, he grabbed the robe he'd tossed across a lawn chair, nearly ripping the fabric in his haste to cover her. He lifted her into his arms, but refused eye contact until he'd pounded up the stairs and kicked open the door of the master suite.

Finally! They'd do the deed and expend the last of their mutual attraction, ending this game of sexual teasing against sins from the past. He laid her on the bed, leaving her to open the robe as he circled around to the footboard, his eyes blazing, his nostrils flaring with unchecked lust.

Then, he was gone. She blinked, unsure that she'd actually seen him turn and leave. She struggled off the bed, her muscles still wavering from the hot water in the tub and the intensity of her self-induced orgasm, and staggered toward the door.

Just in time to hear the click.

She sagged against the carved wood frame, unwilling to shout for her release when she knew he'd never comply, though she pounded her fist on the wood once, an impotent but necessary gesture. Exhausted and angry, but mostly swimming in a wash of desires she needed to exercise out of her system, she shifted until her back rested against the door. The room glowed with candles, flickering seductive fingers of light over the golden bed sheets and intricately woven satin duvet. She staggered back to the bed and tossed the robe aside, climbing between the covers naked. Maybe he'd come to her later tonight, when he'd found some control for the wild emotions she'd caught in his eyes.

Or maybe not. Either way, by tomorrow, she'd end his game, if it was the last thing she did.

d never met
for him based
f which was the f
ined Macy's high
the one to finally give
Dante also had no
Marshall had come
been unorthodo
major incident
Marshall
barely w
door to
dered
sh

"He's here

Dante snapped ...

tors to the speaker on his de...

After flipping the switch so that the im...
searching the billiards room instantly disappeare...,
he slid his chair back, retrieved his jacket from the
brass peg on the wall and slipped his arms into the
silk-lined garment. A tremor of anticipation ratcheted
through his system. Just a decade ago, a meeting
such as this would have been unheard of, but after
receiving the urgent communiqué from T-45, Dante
decided that the time had come for change, especially
under the current circumstances. As far as Dante
knew, Abercrombie Marshall had not returned to the
States since he'd left the Arm, a frustrated African
American agent with skills coveted by every foreig
agency in the spy biz except the one he'd le

...e man, he had the
...on extensive data—not
...ct that Marshall had not
...opinion, but also he'd been
...the woman her due.

...doubt that Macy was the reason
...in person. Their arrangement had
..., to say the least, especially when a
...like a nuclear attack was at stake.

...entered the room without hesitation,
...iting for the agent assigned to open the
...move out of the way. Tall and broad shoul-
..., Abercrombie Marshall wore his hair sheared
...rt, without a single sprinkle of gray at the tem-
...les. His eyes, dark and assessing, crinkled at the
corners and his full-lipped mouth melted easily into
a friendly smile. He held out his hand, which
Dante accepted.

"Mr. Marshall," Dante said. "I'm honored to meet
you."

"Probably more like shocked as hell, but I hear
your manners wouldn't allow you to speak so
freely."

Dante laughed, releasing the man's hand after a
hearty shake. With a welcoming gesture, he directed
his guest toward one of two comfortable leather
chairs he kept in front of his desk. "My manners
ave been exaggerated, sir, I assure you. Plain speak-
g is simply a lost art in our business."

Marshall sat and Dante did the same in the chair next to his. He had no reason to put on some show of superiority with Marshall by resuming his place behind his desk.

"I want to speak with my agent," Marshall demanded.

"I've done nothing to block communications with you. She's sent regular updates."

"Which you've monitored," Marshall pointed out. "Is she a prisoner?"

Dante didn't hide his shock. "Absolutely not, sir. She's working hard, though with frustrating results so far," Dante said, privately noting the double entendre. What he and Macy had shared over the past two days had given new depth to the word *frustrating.* "You may see her immediately, of course."

"Of course," Marshall acknowledged, with a gleam in his eye that told Dante that at this point, he'd see Macy if he wanted to, with or without Dante's permission. "And I will, but not yet. I have a private matter I wish to discuss first."

Dante shifted in his seat, suddenly uncomfortable with Marshall's tone. He sounded less like the head of an international spy agency and more like a concerned father.

"I understand."

"No, I don't think you do. You probably think this old black man has come here to make sure Macy's heart doesn't get broken through your deal, whatever it is. I don't give a damn about her heart." He leaned forward, his large, long-fingered hands braced on his knees. "For all I know, Macy doesn't have a heart. And if she didn't, I wouldn't give a damn because she'd probably be a better agent for it, not that she's lacking in any way. But this mission is critical, and I won't allow one of my agents to have her will broken as a consequence of working with the Arm."

Dante frowned. Under Dante's direction, the Arm had not used the type of tactics Marshall spoke of— at least, never with someone like Macy, a fellow agent. But he had created a scenario where she'd complied simply because he'd given her no choice. Only he'd known that he planned to give Macy access to the house, even if she refused.

"I assure you, sir," Dante said, having to clear his throat of a sudden lump before continuing. "I'd never authorize any type of mind control with Macy. She means a great deal to me. You must know about our past."

Marshall snorted. "Vaguely. She's never volunteered specifics. I know you were once lovers. I know that you did something that royally pissed her off."

To say the least.

"In her eyes, I betrayed her."

"Did you?"

"Yes."

Marshall leaned back into the chair, his hands casually draped on the armrests. "So you've used your position as head of the Arm to manipulate a mission and win her back?"

Dante winced. It sounded so much worse when spoken by someone else. "Yes. It's because of my loyalty to the Arm that I lost her. And I'm a man who gets what he wants. And I want her back."

Marshall's eyes narrowed. "As an agent?"

"I could care less about what organization Macy gives her allegiance to."

"She can't work for T-45 and be personally involved with you. I respect Macy and I trust her with my life, but that's a conflict of interest no organization can ignore. Understand one thing, Mr. Burke. If Macy returns to you emotionally, you'll be asking her to give up her career. She's poised to take a high leadership role with T-45, an honor she's deserved for a long time. Are you promising her something in return that is worth her giving up her life's dream for?"

Little by little, the air deflated out of Dante's chest. What exactly was he offering Macy, other than a slow roll in the hay as opposed to the fast ones they'd shared in the past? He'd attempted to show her how much he'd changed, how much he wanted to pamper her, pay attention to her, concentrate on her and her needs. But she'd need so much more before she could choose him over her cherished career. And he wasn't entirely sure he had anything that valuable to give.

"Your point is well-taken, Mr. Marshall. I will consider what you've said with great seriousness."

"See that you do," Marshall said before his face resolved into a mask of dire seriousness. "Now, on to the real reason I'm here."

Macy stretched, waiting until every disk in her spine had popped before she released a guttural, frustrated groan and threw down her gloves in defeat. She'd had such high hopes for the billiards room. Though the housekeeper had reported that Bogdanov hardly used the room while he'd lived in the house, the nature of the room invited images of numbers, patterns and shapes, all of which could be used to successfully hide a countercode. With the dark, hand-carved paneling and the walls sporting numerous photographs of homes from all around New Orleans—from the French Quarter to the Garden District—she'd had a thousand sound possibilities about where the scientist might have hidden the sought-after sequence.

Unfortunately, none of her theories had held together under careful scrutiny. Her best shot had been a combination built from the addresses and street names of the houses pictured on the walls, but no matter how many times the computer ran the data through, a successful match to the characteristics of known countercodes would not emerge. The clues had been so promising, she'd nearly questioned the accuracy of the software—until she reminded herself that Bogdanov had written the program himself long before his mind had started to wither away.

So she'd worked from sunrise to sundown exclusively in this room, skipping her nap and putting off her search of the library until tomorrow. Now hungry, tired and teetering on the edge of surrender, she flopped onto the overstuffed couch, threw her head back against the cushions and allowed herself to think about Dante for the first time today.

She slipped back to the moment, shortly before dawn, when she'd heard the lock click open on the bedroom door. Instantly awakened by the sound, she'd kept perfectly still beneath the covers. She'd carefully regulated her breathing so she appeared asleep, despite the fact that her nipples had peaked in response and the electric current flowing to her sex sizzled back to life at the mere possibility that he'd enter the room. Several silent, still moments later, she'd finally realized he wasn't coming in to finish what he'd started the night before, no matter how much her body ached for him—or his for her.

The disappointment had rolled with her out of bed in a rush, causing her to jam her arms back into the robe with more force than necessary. She had to hand the man some credit—he'd succeeded in getting under her skin. His inventive and attentive seduction had shown him to be a changed man—a man she could no longer ignore or banish exclusively to her past.

And as for that past, she realized without any sense of defeat that she was finally ready to hear his explanation for why he'd betrayed her.

She shouldn't have run all those years ago, lured by promises T-45 not only made, but kept. She'd had her choice of assignments, world travel, incredible financial reward and access to the world's most advanced technology—all without the red tape and old-boy network so prevalent in the States. She'd blamed Dante for all her frustration over her lack of advancement in the Arm, when, in truth, he couldn't have stonewalled her on his own. And why would he have? The powers that be would never have tapped her for a leadership role over him.

Dante had forced himself back into her life, making her think about their past through eyes unclouded by raw emotions, righteous indignation and anger. She loved her new life. In many ways, her leaving had been the right move—for both of them. Neither she nor Dante had been ready for a real relationship, not with both of them so wrapped up in their ambitions. The Dante she'd known before had never been patient or gentle, as he'd clearly become. The Dante she'd known before had never planned anything in his private life more than a few moments ahead though every special rendezvous they'd shared this week had been orchestrated to the letter. After hours, he used to embrace the spontaneous and the wild because during the day, his career epitomized careful planning and controlled response.

But he'd changed. And so had she.

Damn him. Damn them both.

She hadn't asked him to change. She'd never voiced a single clue that his unpredictable and unbridled ways had bothered her in the least since she'd been exactly the same, but she had to admit that this slow, patient, attentive Dante appealed to her on levels she'd once kept deeply buried. Would his newfound appreciation for relishing the pleasurable and sensuous last once he'd met his objective? Or was this alteration simply a means to an end?

Slapping her hands on her thighs as she sat up quickly, she decided the time had come to find out.

Until now, she hadn't realized that her anger and resentment of Dante had gone beyond the single incident in which he'd taken credit for the intelligence she'd painstakingly gathered on her last case for the Arm—taken credit and thus ruined her career. Maybe because everything about their relationship before had been fast and furious—the way they'd met and fallen into bed, the way they'd jumped into living together, the way she'd left when he'd advanced his career on the back of her hard work— she'd never had the chance to realize the depth of what had been missing from their love affair. Nothing about their relationship had exhibited patience or maturity or selflessness. But in the past two days, Dante had shown her all those things in spades.

She knew she was ready to hear his explanation for what he'd done—but was she prepared to believe him?

Uncomfortable with the barrage of emotions slamming at her from all directions, Macy threw herself into the task of gathering and storing her equipment and filing her reports, which would be transmitted to both Dante and Abercrombie Marshall via secure wireless technology. She had several rooms left to search, but she couldn't help allowing a moment of fatalism to pop into her brain. What if New Orleans was the target of the terrorists, as improbable as that was—or what if the enemy planned to annihilate Washington, D.C., which was much more likely? How would Macy react if scores of innocents died because one expert agent didn't have the right stuff? What if she learned that Dante also died in the attack she failed to prevent?

The thought weakened the muscles in her legs and made her chest ache. She blocked out the innocents. She wasn't ready to give up yet. But, God, she was in deep, deeper than she ever imagined, with Dante. Using sex as his weapon, he had conquered her ability to remain aloof, even though he'd made no secret of his methods or his goals. She'd convinced herself that she was over him—had been for a long time— and therefore, she was safe from his manipulations, but clearly, that wasn't the case.

She needed to end her emotional upheaval. She needed to slice through the tense thread he'd woven around her heart with his sweet seduction. She had only one means to accomplish this goal—she needed to turn the tables.

Determined, she dashed to her tiny bedroom in the back of the house, showered, changed and returned to the billiards room long before anyone had stirred in the house, which she considered odd since night had fallen. She grabbed some fruit from the kitchen and munched while she arranged the billiards room to her liking, wondering where exactly Dante was.

In the floor-to-ceiling mirror, she checked her bold, red lipstick and tore her hands through her hair so that her auburn waves flashed around her face in wild disarray. A touch of black eyeliner around her eyes and she'd re-created the woman Dante once hadn't been able to resist. In tight black slacks and a turquoise tank top that zipped up the front, she loosened the fastening so that her breasts nearly spilled from the material. The look was sleek and overtly sexual.

She'd hear his explanation, and if his words rang true, she'd make him an offer he couldn't refuse— and then she'd know, once and for all, if she was as equally obsessed with him as he was with her or if fast, furious, on-the-pool-table sex would finally scratch the itch that threatened to drive them both insane.

She was on the brink of tapping on the lens of the camera mounted above the fireplace to get Dante's attention when the double doors to the billiards room swung open. Dante stepped in, his brow instantly arched over curious eyes. She spun and stalked toward him with her sultriest strut, stopping fast when Abercrombie Marshall followed Dante into the room.

"Abe?"

Macy swallowed thickly, but her boss had the decency to ignore the seductive nature of her appearance. In fact, his eyes filled with such gravity, she immediately zipped up her blouse and stood ramrod straight. Something was wrong.

"Macy, we have a situation."

He gestured toward the couch, but Macy shook her head. She couldn't imagine her boss would reprimand her for her attempted liaison with Dante. He'd known—if not specifically, then by inference—the price she'd had to pay for access to the house. No, his expression denoted something more dire— something deadly.

"The terrorists have taken a silo?" she guessed.

Gravely, Abe nodded.

Her eyes flashed to Dante, who confirmed Abe's report with the stoic set of his jaw.

"Where?"

"Silo 887, in the Kunlun Mountains in Russian

342

South Siberia. The area is incredibly remote and travel to the region is treacherous."

"The Russian army?" she asked.

"Unable to reach the target area at this time," he replied.

Dante stepped forward. "The Arm has sent in special ops, but initial reports from satellite photos indicate that the terrorists have sufficiently booby-trapped the pass leading to the silo. They have antiaircraft capabilities. Chances are slim that we'll reach the area before zero hour," Dante said.

The impact of her failure knocked her in the gut, but Macy succeeded in standing tall despite the shaking in her arms and legs. The terrorists had the silo, but without the actual launch code, they could do no harm.

Yet.

"What are our options?" she asked, her voice surprisingly crisp.

"We find Bogdanov's fail-safe before the terrorists work out the launch code," Dante answered.

Abe reached out and pressed his large hand on Macy's shoulder, which she suddenly imagined had grown very unsteady. "The operation between T-45 and the Arm just became official. We have to find the code or millions of people will die."

Chapter 8

"All the books have been searched," Dante reported, tearing off his jacket and slinging it over the back of a chair. Time had run out on any goal other than finding the countercode. Once again, he'd been forced to choose the good of the mission over his relationship with Macy. But this time, he'd find a way to control the outcome, if they could simply make sure that millions of people didn't die because they failed.

Macy stepped to the center of the library, her gaze high as she turned around in a tight series of circles, her eyes lowering at every pass. Like a machine programmed to accurately assess the inner workings of some electronic device, Macy focused her finder's instincts on the library with cool precision. After consulting with Marshall, they'd decided against bringing in more agents. The Arm had already completed thorough and by-the-book searches. Only someone like Macy, an expert in pushing beyond the limits of protocol and procedure and one who had studied Bogdanov's life to the point that she likely knew him better than she knew herself, would be able to find the countercode in enough time to avert a disaster.

She had, however, agreed to accept Dante's help, just as he'd agreed to allow a squad of T-45 operatives who'd trained in the Himalayas to join the Arm special ops team in their quest to stop the terrorists at the source. The cooperative nature of this mission would have made history, if either agency ever allowed the pairing to go public, which they wouldn't. T-45 subsisted on its reputation as a rogue operation. As soon as the mission was complete, all proof that it had ever worked alongside the Arm would be effectively erased.

"Not having to go through the books will save time," Macy said, breaking into Dante's thoughts, forcing him to accept that he'd made his decision and the outcome now was beyond his control. His superiors had been alerted. The fallout would be heavy, but he could handle the heat. He had before.

"Besides, Bogdanov didn't read any of these books," she said. "They're all in English. They likely belonged to his wife."

"None in Russian?"

The library easily housed over a thousand books.

Surely a man with Bogdanov's national pride would have a few native novels on his shelves, even if just an original copy of *War and Peace*.

She turned, quirking an eyebrow at him. "Don't you read your own reports? Nothing but English. Bogdanov was proficient in French, German and Latin, but while he could speak well enough, reading English was beyond him."

Dante had read the reports, but such esoteric details tended not to stick. He'd been more concentrated on the bottom line assessment that the code was nowhere to be found.

"Couldn't he have hidden code in an English text, to throw off anyone who might be looking?"

She paced the room while she snapped on her special nylon gloves. "Perhaps, but I don't think so. Your agents checked the books for signs of handling, and most of them hadn't been touched in decades—as if they were simply put here for show."

"So we ignore the books."

"For now. The books are almost too obvious. Besides, I think Bogdanov would keep the code somewhere he could see it. Every day, possibly."

"How did you draw that conclusion?"

Macy's attention focused on a painting, an original by a Dutch master of an austere, upper-class couple. She answered without taking her eyes off the portrait. "When Gorbachev knocked down the Berlin Wall and Communism started to fail, Bogdanov

347

feared that some mad countryman would launch an attack against the United States. He created the countercode so that he personally could stop the destruction. He wanted to save his beloved country from starting World War Three. That's why he hid the code here in the United States rather than in the Soviet Union. This property belonged to his American wife and has been in her family for years."

This much, he knew. "Her murder was no accident. If we hadn't removed the housekeeper, she would have been next."

Macy pursed her lips but didn't speak, smudging her red lipstick while she ran her fingers up and down the picture frame. Damn. Dante knew he shouldn't be noticing something so insignificant right now, but he couldn't help himself. When he'd walked into the billiards room earlier with Marshall on his heels, he'd had an instant to meet Macy's eyes. The way she'd dressed, the way she'd moved—he'd been two seconds away from facing down a woman who'd had enough of taking no for an answer. She'd intended to seduce him and no matter his intention to draw out his teasing one more night, she would have succeeded in changing his mind. Last night, when he locked her in the room, he'd expended the last of his control. With blood rushing to his cock and his brain starving for nutrition, he'd barely put her off for one more evening.

His time had run out. She'd wanted him. And if not for this ominous change in the course of their operation, she would have had him, likely right on the billiards table.

"Have you noticed that everything in the house is antique, or at least fifty years old? Except for a few toiletries, the clothes in the closet, the food in the pantry and the appliances in the kitchen. Even the wiring is outdated, though still up to code."

Dante's men had already pointed that out.

"And?"

She shook her head. "The age of the items in the house is likely inconsequential at this point," Macy said. She moved to a curio case filled with knick-knacks all related to tobacco and smoking. A collection of antique pipes. A snuffbox. A cigar cutter inlaid with genuine mother-of-pearl.

"Bogdanov played chess and his hobbies included puzzles, mainly those in three dimensions," she answered. "I suspect he hid the code by creating a pattern of objects." She marched to the desk and lifted an ink blotter first, then the pen set, then a tarnished silver vase. "And he kept it out in the open."

"Hid in plain sight?" he guessed.

"Yes, but not for the reason you think. I believe that his visual connection to the countercode would have given him comfort. He was a worrier. He often wrote his formulas, even the ones he'd memorized, on large sheets of paper and hung them in his laboratory. That's why I started my search with the kitchen. He loved to cook and spent many hours there."

Dante crossed his arms, fighting the sensation that his presence was completely unnecessary. Before they'd begun, she'd assured him that talking through the dilemma might bring some clue to light that would help, but he wondered.

"So you're searching the rooms in the order of how much time he spent there?"

"With the exception of the billiards room, yes. I went there next on a hunch. You can't imagine how ticked I am that my hunch didn't pan out."

Dante couldn't contain an ironic chuckle. After realizing what she'd had in mind for the evening, he was fairly ticked off himself.

"Okay, then. Let's get to work. Tell me what to do."

She spun and surprised him with a withering look. "If only you'd said that to me before Marshall arrived, Dante, we'd both be smiling like idiots right about now."

Macy stormed out of the library, stalked into the parlor and, because she knew she'd already thoroughly searched the space top to bottom, kicked a small ottoman across the room. She screamed in impotent frustration, dragging her hands through her hair, and toyed with the idea of pulling the strands free so that her head might stop pounding. They'd searched through the night and come up with nothing. Zero. Zip. The code had to be here. It had to be.

Dante approached behind her and she noticed the caution with which he moved. Only years of training had kept them on task during the search. Only once had the traitorous thought occurred to her that if the country was about to descend into chaos, didn't she want one last glorious memory to pull her through? Perhaps a vivid, fresh, intense memory of her and Dante making love?

When he cupped his hand gently on her shoulder, she nearly flew out of her skin. Instead, she whipped around and launched herself against him, capturing his mouth with hers and locking her arms around his neck so that he had no means of escape.

He didn't deny her the kiss she so desperately needed. His tongue battled with hers. They inhaled each other until neither one could take a breath and gasping became the music of the night's dance.

He swung them out of the parlor, and with half a thought, Macy realized he was attempting to direct them up the stairs. To the master suite? She didn't care where they made love, so long as the event happened in the next few minutes. Her flesh flamed, and with one quick tug, she divested herself of her zippered blouse and then tore at Dante's shirt until

351

the buttons pinged along the hardwood floor on their way to the stairwell. Seconds later, her bra flew into the air, hooking on the banister.

Macy locked her legs around Dante's waist, pressing her sex against his hard erection until a liquid agony filled her. She pulled herself high, gasping when his mouth surrounded her nipple and he suckled her to near delirium. They'd both wanted this for too long to deny their intrinsic lust any longer.

Shockingly, Dante stumbled beneath their combined weight on about the third step. With a laughing scream, they ended up on the stairwell, their momentum barely skipping a beat. His pants disappeared first, then hers, along with shoes and boxers and panties. Dante turned, bracing his back against the stairs as Macy climbed over his lap and guided his sex into hers.

The slick sensation spawned renewed fire between them. Macy braced her arms on his knees behind her, arching her back so he could bathe her breasts in hot, desperate kisses. When she thought she'd go insane from his plucking her nipples with his teeth, she returned the favor, yanking his hair into her hands and tugging him close so that no space existed between his body and hers until she found that spot near the base of his neck that always drove him mad. Right when she knew he teetered on the brink, she lifted her body to milk the pleasure from him—and give him so much in return.

The pace intensified. He grabbed her hips and urged her to take whatever bliss she needed—so she did. His sex thickened inside her, and his hands and lips took greedy license, touching and tasting until she was caught up in a storm of sensations. The second she'd neared the edge of her climax, Dante pushed her over fast with the guttural glory that was his release.

Moments passed. Sanity returned. When her chest stopped heaving, Macy realized that more than anything in the world, she wanted to stay right where she was, curled over Dante's lap, connected to him physically, breathing hard while he stroked her hair. He whispered something into her ear that she couldn't understand, which was fine with her, because she didn't want to hear. Words had the power to destroy this tentative truce.

Words, and the fact that they were on the staircase, which while exciting at the moment, was not exactly comfortable. She rolled off of him, but unashamed and with no regret, she snuggled beside him and stared up at the ceiling.

Only there wasn't a ceiling, exactly—it was covered by a long, artfully cut mirror.

She blinked. How odd.

"Macy, I want to tell you about the Chilean operation."

Dante caught her attention and she dragged her gaze away from the mirror hanging above them. For a second, she wondered just how hot Dante had gotten being able to watch her on top of him, but his eyes reflected a seriousness she knew to respect. She needed to hear his explanation—wanted to hear how he justified such a breach of trust. If not for the change in their mission and their sudden surrender to undeniable desire, she would already know the complete truth about his betrayal.

"Why did you pass off my intelligence work as your own?" she asked, cutting to the chase.

"Because Russell didn't trust you."

His admission slapped her in the face. "Russell? He recruited me!"

Dante frowned. "He was also fairly hot for you, but you fell into bed with me."

"Russell?" Macy didn't want to believe what Dante claimed, but in retrospect, she supposed that the attention her former superior had given her might have sprung from ulterior motives. She'd been around men all her life and had learned to ignore most sexual attention and flirting as just natural and without meaning. A guy had to practically hit her over the head to show her that his interest was sincere. Or whip her into a whirlwind of lust and desire as Dante had.

"Russell had the ear of the Joint Chiefs," Macy said, unable to voice the possibility that her name could have been sullied all the way to the Oval Office. "He poisoned their minds against me?"

Dante turned and stretched his legs, balancing on one elbow so he could toy with her hair with his fingers. "Yes, but he tipped his hand when he blamed you for the information that leaked in the Boston operation. Every agent in the field knew that Carlson had blown the deal."

"But Carlson was dead."

"Exactly. And Carlson also trained with all the men who ran the Arm, including the Joint Chiefs, while you were a young, pretty upstart who'd soon surpass them all. Russell couldn't prove his accusations, but he resented you enough to have you redlisted."

Meaning she was an agent to be watched—an agent who might not be trustworthy.

Dante threaded his fingers through hers, working out the sudden attack of tension with a soft massage. "I pulled some strings and kept you on the Chilean project, but when you found the intelligence we needed to break the case, I had to make a choice."

Macy narrowed her eyes. God, how she'd tried not to think about that time, his betrayal, her incredible emotional loss. The case had been sloppy from the start, and now she knew why. The lead operative, Russell Rhodes, had apparently had his mind on other things. She'd been trying to stop an influx of cocaine from being smuggled in by Chilean freighters. He'd been trying to ruin her reputation and get her booted from the Arm.

"The information was risky, I remember," she said, the recollection painful even as a chill skittered across her skin. "I couldn't find a second source to verify the ties between the Chilean shipping company and the Brazilian industrialist we'd had under observation for six months."

"The rich Brazilian industrialist with ties to the president's reelection campaign," Dante reminded her. He rubbed his hand up her arm and, noting the gooseflesh, grabbed his shirt from the bottom of the stairs and wrapped the material around her. "I suspected Russell might have planted the intel to discredit you entirely, so I called his bluff. If the information proved false, I would have been blamed for the bad data. When it proved true and the mission was successful, I finally had the clout to push Russell out of the way. Once I was in charge, I could repair the damage he'd done to you."

She tugged the shirt closed, suddenly vulnerable and yet possessing a clarity that spoke volumes. She'd thought the anger she'd felt toward Dante still simmered beneath her surface, but not a spark of rage vexed her now. She was frustrated, yes. Regretful, absolutely. But angry? Not anymore.

"Why didn't you just tell me the truth?" she asked. "Why did you let me believe for all these years that you'd betrayed me?"

Dante bit his lip in a pained way she'd never seen before. When he glanced up, his eyes reflected the remorse he'd clearly harbored since he'd made his difficult choice. "I never had the chance. You bolted and I had to leave immediately to handle a hostage crisis in Laos. By the time I was back in the States, you were long gone, hidden in T-45's web of secrecy. I wanted to be your knight in shining armor, Macy. For once, I wanted to take care of you. You never allowed that of any man. I wanted to be the one."

She grinned at the irony. "Until this week, no, I never have let a man pamper me, protect me. In my family, with four brothers, I learned to fend for myself."

He slipped his arm beneath her and tucked himself close, both their bodies stretched out down the carpeted stairs, the hair on his legs brushing softly against her own bare skin. In a window just at the top of the stairs, the sunlight had begun to slide fingers of light through the slats in the blinds. They'd been up all night. Together.

"I should have let you in on my plan rather than waiting until I could ride in on my white horse and sweep you off your feet," he confessed. "I had the ring that day, Macy. I was going to explain everything and then ask you to marry me."

"But I was already gone." She reached out and touched his cheek, the bristle of his beard rough and wonderful against her skin. "I should have trusted that you wouldn't have hurt me without having a damned good reason, but T-45 had already been wooing me and I'd been passed over twice for promotions—now I know, thanks to Russell. I shouldn't have let my anger get the best of me."

He smiled. "You have always been a passionate and impatient woman, Macy. We both made mistakes."

He leaned forward and kissed her gently, rolling closer so that she eased onto her back and wrapped her arms around his neck. While her lips engaged in the sweetest, most sensual kiss of the morning, her eyes seemed obsessed with the dawn reflected in the mirror that hung on the slanted ceiling above the stairs. A long pink ribbon of light filtered over the reflective glass, creating an opaque cloud of color. She was staring, entranced, when shapes seemed to form in the glass, lines and curves. Then, they disappeared.

Lines and curves.

She blinked, trying to bring the images back into her sight. Nothing.

Lines and curves.

Numbers.

"Good God, Dante," she said, pushing away from him. "The code. I think I've found it."

Chapter 9

In less than an hour, Dante had every mirror in the house assembled in a line on the floor of the parlor, cradled on a cushioned tarp. Dressed in his crumpled slacks and buttonless shirt, he ignored the stares of his forensic chemical analysis team and continued to pace behind them as they worked their magic. Macy marched into the room moments later, dressed in a sweat suit and looking incredibly sated and satisfied. In the rush since Macy saw the numbers in the mirror, they hadn't had a chance to finish their conversation, but her tiny, private smile spoke volumes.

But his hunger would have to wait. They had a few million lives to save.

"Anything?" he asked.

She handed the computer printout to him. "The housekeeper claims none of the mirrors were original and that nearly every one, so far as she can remember, was shipped here special from Russia."

"They're not Russian."

Sean Devlin strode into the room as if he owned the place, and immediately grabbed a pair of protective gloves from a nearby box.

"Devlin, what are you doing here?" Dante asked.

"Heard there was a breakthrough."

Dante and Macy eyed each other with equal amounts of suspicion. He hadn't called Sean in, and judging by the annoyance clear on Macy's face, she hadn't either.

"We know they're not Russian," Macy snapped. She and Sean had never truly gotten along. For some reason, Macy possessed the antidote to the former agent's killer charm. "They were all produced here in the United States, then shipped to Bogdanov's home in the Russian Swiss Alps. Then, a few months later, they returned to the States. The entire process seemed to take about two years and the timeline coincides with Bogdanov's work on the countercode system in the silos."

Devlin leaned down and looked at the mirror closest to him. "Have you tried smashing them open?"

Macy had Devlin backed against a wall in two seconds flat. "Why are you here? For all we know, you're working for the terrorists."

Dante didn't move, realizing Macy had a point, albeit an unlikely one. His old friend was a lot of things, but mercenary wasn't one of them. "Macy, leave him alone. Sean's probably here because this is where the action is."

Sean's expression was entirely innocent, which clearly meant he was up to something. Besides, Sean had been the best muscle in the business. He could likely snap Macy's neck before anyone saw him move.

"Or not," Dante said, his blood running cold.

Sean rolled his eyes. "I'm only here to deliver a message. A private message, to Dante. I didn't have any idea about the mirrors until I snuck inside and overheard."

"Snuck in?" Macy said, throwing an accusatory glance at Dante.

Sean clucked his tongue. "Cut the guy some slack, Rush. I designed nearly every system the Arm uses. Keeping me out is the least of your worries."

"Here!"

One of the techs working on a small mirror taken from the kitchen raised his hand in triumph. "I've got the formula."

Macy released Sean and the entire group gathered around the tech while he painted a clear, foul-smelling compound across the glass. He then lifted the glass and adjusted a sunlamp positioned above him. A combination of two numbers and a letter became clear.

"We've got it," Macy said. She directed her attention to the other techs. "Get me the numbers and letters in ten minutes." She glanced once at Sean and then speared Dante with a look that said, *Get rid of this guy.* "I'll get the decryption software down here and we'll have the code in fifteen."

His operatives hesitated, but with a nod, they obeyed Macy's directive. The room suddenly swarmed with activity, and when Macy disappeared to retrieve her equipment, Sean and Dante were left alone with nothing to do.

They retreated to the kitchen. Sean poked around in the cabinets, satisfied to remain still only after he found leftover crab and sun-dried tomato ravioli in the refrigerator.

"Why are you really here?" Dante asked, crossing his arms over his chest, which was visible since his shirt had no buttons to fasten, thanks to Macy.

Sean popped a large, cold pasta square in his mouth. "I thought I saw Macy on the monitor the other day. Did some checking around, realized what was really going on. You wanted her back."

Dante rolled his eyes. "Is that any great surprise?"

"After you nearly died, no. Have you told her?"

A lump formed in Dante's throat. Talking about his near-death experiences didn't come easy to him. In fact, except for Sean, he'd discussed the incident with no one outside the official debriefing and the mandatory consultation with the department psychiatrist. "There's been no time. Besides, the Arm went to great lengths to cover up the event. But when this mission is complete, I'll fill her in on everything."

Sean nodded with a resigned acceptance that made Dante furrow his brow. For a man who seemed to care about little except partying, traveling and testing his mettle with extreme sports and high-risk hobbies, his friend had shown a lot of interest in his private life lately.

"If the mission was deemed classified, you can't tell her and keep your job," Sean said.

Dante nodded. He'd broken enough rules already—well, more like created his own. But he hadn't revealed any classified information to an agent from a rival organization, which would be the kiss of death. And rightly so. He'd known the situation might come down to hard choices, but the fact remained that while Macy hadn't yet said the words, he knew she forgave him. They'd made love in their old, hot, wild style, but somehow the passion had run deep into both of them, deeper than either of them ever imagined. She'd listened to his explanation. She'd trusted what he'd said as the truth—which it had been. That alone told him her heart was open to him again. He wasn't going to let something as insignificant as his job stand in the way of their future.

"I'm willing to sacrifice what I have to, Sean. I want Macy back."

With a smile, his friend finished off the last of the

ravioli, wiped his hands on his jeans and then clapped him on the shoulder. "I thought you might be thinking along those lines." He dug into his back pocket and pulled out a tiny purple velvet bag, one Dante instantly recognized.

"Where did you get that?" he said, swiping the small sack out of his hand.

"From your place. The minute I saw Macy on that monitor, I figured you'd need it." Sean grabbed a bottled water from the refrigerator, gave his friend a salute and then let himself out the back door. "Call me when you set the date, okay?"

Once he was alone, Dante untied the gold string and turned the contents of the sack into his palm. Part of him couldn't believe that he'd kept the ring, after all these years. Part of him was terrified Macy would say no. But for the first time in his life, he knew one thing throughout his entire body and soul—he wanted Macy as his wife, even if he'd have to save the world to accomplish his task.

When he heard footsteps down the hall, he pocketed the ring.

"I have the countercode," Macy announced, her face flushed with excitement. "I just transmitted the series to the T-45 operatives at the Russian Central Command. The system will be down in minutes, and from their remote location, there is no way the terrorists can launch the missile. We've won!"

He inhaled deeply and pasted on his dourest face. "That, my dear Macy, remains to be seen."

Macy paced her room, which didn't do much to curb her anxiety since she only needed about three steps in either direction to go from wall to wall. Nearly a half an hour had passed with no official word from Abe or the coterie of agents sent into Russia. Could the computer program have failed to reconstruct the code correctly? Had they missed a mirror somewhere in the house that contained a crucial combination? Fear and doubts swam in her brain, propelled by the most puzzling turn of the day.

Dante's sudden coolness.

She slammed onto the bed, her hands shaking. She'd given him what he wanted by making love with him in the early morning hours. Now that he'd tasted her again, was his appetite satisfied? Could she have been so gullible with her emotions? Now that she knew the truth, she accepted her own culpability in the destruction of their relationship nine years ago. She hadn't trusted that he'd take care of her. She'd abandoned him. She hadn't believed in their love.

Now she did. And she wasn't about to allow misconceptions to ruin her chance at love again. When he finally appeared in the doorway, dressed in casual slacks and a polo shirt, his face clean-shaven and his signature scent teasing her from a distance, she stood, ready to fight for what she wanted.

Dante.

"What's the news?" she asked, her gaze darting to the paper he held loosely in his hand.

"The code worked," he answered simply, his smile so small, an icy stream of dread coiled through her veins. "The system is disabled and the terrorists can't launch the missile. They're attempting to escape. The Russian army has three in custody, picked up just on the other side of the fortified pass."

Strangely, he didn't hand her whatever missive he was holding. A communiqué from Abe? Her orders? A commendation from the president? Or maybe the note had nothing whatsoever to do with her.

From the intense look in his eyes, she doubted that scenario.

"What's wrong?"

Dante shrugged. "It's over. You can go back to France and never see me again."

She stepped back, remembering only after she stumbled that the bed was right behind her. "No, Dante, I can't." With a deep breath, she strode forward, searching his eyes for some clue that would tell her what his assumption was really all about. "You don't really think I can do that, do you? Leave, after what happened between us?"

He folded his arms over his chest. "Three days

ago, you said you could sleep with me and leave without giving me a second thought."

"Three days ago, I didn't know how much you'd changed or how wrong I was about what happened in the past."

His eyes widened, the gray finally lighting with a glimmer of something she'd best describe as hope. "You truly have forgiven me?"

She pressed her lips together. "I was as much to blame as you, for not trusting you. For putting my own career aspirations ahead of our love. The truth was, Dante, I wanted to join T-45 long before Russell screwed me over. When I thought you'd betrayed me, I jumped at the chance to leave. Maybe because staying would have meant I'd have to choose between you and advancing my career."

Which, she realized, she'd have to do right now. As a T-45 agent, there was no way she could continue an intimate relationship with the head of a rival organization.

She looked up at Dante. Obviously, he'd read the writing on the wall, too.

Damn.

Macy slipped back to the bed, sighing as a sudden wash of emotions threatened to swamp her. She wanted Dante, but she wanted her job, too—and she couldn't have both. She'd just begun to shake her head in disbelief at the cruelty of love and fate when he finally handed her the paper he'd been holding.

She scanned the page, then sought his gaze to make sure she could believe what she read. "This is your resignation from the Arm."

He closed the door behind him, then dropped to one knee in front of her. "Yes, it is."

She couldn't catch her breath. Her vision shook, along with her hands. "I don't understand. You're the head of the agency, Dante."

His grin was crooked and brimmed with a singularly suave charm that would make her insides flutter until the day she died.

"And I've had a good, long run," he said. "Nine years on top should be enough for any man, don't you think?"

She crunched the letter as she threw the paper on the bed and then grabbed Dante's hands. "No! You can't give up what you've worked so hard for."

Warmth from his silver eyes nearly melted her into a puddle on the bedspread. "I'm not giving up what I've worked for, Macy. I'm finally taking it. I love you, Macy. I was too stupid to fight for you nine years ago, but now I've learned my lesson. I've had my glory days. The spy business hasn't held any appeal for me for a long time now."

In as few words as he could, Dante told Macy about how he'd nearly died during a covert operation. She nearly held her breath while he opened his heart and, in a rush of honesty, confessed how the one thought that had kept him alive on the operating table and had bolstered his determination during his recovery was the possibility of having her in his life again. "Took a world crisis to give me the opportunity, but I don't care," he concluded. "Please, Macy, give me another chance."

Thankfully, she resisted the nearly insurmountable urge to pace and instead stayed seated when Dante whipped a gorgeous diamond ring from his pocket.

"I really wanted to hide this and then see if you could find it, but I guess you've had your fill of lost items for a while."

He gently took her left hand and slid the impressive gem onto her ring finger. The gold band encircled her perfectly and the weight of the stone seemed to find immediate balance on her hand. "Dante, I—"

"This is the ring I bought you nine years ago, Macy, but I'm grateful that I never had the chance to ask you to marry me then. Neither one of us was ready. Now we know how much we mean to each other, how much we can accomplish together. Please, Macy Rush, would you do me the honor of becoming my wife?"

Before she could reply, an Arm operative knocked on the door and announced a top-secret communiqué from headquarters. Dante told the poor sap to shove it under the door, which he did. With an apologetic shrug, he retrieved the letter, scanned it, and then laughed heartily.

"What is it?" she asked, joining him.

"It's from your boss, or I should say, your former boss."

Macy grabbed the paper and read. Her jaw dropped. When her gaze met with Dante's, the twinkle in his eye made her suspect he'd had something to do with this turn of events. "Did you do this?"

"What? Make Abercrombie Marshall retire and tap you as his successor? No, my dear, even I'm not that powerful. Besides, he's not really retiring. Read the note on the bottom."

In his woefully bad handwriting, Abe had jotted a personal note to Macy, informing her that he'd just been appointed as the new head of the Arm. He was finally returning to the outfit that had drummed him out on account of his skin color thirty years ago—and now he was in charge.

"Bully for him," Macy said. "He'll do wonderful things with your legacy, Dante."

Dante shook his head and shrugged, as if he was pleased but truly didn't give a damn. "Now, back to the proposal on the table."

Macy allowed the paper to drift to the floor and slid her arms around Dante's neck. She saw no reason to beat around the bush. "Yes."

Dante's eyes widened. "That's it? Yes? What's the catch?"

She grinned, remembering how she'd questioned

him similarly just a few days ago. "Catch? Well, there is the fact that I love you, too. And I'm not a patient woman, with time for long engagements. But if you want something more . . ."

He snaked his hands around her waist and tugged her close so that their bodies aligned perfectly. "May I make a suggestion?"

She nuzzled his neck with her nose, inhaling that spicy tobacco scent she'd crave forever, even if he was with her every single day. "Feel free."

"I was thinking that your flat in Paris is much too small for two people."

The warmth of his skin acted like a magnet to her lips. She managed to hum her understanding and agreement as she bathed his neck in slow, erotic kisses.

"So I figured I could fill my spare time looking for an old house to renovate. You know how I love old houses," he said.

She pulled back and eyed him with naughty suspicion. "I don't suppose you'll want a similar deal to the one we had here, do you? Something like, 'I can't spend time in a room until we've made love there'?"

With a chuckle, he buried his nose in her hair and dropped gentle kisses on her face. "Works for me. We could try out multiple rooms in multiple houses, until we find just the right spot. You game?"

Macy laughed, secure in Dante's embrace and certain for the first time that they had a real shot at a future together. "With you, Dante, I'm game for anything."

USA Today bestselling author Julie Elizabeth Leto has built a reputation for writing ultrasexy, edgy stories that push the envelope of traditional romance. And yet she's a die-hard romantic who firmly believes in creating stories about strong, powerful, charming heroes and about heroines who can take care of themselves and embrace their sexuality, even while they are searching for the right guy to share their heart with. A Florida native, Julie lives in her hometown with her husband, her daughter, a very spoiled dachshund named Lady, and a large and beloved extended family. She's written more than twenty romances for various publishers and has her first female action-adventure novel coming out in summer 2005. For more information about Julie's upcoming releases, visit her Web site at www.julieleto.com.

All your favorite romance writers are coming together.

SIGNET ECLIPSE

National bestselling author
JILL SHALVIS
is turning up the heat.

WHITE HEAT

0-451-41142-0

Bush pilot Lyndie Anderson lives only for her plane
and the open sky, and she'd like to keep it that way.
Firefighter Griffin Moore hasn't been himself since
an Idaho wildfire claimed his entire crew. But when
Lyndie is hired to fly Griffin into the heart of a raging
inferno, the sparks of desire begin to fly…

"Shalvis writes with passion and fire."
—*Affaire de Coeur*

**"Jill Shalvis is a breath of fresh air
on a hot, humid night."**
—*Readers' Connection*

And don't miss:
BLUE FLAME

0-451-41168-4

Available wherever books are sold or at
www.penguin.com